Praise for *Captain Wentworth's Diary*

"In this retelling of *Persuasion* we are given a real treat . . . Like the other books in Ms. Grange's series, scrupulous attention is paid to the original, even while interpreting what is not explicitly shown, and some well-known scenes are fleshed out while others are condensed, nicely complementing the original." —*AustenBlog*

"Amanda Grange's retellings of Jane Austen's novels from the point of view of the heroes are hugely popular and deservedly so . . . *Captain Wentworth's Diary* will entrance and enthrall old and new fans alike." —*Single Titles*

"One of those wonderful historicals that makes the reader feel as if they're right in the front parlor with the characters . . . this book held me captive. It is well written and I very much hope to read more by this author. Amanda Grange is a writer who tells an engaging, thoroughly enjoyable story!" —*Romance Reader at Heart*

Praise for *Mr. Knightley's Diary*

"A lighthearted and sparking rendition of the classic love story." —*The Historical Novels Review*

"Charming . . . knowing the outcome of the story doesn't lessen the romantic tension and expectation for the reader. Grange hits the Regency language and tone on the head." —*Library Journal*

"Ms. Grange manages the tricky balancing act of satisfying the reader and remaining respectful of Jane Austen's original at the same time, and like Miss Woodhouse herself, we are given the privilege of falling for Mr. Knightley all over again." —*AustenBlog*

"Readers familiar with *Emma* should enjoy revisiting the county and its people and welcome the expansion of Mr. Knightley's role. Others will find an entertaining introduction to a classic." —*Romance Reviews Today*

"Well written, with a realistic eye to the rustic lifestyle of the aristocracy, fans of Ms. Austen will appreciate this interesting perspective." —*Genre Go Round Reviews*

"A very enjoyable read and an amusing tale." —*Fresh Fiction*

Titles by Amanda Grange

MR. KNIGHTLEY'S DIARY
CAPTAIN WENTWORTH'S DIARY

LORD DEVERILL'S SECRET
HARSTAIRS HOUSE

Captain Wentworth's Diary

AMANDA GRANGE

BERKLEY BOOKS, NEW YORK

THE BERKLEY PUBLISHING GROUP
Published by the Penguin Group
Penguin Group (USA) Inc.
375 Hudson Street, New York, New York 10014, USA
Penguin Group (Canada), 90 Eglinton Avenue East, Suite 700, Toronto, Ontario M4P 2Y3, Canada
(a division of Pearson Penguin Canada Inc.)
Penguin Books Ltd., 80 Strand, London WC2R 0RL, England
Penguin Group Ireland, 25 St. Stephen's Green, Dublin 2, Ireland (a division of Penguin Books Ltd.)
Penguin Group (Australia), 250 Camberwell Road, Camberwell, Victoria 3124, Australia
(a division of Pearson Australia Group Pty. Ltd.)
Penguin Books India Pvt. Ltd., 11 Community Centre, Panchsheel Park, New Delhi—110 017, India
Penguin Group (NZ), 67 Apollo Drive, Rosedale, North Shore 0632, New Zealand
(a division of Pearson New Zealand Ltd.)
Penguin Books (South Africa) (Pty.) Ltd., 24 Sturdee Avenue, Rosebank, Johannesburg 2196,
South Africa

Penguin Books Ltd., Registered Offices: 80 Strand, London WC2R 0RL, England

This is a work of fiction. Names, characters, places, and incidents either are the product of the author's imagination or are used fictitiously, and any resemblance to actual persons, living or dead, business establishments, events, or locales is entirely coincidental. The publisher does not have any control over and does not assume responsibility for author or third-party websites or their content.

A Berkley Book / published by arrangement with Robert Hale Ltd.

Copyright © 2007 by Amanda Grange.
Cover art: *The Proposal* by John Laslett, 1837–1898, courtesy of Fine Art Photographic Library / Private Collection.
Cover design by Monica Benalcazar.
Text design by Tiffany Estreicher.

PRINTING HISTORY
Robert Hale hardcover edition / 2007
Berkley trade paperback edition / May 2008

Library of Congress Cataloging-in-Publication Data

Grange, Amanda.
      Captain Wentworth's diary / Amanda Grange.—Berkley trade pbk. ed.
         p. cm.
      ISBN 978-0-425-22352-9 (pbk.)
      1. Wentworth, Frederick (Fictitious character)—Fiction.   2. England—Fiction.   I. Austen, Jane,
1775–1817. Persuasion.   II. Title.

PR6107.R35C37 2008
823'.92—dc22   2007049422

PRINTED IN THE UNITED STATES OF AMERICA

10   9   8   7   6   5   4   3   2   1

Captain Wentworth's Diary

1806

JUNE

Thursday 5 June

At last I am on my way to Somerset!

Harville and I travelled from the coast together, marvelling at how strange it was to see green fields as we went along, rather than the blue sea. Apart from the ground's alarming tendency to stay still beneath us, instead of rolling and dipping like an honest element, the journey was not uncomfortable, and we managed to while away the time by regaling two governesses, the Miss Browns, with our recent adventures at sea. Or rather, I did, for Harville said little, and it fell upon me to astonish them with tales of the dangers we had passed through in our efforts to protect them from the French. I was rewarded by their horrified gasps and grateful thanks.

As they left the coach, I rallied Harville, telling him he was a fool to exchange the smiles of a country full of women for the shackles of one, and asking him if the elder Miss Brown was not the most beautiful girl he had ever seen. He acknowledged that she was very pretty, but not as pretty as his Harriet, and he would not be dissuaded; he is still determined to ask her to marry him as soon as he gets home.

We found a comfortable berth at the Cow and Calf, and now here I am in my room, sitting by the open window, looking out over fields. I have not yet accustomed myself to the country, with its rich smell of flowers and grass. It seems strange to me after the salt tang of the sea, but I will grow used to it before long, I dare say, and I have no doubt I will soon be revelling in the joys of shore leave.

Friday 6 June

Harville and I made a good breakfast, and then we parted, he to go to Wiltshire, and I to go to Monkford. He left first, on the stage, and I had to wait an hour for the coach that was to carry me onwards. It arrived at the inn in a great hurry, pausing only long enough to change horses, disgorge three passengers, take up two more, myself and a young man who sat outside, and then depart at the same riotous pace. I took my place inside, being in funds, and was soon thrown about by the speed and the poor condition of the road, but as a very pretty farmer's daughter was thrown into my lap I could not regret it. Her mother looked at me disapprovingly, but we could none of us help laughing when another pothole sent *her* into my lap as well! Restraint being thus broken, we began to talk, and it soon emerged that they had a cousin at sea. The time passed quickly as we talked of battles and promotion, and it was a surprise to me when it was time for me to leave the stage.

I looked about me, to get my bearings, and found I had some distance to cover on foot, but I was glad of the exercise after spending so long confined. I passed through Uppercross, which I had expected to be larger from my brother's description, but which turned out to be merely a moderate-sized village, with yeomen's houses, a high-walled mansion, and a parsonage. I wondered if my brother lived in something similar, and hoped it was so, for although the parsonage was a small house, it had its own neat garden, with a vine and a pear tree trained round the casements.

I came at last to Monkford, and found myself a subject of interest to the two dames and three little boys I passed, the latter falling into line some way behind me. I looked about me for my brother's house, and at last I asked a gentleman coming towards me where Mr Wentworth, the curate, lived. He gave me directions, and I soon found myself at the gate.

My eye ran over the house with interest. It was not as fine as the parsonage at Uppercross, being much smaller, and without a vine, but it had a good aspect, and I was in high spirits as I knocked at the door. The servant answered and told me that his master was not at home, having not known exactly when to expect me, but that he could be found in the church. I left my belongings in the hall and went in search of him.

The church was a modest size, but in a good state of repair, which spoke well of its parishioners. As I went in, Edward saw me and gave me a hearty welcome. He finished his business, and then we left the church together.

As we walked back to his house along the dusty road, I told him all my news, of the ships I had sailed in and the captains I had sailed under, of the battle of St Domingo and my promotion to commander, and in return I listened to his tales of sermons and services, of neighbours and parishioners. I could not help laughing at the difference.

'What! One of your neighbours climbed over your wall uninvited last month? What a calamity! I do not know how you survived the excitement!'

'A pretty time you have had of it!' Edward retorted. 'Never knowing where you would be in a few hours' time, and whether you would be alive or dead. I would rather be safe in my parish with my garden and my books, my home and my church, than tossing about on the open sea in a flimsy wooden boat. You were always the bold one, Frederick.'

'And why not? The war has made it possible for men of ability and ambition to rise in the world, and I mean to use the opportunities it has given me to make my fortune. Ah! the limitless horizons, both at sea and on land, the battles to be fought, the prizes to be won. I will be a wealthy man soon, and I mean to own an estate before I am done.'

'And then be off again the minute you have bought it! You will never settle on land, you will find it too dull. I believe you will scarcely be able to tolerate your shore leave. I can offer you no battles, unless you wish to frighten my parishioners into listening to my sermons instead of whispering about each other's bonnets, and I can offer you no glory, save the glory of being a novelty, to be examined and talked over like a prize bull at a fair.'

'It is enough. I have had my fill of battles for the time being, and I am ready for variety. A man may grow weary of the sea as well as anything else, and I will fight all the better for the change. Besides, I mean to enjoy myself whilst I am here, and to do all the things I cannot do on board ship. I mean to ride and walk and explore the countryside, and I am looking forward to meeting your neighbours. You have told me a great deal about them in your letters and I cannot wait to make their acquaintance. I hope there are some pretty girls hereabouts!'

'I have never noticed.'

'Come, now, even a curate notices a pretty face,' I said.

'If you had been plagued by every spinster from sixteen to sixty for the last twelvemonth, as I have, you would not be so eager to attract their notice. If they are not offering to arrange flowers in the church, they are baking me cakes, much to my housekeeper's annoyance. "Do they think I don't know how to bake a cake?" she asks. It is all I can do to keep her from leaving me; I have to soothe her ruffled feathers at least once a week.'

'They may bake as many cakes for me as they wish, though I wonder they do not have servants to do it for them.'

'They are most of them too poor to employ more than a

maid of all work, so that most of them take their turn in the kitchen from time to time,' said Edward.

'And which of your spinsters is the prettiest, do you think?'

'If you must have it, Miss Welling is thought to be very pretty, and Miss Elliot is held to be handsome. She, though, is a baronet's daughter, and I doubt if she has ever seen the inside of a kitchen in her life. She will not pay any attention to you, commander or no. You will be beneath her notice.'

'Ah, yes, I recollect you mentioning the Elliots. It was Sir Walter Elliot who asked you if you were a member of the Strafford Wentworths, I recollect, and cut you when you replied that you were not,' I said.

'He did not cut me, he simply remarked that he was astonished the names of the nobility were becoming so common, and then passed on.'

'Fine talk, when he is nothing more than a baronet. I have no time for such people. They do nothing useful, but give themselves airs because of the achievements of their ancestors. They are a spent force.'

'Then I pray you will tell him so, and ruin my standing in the neighbourhood.' Edward snorted.

'Never fear, the Navy has not rid me of all my manners, or all my common sense, but I will take the liberty of thinking it.'

Upon asking him when I might have a chance of seeing Miss Elliot for myself, he told me that we were invited to a soirée tomorrow evening, and that Sir Walter intended to grace it with his presence.

'And has Miss Elliot any handsome sisters?'

'Two. Miss Elliot—Elizabeth—is the eldest, after which come Miss Anne and Miss Mary, though the latter is very young and is away at school.'

'And Miss Welling? Does she have any sisters?'

'An elder sister, who is married, and a younger one, who is not.'

'Splendid! Four handsome young ladies to meet. I believe I am going to enjoy my time here!'

Saturday 7 June

I rose with the dawn and went to the stables, but nothing there took my fancy and I decided to buy a horse. I told my brother of my intention and he said it was hardly worth my while as I will soon be back at sea, but I was determined to have one, and I walked into Crewkherne after breakfast for that very purpose. I saw several horses, but none of them caught my eye, and I was about to walk away when Limming, who was conducting the auction there, told me of a chestnut he knew, which was to be sold on account of its owner having lost heavily at cards. He promised to have the animal for me on Monday, and I agreed to take a look at it.

When I returned to Monkford I had luncheon with my brother and I told him about the horse.

'And can you afford it?' he asked.

'Of course I can. I have my prize money. I can afford ten such horses,' I told him.

'You do not think it too extravagant?'

'What is money for, if not to spend and enjoy?'

'To give to the poor,' he said, taking another glass of wine.

'It is a wonder to me how our mother could have had two such different sons!' I exclaimed. 'But to please you, brother, I will make a contribution to the poor-box. Are you satisfied?'

'For the time being,' he said.

After our meal, I explored the countryside whilst he attended to his duties in the parish. We met again in the evening and prepared to attend the party at the Honourable Mrs Fenning's.

'A new suit of clothes?' he asked, as he cast his eye over me from head to foot when I joined him downstairs. 'No, do not tell me,' he said, as I opened my mouth. 'Prize money!'

'It is there for the taking, if a man has courage to fight for it. There are French ships just waiting to be captured, and as soon as I have my own vessel, I mean to take a dozen!'

'You will need a steady supply if you continue to spend your money as quickly as you make it.'

I laughed at him and his caution and clapped him on the back, and told him to join the Navy and sail the seas with me. He returned with a desire that I would remain ashore and give myself to the church, and we set out for the party in perfect amity.

The Honourable Mrs Fenning's house was a large mansion on the outskirts of Monkford, not as grand as the mansion house at Uppercross, but impressive nonetheless. I looked about me as I went in, thinking that I would like to buy something similar when I had taken a few more French ships. Mrs Fenning welcomed us cordially, and my brother and I went into the ballroom. I glanced around, and saw that there were already a number of people there.

'And who are all these people?' I asked my brother, then said: 'No, let me guess.' My eyes alighted on a good-looking man of perhaps forty or forty-five years of age. His hair was swept back in the latest fashion and he was dressed with the greatest style. 'That must be Sir Walter Elliot,' I said. 'And the gentleman next to him is . . . ?'

'Mr Poole, with his daughter, Miss Poole.' Miss Poole was a plain lady of indeterminate age. 'And the young lady next to Sir Walter—'

'Is his daughter Elizabeth,' I said. 'You are right, brother, she is very handsome.'

Edward was uncomfortable, and said with an embarrassed laugh, 'That is not Miss Elliot. Sir Walter's daughters are not here tonight, they are indisposed. A soaking at a picnic has given them a chill. No, the lady next to him is Miss Cordingale. We all thought he would marry Lady Russell when his wife died, for Lady Russell is a widow, they are old friends and they are of an age, but—'

'Sir Walter, like many men before him, wanted a younger wife. It is the way of the world,' I said.

Mr Poole stepped forward and spoke to my brother, then

greeted me. We exchanged pleasantries, then he introduced me to Sir Walter.

Sir Walter looked at me with a critical eye.

'You have just won your promotion, I am told,' he said, in a stately manner. 'I must congratulate you . . .' I was about to say that it was nothing, that I had only done what any sailor would do, and that I was proud to serve my country, when he continued: '. . . you have kept your complexion remarkably well. There are signs of leatheriness, of course, but it is not yet ruined. It will soon be destroyed, however, for an outdoor life is, above all things, an enemy to the skin. I would advise you to wear a hat, sir, and a veil, when in sunny climes.'

'Thank you, but I believe I must carry on without them, for there is no time to think about veils in the heat of battle. There is a ship to be manoeuvred and an enemy to subdue.'

'A sad comment on the preoccupations of the naval man,' he said. 'With a tolerable figure, the uniform is not unbecoming, but a ruddy complexion ruins all.'

'But think of what good work the Navy does in protecting us!' said Mr Poole, turning to me apologetically. 'Without such courageous men, we would have been overrun by Napoleon long ago.'

'So the newspapers would have us believe, but who writes them? Gentlemen? I think not,' said Sir Walter. 'There is not a single man of note amongst such scribblers.'

'So there is not,' said Miss Poole, much struck. 'You are right, Sir Walter, there is not a one.'

'Believe me, Mr Poole, it will take more than a French rabble to overrun England. One Englishman is worth ten Frenchmen,' said Sir Walter.

'Ordinarily, perhaps, but under the guidance of Napoleon Bonaparte, who knows? He seems intent on subduing Europe, and so far, he is succeeding. The man is a monster!' Mr Poole was brave enough to remark.

'How can one expect otherwise, when his father is a lawyer?' returned Sir Walter, not to be outdone. 'It is not to be supposed that he would act with propriety. On the contrary, he was destined from an early age to run contrary to everything that is decent and good.'

Miss Poole bobbed and smiled at Sir Walter's side in silent flattery, mutely agreeing with every word, whilst Mr Poole looked as though he was about to speak and then thought better of it.

'Nevertheless he has managed to make himself emperor,' I remarked.

'Any man may make himself an emperor, but an emperor is not a king. It takes centuries of breeding to make a king,' returned Sir Walter.

'And to make a baronet!' remarked Miss Poole breathlessly.

Sir Walter rewarded this perspicacious remark with a regal smile, and I made my bow and moved on, glad to leave Sir Walter behind.

I was introduced to a succession of other guests, amongst whom were Mr Shepherd, a local lawyer, and his daughter;

Mrs Layne; and Mr Denton. Then I took my place, for the music was about to begin.

Mrs Fenning had hired a harpist and I listened attentively, until the sight of Miss Welling dropping her fan attracted my attention. From her glance in my direction, I suspected the incident was not altogether accidental, and that it had been intended to attract my notice. She was a very pretty young woman, as my brother had said, with soft fair hair and a most engaging figure, and I looked forward to speaking to her after the music was finished.

I was not disappointed, and we engaged in an agreeable flirtation before the evening came to an end.

Sunday 8 June

The worthies of the neighbourhood were all at church today, with Sir Walter paying a great deal of attention to Miss Cordingale, much to Miss Poole's chagrin. However, as Miss Cordingale blushed prettily when Mr Sidders glanced in her direction, and as Mr Sidders is a young man of about her own age, very handsome, and with a large fortune, I fear Sir Walter will have to look elsewhere for a bride. Perhaps Miss Poole will have him yet!

There were some pretty farmers' daughters in church, and three young ladies whose smiles brightened the morning as I was introduced to them outside, after the service. To my surprise, I found I was enjoying my shore leave even more than my time at sea!

Monday 9 June

I saw the chestnut this morning and was very taken with it. The price asked was too high, but after some haggling I bought it for a reasonable sum. My brother shook his head, asking what I would do with it when I returned to sea, but nevertheless, he had to admit it was a fine animal.

This evening we attended a private ball at the house of Mr and Mrs Durbeville, a couple of impeccable ancestry and fortune, or so my brother informed me. I found them to be agreeable people, and not above their company, for they welcomed me warmly and hoped I would enjoy the ball.

I recognized a number of people as I walked in. I saw the Pooles, and then my eye fell on one of the pretty young ladies I had met outside the church, Miss Denton, and I led her onto the floor. So well did I like dancing with her, that I asked her for another dance later in the evening. She blushed prettily and expressed herself delighted to accept.

There followed a minuet with Miss Welling, who flirted most agreeably, but alas! the farmers' daughters were not there, so I had to content myself with Mrs Layne for the next dance. She regaled me with talk of her children, and I believe I managed to sound interested in all their myriad virtues, before the dance was over and I found myself once again standing with my brother at the side of the room.

I soon found my eye drawn to Sir Walter Elliot, who had just arrived, and who was standing next to Mr Poole at the other side of the room. He was marvellously turned out again, his clothes just so, and topped with a handsome head that had been primped and preened by his valet. There was a handsome young lady next to him, and I remarked to my brother: 'Another of Sir Walter's amours?'

'No, that is his daughter, Miss Elliot.'

I could see why she had a reputation for beauty. Her face and figure were both good, and there was something about her carriage that showed she knew her own place in the world. I was much taken with her, and began to cross the room, intending to ask Mr Poole to perform the necessary introduction. As I approached, however, I heard her speaking to her companion, a poor, dowdy creature, in the most slighting way. Her father encouraged her in this behaviour, and it gave me such a disgust of them that I changed the direction of my steps ever so little, and approached the companion instead. A set was forming, and I asked her, 'Might I have the honour of this dance?'

Sir Walter looked at me as though I had confirmed all his worst suspicions about those beneath the rank of baronet, and his daughter was no more pleased. The companion started, coloured slightly, looked doubtingly at Miss Elliot, and then, with a hesitant 'Thank you,' took my arm.

I noticed several surprised glances from those around us as I took her onto the floor.

'You should not have asked me to dance,' she said mildly, as we took our places in the set. 'We have not yet been introduced.'

'Then why did you accept?' I asked.

She coloured, and I thought that, although she did not

have Miss Elliot's striking beauty, she was extremely pretty, with her delicate features and dark eyes.

'I hardly know, unless it is because I have so few opportunities to dance that I cannot afford to ignore one,' she said.

I was about to feel sorry for her, when a spark in her eye showed me that her words, although no doubt true, were uttered with a spirit of mischief, and I found myself growing more pleased with my choice of partner.

'You should not allow your mistress to dictate to you. Even a companion has a right to some entertainment once in a while,' I said, as we began to dance.

Her eyes widened, then she said, 'What makes you think I am Miss Elliot's companion?'

'I have not been at sea so long that I have forgotten how to detect a difference in rank,' I said. 'Even to my unpractised eye it is obvious. Your dress, whilst well cut, is not as elegant as Miss Elliot's. You do not have her confidence or her air, and she speaks to you as though you are beneath her notice. Her father supports her in this, and encourages her to slight you. And then there is the fact that, as we walked onto the floor, you did not receive the deference from others that is her lot, indeed, they looked surprised to see that you had been chosen. You also have a shy and retiring disposition, suited to your role in life. But never fear,' I went on kindly, 'you are no doubt far more interesting than the beautiful Miss Elliot, for all she is the daughter of a baronet. And now, let us have done with Miss Elliot, I would rather talk of you. Have you lived in the neighbourhood for long?'

'I have lived here all my life,' she replied gravely.

'That is a mercy. At least you have not been separated from your friends and family, in keeping with the cruel fate of most of your kind. Your mother and father are pleased to see you so well settled, I suppose?'

There was a small silence, and then she said: 'My mother is dead.'

I cursed myself for my rough manners.

'Forgive me. I have been a long time at sea, and I have forgotten how to behave in company. I have presumed too much on our short acquaintance, but please believe me when I say that I did not mean to distress you. Do you enjoy balls?' I asked her, thinking that this would be a safe topic of conversation.

'I like them very well. But you do not need to change the subject, and you must not worry that you have wounded me. My mother has been dead these five years. I miss her, but I have grown used to the pain.'

I was relieved, for I did not want to wound so delicate a creature.

'And is your father living?' I asked her, hoping that she was not an orphan, for then her lot in life would be hard indeed.

'He is.'

'That is a blessing. He is pleased to see you living at Kellynch Hall, I suppose?' I asked.

'Certainly. He regards it as the finest house in the neighbourhood.'

'And he approves of the Elliots? He shares Sir Walter Elliot's opinions and beliefs?'

'I believe I may safely say that their thoughts coincide in every particular,' she said.

Poor girl, I thought, if her father is another such a one as Sir Walter, but I did not say it. Instead, I asked her to tell me something of my new neighbours, in order to put her at her ease.

'The lady to your left is Miss Scott,' she said, indicating an elderly spinster of a timid disposition. 'She is easily alarmed, and it is better not to speak to her about the war, for she lives in fear of the French invading England. Her sister sends her newspapers every month, telling her of some new threat, and I believe she will not rest easy until peace has been declared. Opposite is Mr Denton; he lives at Harton House. Next to him is Mrs Musgrove, and beyond her is Miss Neville.'

The dance was over all too soon. She had a surprising grace when she danced, which I found pleasing, and as a result of my attentions she had lost her downtrodden look. By the end of the dance, there was a light in her eye and some colour in her cheek, so that she was almost blooming. I escorted her to the side of the room and left her, reluctantly, with a displeased Miss Elliot, before rejoining Edward.

'And what do you think of Miss Anne?' he asked me.

I regarded him enquiringly.

'Miss Anne Elliot,' he elaborated.

'I have not seen her. I assumed she was still at home with a chill,' I said. 'You must point her out to me—though if her father and sister are any indication, I do not think I wish to meet her. She will, no doubt, be proud and disagreeable, full of her own beauty and importance, and holding other people in contempt.'

'But you have just been dancing with her!' he said.

I was astonished.

'What?'

I looked across the room at Miss Anne. She happened to glance round at that moment, and I caught her eye. Upon seeing me, she smiled and turned away.

'So, that is Miss Anne!' I exclaimed, as our conversation took on a whole new meaning. I could not help laughing. 'I am beginning to enjoy my shore leave.'

'I hope you are not thinking of a flirtation,' said my brother. 'She is very young, only nineteen, and no match for a man of your age and experience.'

'Is she not, though? I think she is a very good match indeed. She has already given me one broadside, and I suspect she would be capable of giving me another.'

My brother looked at me doubtfully, but I clapped him on the back and told him not to worry, saying that I had no intention of harming the lady, but that a mild flirtation would help to pass the time until I return to the sea.

I am looking forward to it. I believe it will provide her with some much-needed attention, too. There is nothing like being singled out by an eligible bachelor to raise a young lady in the estimation of her friends.

Wednesday 11 June

I fell in with my brother's idea of joining him on his duties around the village this morning, for I had nothing else to do. Whilst he pointed out the houses of every member of his congregation, and introduced me to those who were at their windows or in their gardens–which seemed to be all of them–I found myself wishing for a sight of Miss Anne Elliot. Unfortunately, the closest I came to such an encounter was when Sir Walter and Miss Elliot drove by in their carriage, going through a puddle and splashing my boots. Edward laughed, but I was not amused, for I had no servant, and when we returned to his house, I had to polish them myself.

This afternoon, after putting the shine back on my boots, I rode out into the country. I was enlivened by the sight of a milkmaid with rosy cheeks, who was carrying two pails across her shoulders by means of a yoke. I helped her to put it down as she took a drink at the well, and was rewarded with a kiss and a smile.

I was beginning to think that life in the country was very pleasant, and to understand why Edward had chosen to stay on shore, when an evening playing whist with the local worthies reminded me why I went to sea.

Friday 13 June

I rose early, full of energy, and was soon out of doors. How my brother could bear to lie in bed on such a beautiful morning I did not know. I walked through the village and then on into the country, going through fields and copses until I came to the river. I jumped it at its narrowest point, in the exuberance that comes with an early morning in summer, and went on, through verdant fields. I had just come to a small weir when a familiar figure came into view. Miss Anne Elliot was walking there, and she was coming towards me.

'Commander Wentworth,' she said.

There was a smile around the corners of her eyes, and it was clear she was thinking of our last encounter as much as I was.

'I am surprised to see you here,' I remarked as I drew level with her, determined to pay her back in her own coin, 'for I was sure your duties as a companion would keep you inside, even on a morning as beautiful as this one. Can it be that Miss Elliot did not need you, or have you slipped out of the house whilst she is still abed? Do not neglect your obligations, I beg of you, lest you should find yourself turned out of the house. I would not like to see you made destitute for the sake of a morning's stroll.'

She laughed up at me.

'Are you very angry with me?' she asked.

I smiled.

'How could I be angry with you when you bested me in a fair fight? You would be of great value aboard a warship, Miss Elliot. Your tactics have the advantage of being both original and efficacious.'

'It was too tempting!' she said.

'But what are you doing out at this hour, alone?' I asked

her. 'I cannot believe your father would be pleased if he knew you were walking without a chaperon.'

'On the contrary, he has no objection to my walking alone when I am on Elliot land.'

I started.

'Yes, sir, you see, you are trespassing. The land as far as the river belongs to us.'

I thought of my leap across it, taken without any idea I was entering private lands.

'I am glad I did not know, or I would not have come so far,' I said. 'But you are within your rights to throw me off. Well, are you going to call one of your gamekeepers to eject me, or are you, perhaps, going to rout me yourself?'

'I believe I will ignore it for the moment,' she said consideringly. 'You have, after all, saved us from Napoleon. It was a great service, and as our fields still belong to us, rather than belonging to the French, then the least we can do in return is to allow you to stroll in them from time to time.'

'Then, if you permit, I will accompany you on your walk.'

She nodded gracefully and we fell into step together. I limited my stride so that I could accommodate her own smaller step, and as I looked down, I noticed that she had small and very pretty feet, encased in blue kid shoes.

'Do you often walk in the mornings?' I asked her.

'Always, if the weather permits,' she said.

'The exercise seems to suit you,' I said, noticing the air of vitality about her. 'Are you always so animated, so early in the day?'

She coloured slightly, and I confess I felt a surge of vanity, as I guessed it was my attentions, and not the earliness of the hour, that had brought the bloom to her cheek. I took pity on her embarrassment, however, saying: 'Perhaps you are remembering the assembly on Friday, and how enlivening it was? Or can it be that you are one of those souls who are always happier out of doors?'

'I believe I do prefer it,' she acknowledged.

'And I. I feel trapped indoors, hemmed in, but then I am used to the open sea and the endless horizon. Have you ever been to sea, Miss Elliot?'

'I have been on pleasure trips around the bay at several beauty spots, but never any farther.'

'And how did you like it?'

'I liked it very well. It was invigorating to feel the wind in my face, and to feel the spray. I wondered, at the time, whether life was like that for sailors, who live on a ship all the time, or did it become commonplace? Do you take pleasure in the elements, Commander Wentworth, or are they something to be battled against, or simply ignored?'

'On occasion the sea is our enemy, but usually the open air, the wind and the sun are exhilarating.'

'But is it not confining, also, to be on board a ship? It must be frustrating to be full of energy and yet unable to go anywhere.'

'Unable to go anywhere?' I exclaimed. 'I cannot allow it. On a ship, one is able to go everywhere!'

'I mean that you cannot walk very far, for if you do so, you will fall overboard.'

'There is something in what you say, though with new sights always on the horizon, there is never any urge to walk very far.'

'I can understand it must be so when you are within sight of land, but surely it is not the same when you are in the middle of the ocean?' she asked.

'Yes, even there. Every wave is different—a different colour, a different size—and the sails are constantly changing as they belly out or shrink with the wind. And then there is the thrill of knowing that at any minute an enemy ship might come into sight and chase us, or else present us with a tempting target to run down.'

'I confess I should find that alarming.'

As she said it her shawl slipped down into the crook of her elbow, and I was distracted by the smoothness of her arm, so that it took me some time to answer. She turned questioning eyes on me, and I noticed how deep-set they were, and how attractive.

'Do you not find it alarming also?' she asked.

'Not at all!' I said, recollecting myself. 'An enemy ship is nothing very terrible. On the contrary, it offers a man a chance to defend his country, and to seize a prize. There is a great deal of prize money to be won on the high seas, Miss Elliot, and, with the war, promotion comes quickly to those who are willing to take advantage of the opportunities on offer.'

'You have already taken advantage of them, I believe. Your brother told us that you have been recently promoted.'

'That is so.'

'It was in consequence of the action off St Domingo, was it not?'

'Indeed. Ah, that was a battle! The French were aiming to disrupt our trade, for there was little else they could do after we had decimated their fleet at Trafalgar. With their plans of invasion destroyed, they sailed for the West Indies. We gave chase, and at last we caught up with them. Then there were some spoils! Five French ships, all captured or driven ashore. A good day for England.'

'And a good day for you.'

'Yes. I was awarded my own command, and I had my share of the prize money.'

She listened attentively, and then said, 'I hear the action crippled the French Navy.'

'You seem to be knowledgeable about the war,' I said, surprised at the depth of her information, for few young ladies had any interest in anything beyond their immediate neighbourhood.

'I can hardly fail to be interested, since my fate and the fate of all around me depend on the outcome. If Napoleon invades, I fear England will be very different, and I, for one, should not like to see it.'

'Have no fear, we will keep you safe,' I assured her. 'The French Navy is not completely destroyed, alas, for they still have more than thirty ships, and they are building more to replace those they lost, but the threat of invasion is behind us, at least for now. It will take them a long time to recover from the recent blows we have dealt them, and you can continue to take your walks in peace.'

'I confess I am glad.' She stopped and looked about her. 'I like nothing better than to stroll out of doors in the summer.'

It was easy to see why. The English countryside, in all its verdancy, was encompassed in her gaze. There were fields and hedgerows, and the winding river flanked by placid banks. A small beach of sand was set in a hollow where the river curved, and, farther along, the water was transparent as it flowed over shallows, revealing the white and brown pebbles that littered the bottom.

'This is the end of Elliot land,' she said.

'Then I must take my leave.'

I was reluctant to do so, however, and delayed my departure by asking her if she would be at the assembly rooms tomorrow. She replied that she would, and, able to find no reason to detain her further, I expressed a hope of seeing her there and made my bow.

As I walked away from her, I resisted the urge to look back, though I was sorely tempted. I wanted to see her standing there in her sprigged muslin, with her shawl draped over her arms, and the sunlight catching the side of her hair. I wanted, too—let me confess it!—to see if her eyes followed me.

I made my way to Edward's house, and found him at breakfast.

'Where have you been so early?' he asked.

'For a walk.'

'I wish I had half your energy. I have a busy couple of days ahead of me, and I think I will forgo a visit to the assembly rooms tomorrow.'

'Come now, you cannot ignore your neighbours, and who will the ladies dance with if you deprive them of two bachelors, for married men scarcely ever take to the floor?'

'Most of the married men hereabouts are agreeable to dancing,' Edward said.

'Nevertheless, I must have you go.'

'And why, pray, is that?' he asked, helping himself to a rasher of ham.

'It is only polite. Besides, I met Miss Anne Elliot whilst out walking, and discovered that she will be there.'

'I hope you do not mean to pursue her, Frederick. It can come to nothing, and might harm her reputation.'

'You think too much of such things. All right! All right!' I laughed, as I saw him about to give me a sermon. 'I will not damage her reputation, you may be sure. It will tread carefully, and treat her with the utmost respect. It will not ask her to dance more than twice, and I will not seek her out, or at least, not any more than is consistent with propriety. But I have a mind to dance with her, and as it would look odd if I were to go to the assembly rooms without you, I must beg you to find the energy.'

'I am surprised at your preference. I cannot think what you see in her. I thought Miss Neville would be more to your taste,' he remarked.

'I like Miss Neville, too,' I said, 'but Miss Anne is better informed, and likes the sea very well!'

'But will not live on it.'

'You mistake the matter if you think I have marriage in mind. What, to throw myself away at the age of twenty-three, with ten years of danger and excitement before me? But I like the way she looks at me when I talk of the battles I have seen, and the ships I have captured. She is a very intelligent girl.'

'Ah, I see, you fancy her a Desdemona to your Othello, a young girl enraptured by your tales of adventure in far away lands. Now I understand.'

'I hope not,' I said with a laugh, taking a slice of beef as I found myself hungry after my walk. 'I am not a general, nor am I very much older than Anne. And if I ever show any inclination to strangle her, I hope you will knock me down! But come, Edward, I have given you my word I will not harm her. Indeed, I have no doubt my attentions will do her a world of good. They will give her confidence, and show her that her family's estimation of her worth is not a general thing.'

'If I had known your intentions were so charitable, I would not have objected in the first place. It is very kind of you to take such trouble over a downtrodden young lady,' remarked Edward ironically.

'Would you have me forgo the pleasure of getting to know her? You have always wanted safety, Edward, and I have never stood in the way of that, but I have always courted adventure. Let me make it where I may.'

'If you can find it at the assembly rooms, then you are welcome to it!' he retorted.

'Rest assured, I will.'

They may not be as stimulating as a naval battle, but my encounters with Miss Anne were proving to be just as enjoyable, in their own way.

Monday 16 June

I found myself thinking of the assembly with some anticipation, and as the afternoon wore on, I became impatient for the evening. I was disappointed when I walked into the rooms and saw that Miss Anne Elliot was not there.

I overcame my disappointment, however, and passed the first two dances pleasantly enough by dancing with Miss Riversage. Her wit made her an agreeable partner to begin with, but it descended into spite before the dance was over, and I was glad to lead her from the floor.

Miss Welling caught my eye, and I could not resist the unspoken invitation. Her elegant figure made her an agreeable partner, and her dancing did not disgrace me. On the contrary, not a few eyes followed us down the room. She had a great deal of charm as well as beauty, and entertained me with talk of art and books. I was about to continue our conversation at the side of the room, but her mother's speculative eyes upon me showed me that I was in some danger of being regarded as a suitor, and that was something I did not want.

So, after thanking her for the pleasure of dancing with her, I beat a hasty retreat.

'What! Are you afraid of Mrs Welling?' asked Edward, much amused at my sudden appearance by his side.

'She has a calculating look in her eye. I went into the Navy of my own free will, and I have no intention of allowing myself to be press-ganged into marriage,' I returned.

The next two dances I danced with Miss Bradley, whose company was all the more agreeable to me when I learned that she was all but engaged, and then I retired to the side of the room. As I took a drink from the tray of a passing footman, I found myself at the edge of two groups, and I could not help overhearing both conversations.

'. . . he is the best son a mother ever had. Ay, my Dick is a handsome lad, and as good as you could wish for,' said a proud woman of middle age, who was standing to my right.

A gentleman to my left was not so fortunate in his offspring.

'. . . the boy's always in trouble,' I heard him grumble. 'If it is not one thing, it is another . . .'

'. . . not that he is perfect,' continued the fond mother. 'I would not wish any mother a perfect son. He is not above a bit of mischief, but that is all it is, and what I say is, a boy isn't a boy if he doesn't get into mischief now and again . . .'

'. . . his mother is far too complacent, she refuses to see that the boy is getting out of hand and needs discipline. It is all very well sending him to school, but when he is at home in the holidays he is getting beyond control. I am all for sending him into the Army, or better yet, the Navy. That will stop him trespassing on other people's property . . .'

'. . . he can climb any wall, no matter how high. A boy should be able to climb, and he's so good at it, he never takes a tumble, but his father is always complaining . . .'

'. . . going into our neighbours' gardens and stealing apples . . .'

'. . . never takes anything from the tree, of course, it's nothing but windfalls, but his father will make a fuss . . .' she said.

'. . . fighting with the other boys . . .' remarked the father.

'. . . very good at his boxing, I do think it is so important for a boy to know the gentlemanly arts. Ah, yes, my Dick's a good boy . . .'

'. . . and I intend to pack Dick off to the Army or Navy before the year is out, whether his mother likes it or not . . .'

I began to laugh as I realized that the two sons were the same, viewed from a mother's and a father's point of view. I hoped Master Dick would not find himself in the Navy, where he would no doubt plague his captain—though if he was good at climbing he might, perhaps, be useful in the rigging!

I was about to return my empty glass to a passing footman when I caught sight of something much more interesting out of the corner of my eye: Miss Anne Elliot. She was being ignored by her father and sister, who were congratulating each other on their looks, and was standing quietly by their sides.

I went over to her.

'Something has amused you,' she said, when I had made my bow.

I told her about the excellent and troublesome son, and she told me that the happy couple was Mr and Mrs Musgrove, who lived in the Great House at Uppercross, and were newly returned from Clifton. She further enlightened me that Dick was the boy who had trespassed on my brother's property a few weeks ago.

'I had no idea this was such a place for criminal activity. You must tell me more about it whilst we dance, for I need to be prepared,' I said.

'You have not asked me yet,' she returned.

'Would you do me the honour?' I asked her.

'Thank you,' she said, making me a curtsey, and we went onto the floor in high spirits.

I danced two dances with her, and found that we drew many eyes, some curious, some pleased, and some—those of Sir Walter and Miss Elliot—contemptuous. Anne took no notice of them, however, for she never faltered, and I found her company as well as her dancing exhilarating. We never stopped talking, about art, about music, about her work in the parish and my life at sea.

I was forced to relinquish her hand to a lawyer, a dull fellow, when our dance was over, and then she danced with a baronet. I was far less pleased with this partner for her, and I found it hard to take my eyes from them.

'You had better look elsewhere,' said my brother, coming up to me. 'Your attentions are starting to be marked.'

'I may look at the dancers, I suppose. It is only what everyone else does.'

'The dancers, yes, if it is all of them, but you do nothing but look at Miss Anne—and scowl at her partners, I might add.'

'I do nothing of the sort.' I tried to turn my eyes away from them, but found it impossible. 'Who is he?' I asked.

'Sir Matthew Cruickshank. He is visiting relatives in the neighbourhood.'

'So he is not resident here?'

'No, he resides in Gloucestershire. He will be returning tomorrow.'

'He looks a very agreeable man,' I said, in high humour at the knowledge that he would soon be leaving, particularly as it was evident that he and Anne had exhausted their supply of pleasantries, and had nothing further to say to each other.

'Will you be taking her in to supper?' asked Edward.

'Of course.'

'Then make sure you talk to your neighbour at the other side of you as well,' he cautioned. 'You do not want to draw attention to yourself, or to her.'

'I hope I know how to behave.'

'So do I,' he remarked, and was then claimed by Mr Cox, who wished to introduce him to a young lady visiting relatives in the neighbourhood.

As I approached Miss Anne, I was gratified to see an increase in her animation as she saw me walking towards her, and to know that she wanted to go in to supper with me, as much as I with her.

I remembered my brother's words, and I engaged my neighbours in conversation, which was not difficult as the subject under discussion was a general one, that of Napoleon.

'There will be no easy victory, I fear,' said Miss Anne.

'On the contrary, the war will be over by Christmas,' asserted Sir Walter, showing no compunction in silencing her in front of the assembled company. I saw her flush, and I felt I would like to have Sir Walter on my ship for a few weeks, to show him the meaning of hard work and the value of respect.

As that was impossible, I came to Anne's defence, saying, 'I hope it may be so, but Napoleon is not the type of man to surrender, and his influence is spread so wide, that I believe the war will last for at least the next few years.'

She flashed me a smile of thanks, which more than recompensed me.

Sir Walter, however, was not pleased to be contradicted.

'Depend upon it, he will be defeated by Christmas,' he said, more firmly than before.

'Oh, yes, by Christmas,' said Miss Poole, nodding vigorously. 'You are so right, Sir Walter, I am sure it must be so. With our splendid officers fighting against him, it cannot be long before he sues for peace.'

Anne looked down at her plate, but I could see that she was smiling at Miss Poole's blatant flattery.

'I cannot abide to talk about war,' said Miss Elliot, stifling a yawn. 'It is the most boring of subjects. I believe we must have the yellow room redecorated, Papa, for Mr Elliot's visit. It is looking shabby, and besides, there is some wallpaper I have seen in Ackerman's Repository that would look very well. We should have the bed-hangings replaced, and a new carpet as well.'

'Yes, my dear, I believe you are right. We must not neglect to show him any courtesy, for we do not want him to think that Kellynch Hall is deficient in any way. As the heir presumptive, he will have a natural interest in its upkeep. I believe we should have the drawing-room redecorated as well.'

They continued to discuss their ideas for the improvement of their ancestral home, whilst Miss Poole nodded vigorously and interjected, 'Oh, yes!' or, 'How wonderful!' every few minutes, and I was free to turn my attention back to Miss Anne.

We had an interesting discussion of the latest books, comparing Scott's *Minstrelsy of the Scottish Border* with his latest work, *The Lay of the Last Minstrel.* It would have been less invigorating, however, if it had not been accompanied by her changing expressions, sparkling eyes and frequent smiles.

All too soon, supper came to an end. Reluctantly, I gave up her company as we returned to the ballroom, and I saw her dancing with a fellow called Lauderdale. I was introduced to two young ladies whose names now escape me, and I did my duty, partnering them on the dance floor, but my heart was not in it, and I made a poor companion.

The evening came to an end. I hoped to snatch a few words with Miss Anne, but it was impossible, and I could do no more than catch a glimpse of her as she left, looking as pretty as she had done when she arrived.

Tuesday 24 June

This morning brought a letter from Sophia.

'I wish our sister would not sail the high seas with her husband, but would settle down on shore,' Edward grumbled, as he took the letter from the salver. 'I do not say she should have remained at Deal, but she should have settled near here, in Plymouth, perhaps. It is a fine port, with some respectable houses, and she would not have been lonely, for I would have been able to visit her regularly.'

'As if the occasional visit from a brother could compensate her for the lack of a husband!' I snorted, as I helped myself to a plate of ham and eggs. 'She did not marry Benjamin only to part from him. You know how much she worried when he was away in the North. She could not sleep at night for anxiety about him, fancying him lying on deck, injured or dead, and in the daytime it was no better, for she could not eat because of the same fears. I stayed with her when I had a spell of shore leave, you will remember, and she had never looked paler or thinner. She suffered from all manner of imaginary complaints, and I believe she would have worried herself to death had she not decided to go with him the next time he sailed.'

'But the seasickness,' Edward protested.

'She never suffers from it, at least not after the first twenty-four hours, and there is no healthier life than a life spent at sea.'

'It must be very uncomfortable for a woman, whatever you say,' he remarked.

'Sophia is not just any woman, she is my sister, and she has her share of the Wentworth spirit—'

'Which I have not?' he interjected.

'We cannot all be the same,' I said kindly, feeling sorry for him that he did not have our bravery.

'Thank you,' he returned drily.

'Besides, I am beginning to think it is a good thing you have no taste for the ocean. With our parents dead and Sophia at sea, where would I go on my shore leave if you were not on dry land?'

'I am glad I can be of service to you. I took the curacy on purpose,' he remarked, as he spread out the letter next to him and helped himself to another rasher of ham. 'I confess, though, that she seems happy. I thought she would soon tire of the life, and urge her husband to put her ashore, but her letter is cheerful enough,' he went on, beginning to read it to me.

'And why should it not be? Think of all the places she has seen, and all the things she has done. She has experienced far more of life than she would have done if she had married Mr Wantage, as you wished.'

'I? Wish her to marry Mr Wantage? You jest. I never liked him. It is just that I thought she would be safer with a lawyer than a sailor. Even now, I cannot think a warship is a suitable accommodation for my sister.'

'There is nothing finer. She will live like a queen,' I assured him.

He continued with the letter, in which Sophia mentioned my visit and said that she hoped I had arrived safely, before passing on her hopes that I would soon be given a ship of my own, then she concluded her letter with her best wishes for our health and happiness.

Having finished his breakfast, Edward penned a reply. I added a postscript and it was sent without delay.

'Though when it will reach her, I am sure I do not know,' he said.

'Depend upon it, it will be welcome whenever it arrives. There is nothing better than a reminder of home when one is on the other side of the world. It brings back pleasant thoughts of friends and family, and is treasured up to be read again in quiet moments.'

We talked over our plans for the morning, and I left my brother to his parish duties whilst I set out for a ride. It took the edge off my energy, and this afternoon I went into town to see to some business. I had hoped for an outing this evening, but, no invitations having been issued, I spent a quiet evening with my brother, playing chess. It was a novelty, but, I confess, many such evenings would try my patience sorely. It is a good thing my brother went into the church, and not I!

JULY

Wednesday 2 July

I was walking through the village this morning, when I was agreeably surprised to turn a corner and find myself following Miss Anne Elliot. She was in company with her sister, Miss Elliot, and Miss Shepherd. They stopped outside Clark's shop, there was some conferring, and then Miss Elliot and Miss Shepherd passed into the shop and Miss Anne crossed the road, walking towards a small cottage.

I recognized it as the house of Miss Scott, and guessed that Miss Anne was going to pay her respects. I turned my steps in the same direction and we arrived on the doorstep together. She looked up, surprised, and I made her a bow, remarking that we seemed to be intent on the same purpose. She smiled, and we exchanged pleasantries. She was looking remarkably well, with a bloom on her cheek and a look in her eye that showed me she was not averse to teasing me if the occasion arose.

I was just about to make some remark when we noticed that the door was ajar. Miss Anne looked at me questioningly and I pushed the door open, whilst Miss Anne called out our names so as not to alarm anyone in the house.

We went in, expecting to find the maid, but no one was there, and so we went through to the parlour, where we were confronted by Miss Scott, brandishing the poker.

'Oh, my dear, I am so sorry, I thought you were Napoleon,' she said.

She returned the poker to its place by the fire, whilst Miss Anne behaved as though she was mistaken for the scourge of Europe every day, and asked Miss Scott how she did.

'Very well, I thank you, my dear. It is very good of you to call.'

Miss Anne remarked on the open door, and Miss Scott tutted, and said she had had problems with her new maid, a young girl who spent more time flirting with the baker's boy than she did in attending to her mistress.

We sympathized with her, and Miss Anne promised to speak to the girl.

'My dear, I will be so grateful, for I am sure she will listen to you. I have told her until I am blue in the face that the French will be here at any moment, but she does not believe me.'

She went on to regale us with an account of her ailments and her sister's ailments, before asking after Sir Walter's health, Miss Elliot's health, Miss Anne's health, and Miss Mary's health.

Miss Anne and I eventually took our leave, and we had just reached the doorstep when my brother happened by. I was disappointed, for I would have liked to savour my last few minutes alone with Miss Anne, but I hid my feelings, and my brother and I escorted her back to the shop together. We parted from her outside, she to go in to her companions, and we to continue on our way.

'It was very noble of you to call on Miss Scott,' said my brother, as I walked on with him, 'or could your visit have had another purpose?'

'It was entirely prompted by charity,' I told him.

He did not believe me, but he let it pass, and we went to luncheon together.

Friday 11 July

This morning brought a letter from Harville, telling me that his beloved Harriet had accepted his proposal, and that they had agreed to marry at the start of September.

'Will you go to the wedding?' Edward asked me.

'Certainly. He asked me to stand up with him.'

'He seems rather young for such as undertaking. He is no older than you, I believe, and you are only three-and-twenty. It is far too soon to be taking a wife.'

'I agree with you, and I have told him so, many times, but he is determined on the match, and nothing I can say will change his mind.'

'Can he not put it off? He would do better to enter into an engagement than a marriage at his time of life. Marriage brings with it burdens and responsibilities, and they would only weigh him down.'

'He has a distrust of long engagements, and, having made up his mind, he feels that he cannot marry too soon, for he could be called back to sea again at any time. I dare say that Harriet does not want to wait any more than he does, and if they miss this opportunity, who knows when he will be at home again? He asks me to go and see him, so that I can meet Harriet,' I said, folding my letter. 'I will go next week, if you are agreeable.'

'Pray do not consult my wishes, I am only your host.'

'You may pay me back when I buy my estate,' I said. 'You may visit as often as you like, and come and go as you wish, without ever giving me word.'

'When you but your estate, if you want to please me—'

'It will be my first consideration.'

'—I beg you to buy one with a living attached, and give it to me,' he said. 'Waiting for one to fall vacant is slow work, and with no one to speak for me, I fear I will be a curate 'til I am seventy.'

'I will do my best,' I promised him.

'And make sure it is a good living, with a fine house attached, nothing poky or dark, with plenty of land.'

'Have you anything else to add?'

'I would not object to a stretch of river, and a fine library.'

'And a house in town as well, I suppose.'

He laughed, and said that if he was dreaming, he might as well do it in style.

'Even so, I wish you might find promotion, and find it soon. Is there no one to speak for you?' I asked.

'The bishop is a friend of Melchester's wife—you remember Melchester? We were at Cambridge together.'

'Yes, I remember him. A stout fellow, with a liking for port. So will the bishop speak for you, do you think?'

'He will if he can, but he has his own relatives to think of first, and two of them have entered the church. So you see, it is not very promising.'

'And is there nothing you might do on your own account?'

'I am doing all I can. There are one or two possibilities. Mr Abbott, the curate of Leigh Ings, has just been given a living by one of his cousins, and I believe I have a chance of adding the vacant curacy to my own. The duties are light, and it would mean an increase in my stipend. There is also the possibility of a living in Trewithing becoming available, and as there is no one waiting for it, it might fall to me.'

I expressed the hope that it would be so, and then I set about making my arrangements for visiting Harville. I am looking forward to meeting Harriet, and seeing what sort of woman has won the heart of my friend.

Wednesday 16 July

We dined with the Grayshotts this evening, and after dinner the ladies entertained us with music. Miss Denton was persuaded to perform by her mother, and proved herself a great proficient. After being encouraged by her mother to play a second sonata, she relinquished the stool, entreating Miss Anne to play. More hesitantly, Miss Anne approached the instrument. Her father looked up as she began to play and I thought here, at last, was some evidence of paternal feeling, but he turned his attention back to his conversation and continued to talk through her performance. Miss Elliot did not even do that much, and never once glanced in her sister's direction.

As Miss Anne's song continued, I was drawn over to the pianoforte, for her voice was sweet and her playing showed a superior taste. I listened with pleasure, and when she had done, I asked her to favour us again. She looked surprised, then she flushed with gratification and began another song. I sang with her, and we entertained ourselves as well as others.

Friday 18 July

I went into town this morning, and on my return I happened to pass a small house, from which came the sound of wailing. I hesitated, but upon hearing Miss Anne's voice coming from inside I went in, and a strange scene met my eyes. A buxom woman was sitting in the corner of the room with her apron over her head, whilst seven children were rioting by the hearth. Miss Anne, having evidently just arrived, was speaking quietly but firmly to the children, who, it became plain, were arguing over a scrap of a puppy.

She picked the puppy up and cradled it in her arms, for it had been overwhelmed by the boisterous children. The older children jumped at it, but she reprimanded them until they stood quietly, then she soothed the younger children, who were in tears, and spoke bracingly to the woman, who, at last, emerged from behind her apron.

Within a few minutes harmony was restored, or what appeared to pass for harmony in the house, the puppy was placed in the loving arms of the youngest child, and Miss Anne and the woman had the luxury of looking round. This had the unwelcome effect of making my presence noticed.

'I heard a commotion, and wondered if I could be of any assistance,' I explained.

The woman said there was never a commotion in her house, I apologized, and I was about to leave when it transpired that Miss Anne was going into the village, and that the eldest girl was to go there also. I offered to escort them, they accepted my offer, and we set out together. The girl soon trailed behind, for which I was not sorry, as it meant I was able to talk freely to Miss Anne. I told her of my forthcoming visit to see Harville.

'We were at the Naval Academy in Portsmouth together,' I said. 'Two young boys, eager to be at sea. I can hardly believe it is ten years since I went there, at the tender age of thirteen.'

'You must have made many friends there,' she said.

'Yes, I did,' I told her. 'Benwick, Jenson and Harville. Benwick was younger than the rest of us, joining the academy later, in 1797, but somehow he became one of us. Not that we stayed in the academy all the time. We were put on board ships to gain experience, and very valuable it was.'

'It sounds exciting,' said Anne. 'Very different from my own schooldays.'

She asked me about my training, and about my time as a midshipman, and then she told me about her times at school: her lessons, her masters, her friends—Miss Vance, who had returned to Cornwall to live with her parents; Miss Hamilton, who had married a Mr Smith and gone to live a life of gaiety in London; and Miss Donner, who had married a country squire.

At last we reached the village. I made my bow and left the ladies, returning home to lunch.

Tuesday 22 July

I set out early and arrived at Harville's this afternoon. Harville greeted me warmly, and could not wait to introduce me to Harriet.

I found her to be a taking young thing, without the intelligence of Miss Anne Elliot, perhaps, and without her dark eyes, but pretty all the same. She seemed to be a degree or two less polished than Harville, but she was evidently very much in love with him, and I was glad to wish him all the happiness the occasion demanded.

I had little chance to talk to him of anything else, for when we returned to his lodgings, he would do nothing but sing Harriet's praises. In vain did I try to talk to him about our adventures, past and future, for after answering a question sensibly, he would then sigh, and say that Harriet had the prettiest eyes or the tiniest feet or the tenderest heart, and I spoke about battles in vain. I laughed at him for it, but he only bade me wait until I was in love, whereupon I remarked that if love made such fools of men, I would sooner not succumb. He smiled, and said he pitied me, and then said that Harriet's smile was brighter than the sun.

'You have missed your vocation. You should have been a poet,' I told him.

'Perhaps I will become one yet!' he said. 'I am sure poets have an easier time of it than sailors.'

'Though the pay is even worse,' I said.

He laughed, and said that, on consideration, he would remain with the Navy.

I tried to go to bed three times, but he would not stop talking, and it was late before I returned to my chamber. I fear I will have little rational conversation over the next few days!

Wednesday 23 July

Harville took great delight in seeing me with his friends and family, and I took no less delight in their company. I had not seen them for three years, and, with regard to his sister Fanny, it was longer, for she was at school the last time I visited. Her appearance was a surprise, for she was no longer a child but a young woman, and a very superior young woman at that. Her mind was cultivated and her wits quick. Her face and figure were such that I knew she would soon have many admirers, and I said as much to Harville.

He seemed much pleased, and to begin with I took it as nothing more than brotherly pride, but as the day wore on, I began to think it might have something more at its root, for when we went out for a stroll, Harville and his family gradually fell behind until I was walking ahead with Fanny alone.

Again, when we returned to the house, there were occasions when we found ourselves sitting alone, on account of the others moving to the far end of the room. In short, they were giving us an opportunity to get to know each other, and the reason was not difficult to find. Harville and I being great friends, and Fanny being seventeen, it was in their minds that we might, one day, marry. But, despite her superior mind and her undoubted beauty, she awakened nothing more in me than brotherly sensations, and I am persuaded that I awakened nothing more than sisterly feelings in her. Harville was sensible enough to see it, and, as we took a turn out of doors together after dinner, he soon gave up hinting at anything between us and returned to his favourite topic of conversation, Harriet.

I let him talk, and I did not begrudge him his happiness,

for we have always been the best of friends, but I am glad the visit will be over tomorrow. A man so newly engaged is not good company for anyone except the object of his affections!

Thursday 24 July

I spent the morning with Harville, Harriet and Fanny, and the three of us walked out into the country together. The sun was hot, and the ladies twirled their parasols over their heads as they went along. Harville and I teased them, saying that we had had no such shelter as we toiled under the strong sun of the Bahamas. We regaled them with tales of our water running low on board ship, saying that we often had to sail with parched throats, and by the time we returned to the house, we were all ready for a cooling drink.

I set out for Monkford late in the afternoon, leaving Harville and Harriet making plans for their wedding breakfast. The ride was enjoyable to begin with, as my way took me through varied countryside, but it was marred by a sudden downpour when I was three miles out of Monkford and I was glad to get indoors.

Edward was curious to know about Harville's chosen bride, and I satisfied him as to her character and habits as soon as I had changed out of my wet clothes.

When I had done, he remarked that, in my absence, we had been invited to a picnic, and that he had accepted on both our behalfs.

Saturday 26 July

I am getting to know the neighbouring countryside very well, and already I feel quite at home here. I had my ride this morning before breakfast, as usual, and, later on, I paid some morning calls. After lunch I went into town for a new hat. I had a faint hope that I might see Miss Anne Elliot. I have seen little of her recently, for she has not attended any gatherings at which Edward and I have been present—they have not been smart enough for the Elliots—but I did not have the good fortune to come across her.

Tuesday 29 July

I saw Miss Anne this evening and I was surprised to discover how much I had missed her company.

I was about to ask her if I could escort her in to dinner when, unluckily, my hostess asked me to escort Miss Barnstaple instead. I bowed, and declared myself delighted, but although Miss Barnstaple was an engaging companion, my eyes were constantly drawn to Miss Anne.

She was seated next to a young man who looked to be a perfect fool, the sort who would not know a mast from a yardarm. I thought she looked bored, but to my surprise, Miss Barnstaple said, 'Anne seems to be finding her partner amusing. He is much liked by the ladies, not surprisingly, for he is very handsome.'

I was not struck by his looks myself, for they seemed too

soft to me, and his conversation, snatches of which reached me in quiet moments, did not seem to be anything very remarkable. But I could not say so, for Miss Barnstaple might have construed my remarks—quite wrongly—as jealousy.

I could not help my eyes being drawn to his group from time to time, though, and I was gratified to find that Miss Anne's gaze sought me out on more than one occasion. This small circumstance raised my spirits and allowed me to flatter myself that she would rather be talking to me.

As soon as supper was over, dancing was announced, and I went over to her and asked for the pleasure. She smiled, declared herself delighted, and put her hand in mine. I felt a sense of pride as I led her towards the set that was then forming. It was small, for the room only had space enough for five couples, but I was glad of the opportunity it gave me to talk to her.

'I have not seen you for . . .' I was going to give an exact number of days, when I thought it might seem too particular, so I said, '. . . a while. Have you been mistaken for Napoleon again in the meantime?'

'No, not recently,' she said, as the music began. 'Miss Scott has seen very little of the newspapers, and has grown calmer as a consequence, so that she is able to think of other things. Only yesterday she told me she had planted three new shrubs in the garden.'

'Then you have escaped being attacked with the poker.'

'For the time being, until the next newspaper arrives,' she said. The dance parted us, but when it brought us back together again, she went on, 'You have been away, visiting a friend, I understand?'

I was pleased to know that she had noticed my absence, and I began to tell her about Harville. As I related his plans, for the first time it did not seem so strange to me that he had chosen to shackle himself at an early age, and I supposed the change in my opinion must mean I was getting used to the idea; either that, or, having met his Harriet, I thought they would be happy together.

When I had finished telling her about Harville, I asked her casually, 'Who was the young man you were sitting next to at dinner? I do not believe I know him.'

'That was Mr Charles Musgrove,' she said.

'And is he a particular friend of yours?' I could not help asking.

'His family and mine are closely acquainted. The Musgroves live at the Great House at Uppercross.'

'Ah, a family friend,' I said, relieved. 'I remember his parents,' I continued, feeling suddenly in charity with young Mr Musgrove, and inclined to be expansive. 'I overheard them once, talking about another son of theirs, Dick. Do they have any other children?'

'Yes, they do, but they are all younger than Charles, and still in the schoolroom.'

As we talked, I noticed a well-dressed woman at the far side of the room, who was watching me with unfriendly eyes. I was surprised, and turned away, but I was conscious of her eyes on me for the rest of the dance.

When it was over, I reluctantly relinquished Miss Anne's hand and returning to my brother, asked him, 'Who is that lady?'

'Which one?'

'The one over there, on the other side of the room, well dressed, in an amber silk. Do you see her? She has been watching me as a captain watches an unpromising midshipman, and I am sure I cannot think why. It is impossible for me to have offended her in any way, for I do not know her, indeed I have never spoken to her in my life.'

His eyes turned towards her, and he said, 'That is Lady Russell.'

'The widow who was destined by her friends to marry Sir Walter Elliot, after his wife died?' I asked.

My brother nodded.

I was thoughtful, but still could not think why she had been watching me with hostility.

'I could understand her looking at me like that if I was Miss Cordingale or some other young beauty, and was intent on stealing Sir Walter away from her,' I said, 'but as that is not the case, I cannot think what she is about.'

'Can you not? Then I will tell you. She is an old friend of the Elliot family, indeed, she was Lady Elliot's best friend, and she is Miss Anne's godmother. She has taken an interest in the Elliot girls for the last five years, since Lady Elliot's untimely death, and she is especially fond of Anne, who favours Lady Elliot in both appearance and character. She is concerned that you are paying her too much attention.'

'Ah, I see, she is worried that my intentions are not honourable,' I said, understanding the dark looks she had been casting in my direction.

'Quite the contrary, she is worried that your attentions *are* honourable. She wants something better than a commander for her god-daughter.'

I was affronted, but quickly came about.

'She need have no fear. I do not have marriage in mind,' I remarked, although, as I said it, I thought there would be worse fates than to marry Miss Anne Elliot.

'Then I would advise you to be more circumspect. You are singling Miss Anne out for your attentions, and it will soon be noticed by other eyes than mine. You must not make her the subject of gossip, Frederick.'

'I have scarcely seen her this last fortnight,' I protested.

'But you are making up for it this evening.'

'I have danced with her only once, and I sat next to Miss Barnstaple at supper.'

'But you did not look at Miss Barnstaple as you look at Miss Anne, with such absorption. No, do not bite my head off,' he said, as I began to protest, 'all I am saying is that you should take care. You are not on the high seas now, but in a country village, and you must be careful of her reputation.'

'I will avoid her for a week, if that is what you wish,' I said jovially.

'It might be sensible,' my brother said.

I had not expected him to agree, for I had spoken in jest, and I felt all the irritation of a person who has to carry through a promise that was not made in earnest. I had to watch Miss Anne accept the hand of Mr Charles Musgrove, and had to offer my own hand to several other young ladies who interested me not at all, in order to reassure my brother—and Lady Russell, whose eyes still turned towards me from time to time.

One such partner was Miss Elliot. I could not help thinking that an Elizabeth was a poor substitute for an Anne, but she was presented to me as a partner in such a way that neither of us could refuse, and it was difficult to know which of us felt they had made the worse bargain: Miss Elliot, who was forced to dance with a sailor, or I, who was unable to prevent myself from comparing Miss Elliot with her far more agreeable sister.

However, I achieved my purpose, for I had protected Miss Anne from gossip, and Lady Russell eventually looked away.

'Lady Russell does not seem to watch Miss Elliot as jealously as she watches her sister,' I remarked to my brother, when the dance was over. 'She seems to have no apprehensions there. I suppose it is because Miss Elliot would never condescend to join herself to a mere sailor?'

'That, and the fact that Miss Elliot is self-destined for the heir presumptive, William Walter Elliot, Esq.'

'Ah, I see. By marrying him, she will retain her position as the first lady of the neighbourhood, and she will also retain her home on her father's death. And does the heir presumptive know of her plan?'

'He must have some idea, for Sir Walter and Miss Elliot have twice sought him out in London, whither they bend their steps every spring. On each occasion, they invited him to Kellynch Hall. His coming was spoken of as a certainty the first time, and we all looked forward to seeing him here. We were eager to meet him, for it would have fuelled many a pleasant evening's conversation, when there was little else to talk about. The gentlemen could have contented themselves with talking over his habits, whilst the young ladies' mothers could have put all their ingenuity into schemes for taking him away from Miss Elliot. It was the dearest wish of all of them that they should secure him for one or the other of their daughters. But alas, he disappointed us all, and he did not come. He was invited again the following year, but again he did not arrive. I do not believe Miss Elliot has quite despaired of him, nor do I believe she will, not until she knows him to be lost forever by virtue of his taking another to wife. But he does not seem to be in any hurry to visit Kellynch Hall.'

'Is he a young man?' I asked.

'I believe so. He is engaged in the study of law.'

'Then he is young indeed. It is no wonder that he does not wish to saddle himself with responsibilities at so early an age—though perhaps it is strange that he means to fit himself for a profession when he is destined to inherit so much.'

'It will not be for some time. Remember, he will not inherit anything until Sir Walter's death, which will not be for many years, and even then, he might be robbed of everything at the last, for it is possible that Sir Walter will remarry and produce a son.'

'Thereby depriving Mr Elliot of his inheritance,' I said

thoughtfully. 'He is prudent then, Mr Elliot, and does not rely upon his expectations, but, rather, he wishes to secure a future for himself, irrespective of his claims. I like him.'

'How can you say so? You have not even met him. He might be a scoundrel,' said Edward.

'My dear Edward, if he is training for the law, then of course he is a scoundrel, but he is not an idle scoundrel, at least!' My eyes turned to Miss Elliot again. 'Does Miss Elliot know he is studying for the law?'

'Indubitably. But she expects him to give it up, no doubt, if he marries her. Perhaps we may see him in Uppercross yet.'

I wondered what such a marriage would mean for Miss Anne. Would she be more thought of by her father, if her sister was married, or less? I was tempted to ask her to dance again, but mindful of my brother's caution, I danced with Miss Shepherd instead. I relinquished her to a Mr Clay, who was staying in the area, when the dance was over, and performed my duty by dancing with a number of other young ladies before it was time to go home.

AUGUST

Tuesday 5 August

I have kept my word to my brother, and I have not seen Miss Anne for a week. As the Elliots do not intend to go to the picnic, that will account for another few days out of her company, and after that, I believe I may safely speak to her again without arousing suspicion.

Friday 8 August

There was a heat haze shimmering over the fields when I rose this morning. It made me wish for the sea, for there is nothing better than a fresh ocean breeze on a hot summer's day.

I rode out before breakfast and revelled in the feel of the wind on my face. It reminded me of the exhilaration of standing on the prow of a ship in the early morning, with the air rushing by, and I found myself wondering which ship I would be given to command. I felt myself growing restless for a return to the sea. My own ship! My own crew! A new life, and new challenges, with all the world before me, mine for the taking.

When I returned home, however, my restlessness vanished, for my brother remarked that the Elliots would be joining us on the picnic after all.

'It seems they have heard a rumour that Mr William Walter Elliot will be in the neighbourhood of our beauty spot, and they wish to stage an accidental meeting, no doubt to invite him to Kellynch Hall again,' he said.

'Where do you hear such things?' I asked him in surprise.

'I have just come back from a visit to old Mrs Winters, who is bedridden, and who always enjoys my company. Her daughter is a maid at Kellynch Hall, and, it being her afternoon off yesterday, she told her mother all about it.'

'Do servants know everything?' I asked.

'You have been too long at sea if you do not know the answer to that question!' he said.

'It will be interesting to see him, and to see how he behaves,' I said thoughtfully. 'Will he welcome the meeting or will he be annoyed by it, do you think?'

'He will be surprised, whatever the case, and surprises are always awkward things,' said Edward. 'I wish they had stood by their decision not to come.'

I could not agree with him, and so I kept my peace.

We set out, I riding my chestnut and my brother on a hired mount. I offered to buy him something better with the remains of my prize money, but he would not hear of it, saying he rode seldom and could not afford to keep a horse even if I gave one to him.

We joined the rest of the party in the centre of Uppercross, and set off in procession. I resisted the urge to ride beside Miss Anne's carriage, though I was sorely tempted, for she was wearing the freshest gown of white muslin. I noticed her hands particularly, in their white gloves, and I thought how I could easily enfold both of them in one of mine. My eyes rose to her face, which was framed by her hat, and I thought I had never seen her look more enchanting.

When we arrived at the beauty spot, I could wait no longer and, having given my horse into the care of one of the grooms, I went over to her and asked her how she had liked the journey.

'Was your carriage comfortable?' I asked her.

'Yes, thank you,' she said with a smile.

'You were not jolted over too many potholes? That is the worst of a dry summer, the roads are rutted and full of holes.'

She assured me she had not been thrown about.

'Would you care for a walk?' I asked her. 'It is refreshing, after an hour spent in a carriage.'

'Yes, I believe I would.'

I offered her my arm. She took it, and as her fingers closed about it, I found myself rejoicing in the day; so much so, that Lady Russell's disapproving look did not pierce my glow of happiness.

'You have been here before?' I asked her, as we began to take a stroll, whilst the servants took the rugs out of the carriages and the grooms took the horses out of the shafts.

'Yes, several times. The view from the top of the hill is renowned for its beauty. It draws people from miles around, particularly in the summer months when the fields are at their brightest.'

'Then let us go and see it.'

I was hoping that the others would find the prospect of a walk up the remainder of the hill too much, but the Pooles and the Laynes fell in with us, saying that they felt the climb would be worthwhile in order to see the view. We set out together, whilst the rest of the party contented themselves with strolling beside the picnic spot.

Mrs Layne grew tired before we reached the top, and she and her daughter said that they would remain where they were and join us again on our way down. Miss Anne and I, together with Mr and Mrs Poole, went on to the summit. The view was indeed splendid, showing us the land for miles about, and, far off in the distance, we could just make out the shimmer of the sea.

'It must be strange for you to find yourself on land after so long at sea. Do you miss it?' Miss Anne asked me.

'Yes, I do,' I admitted. Then I turned to look at her. 'But not at this moment.'

She flushed, and looked down, and I thought she had never looked prettier.

Mrs Poole quoted a few lines of poetry. Mr Poole said,

'Quite, quite!' and then, having looked our fill, we set off back down the hill again.

We were soon joined by the Laynes. They were refreshed by their rest but, as Mrs Poole was by this time growing fatigued, they walked slowly, so that they could indulge her with conversation. Miss Anne and I outstripped them. Having already talked of the countryside and the weather, we had a chance for something more interesting, and out conversation turned to other outings and visits we had experienced. This led to our speaking of London, where I had been many times.

'I would like to see London,' she said.

'But you have been there, surely?' I asked.

'No, never.'

I was astonished.

'But I thought you went there every spring?'

'No. My sister and my father go, but not I,' she replied.

'This is monstrous! You must have your share of the pleasure as well as they. The next time they go, you must go with them.'

'They will not wish it.'

'And are their wishes the only ones to be consulted? You must tell them to take you.'

'It would be impossible,' she said.

'Nonsense. There is nothing easier,' I returned.

'For you, perhaps, but not for me. I am not a naval commander. I am not used to giving orders, nor to having them obeyed.'

'Then it is time you became used to it. You may start with

me. Give me a command, and I will obey it. You will soon learn how easy it is.'

She smiled, but only shook her head and said nothing.

'I am waiting,' I told her playfully.

'I cannot think of anything,' she said.

We were nearing the picnic spot, where the food was already laid out. Our fellow picnickers were gathered together, sitting on rugs beneath a shady tree, and waiting only for our arrival so that the picnic could begin. Sir Walter and Miss Elliot were sharing a rug with Lady Russell, Mr and Miss Shepherd. Miss Scott was on a second rug with Mr and Mrs Oldham, whose three young children were playing nearby, and two further rugs were vacant.

I led Miss Anne to a vacant rug, where we were joined by the Laynes, whilst the Pooles went to sit with the Oldhams. There were the usual pleasantries as the rest of our party asked us how we had liked our walk, and what we thought of the view, then the gentlemen began to serve the ladies, giving me the perfect opportunity to continue with my theme.

'Miss Anne, what would you command me to bring you?'

She smiled, and said, 'A little chicken, if you please.'

'Are you sure you would not rather have the artichoke pie? It looks very good.'

She hesitated, then caught my eye and said, 'No, thank you. A little chicken.'

'Or perhaps the lobster? There is nothing better than lobster on a hot day, it is very refreshing. Let me tempt you, Miss Anne.'

'Thank you, no, I will have some of the chicken.'

'The cold beef looks very good—'

'Commander Wentworth, bring me some chicken,' she said severely.

'There,' I said with a laugh, 'that was not so difficult, now, was it?'

'With you, perhaps not,' she said.

'You need only a little more practice, and you will not find it difficult with anyone. You have only to speak boldly, and not stop until you have carried your point. If you apply yourself to my teachings, you will visit London, with all its many attractions, the next time your father and sister go there!'

I saw Lady Russell's mouth harden as she watched us, and I knew that she was displeased to see how much time I was spending with Miss Anne, and how much Miss Anne was blossoming in my company, but I took no notice, for I was far more interested in seeing the colour spring to Miss Anne's cheeks, and in seeing her eyes glow.

Our conversation being remarked by more than Lady Russell, however, I began to join in with the general talk, praising the food, the fineness of the day, and remarking on the pleasure of eating out of doors with friends.

When we had all eaten our fill, we split into different parties. Miss Scott went into the neighbouring copse to collect wild flowers, the Shepherds took a stroll down the hill, and the rest of the party remained on the rugs beneath the trees, answering riddles in a desultory fashion, as befitted a hot afternoon.

Mr Layne had just posed a riddle when Mr Poole, happening to look in the direction of the copse, said, 'Hullo! What is this?'

I followed his gaze, and saw Miss Scott running towards us in a state of agitation.

'The French,' she cried, as she approached us, waving her arms. 'Oh, heaven help us, do something, someone! Commander Wentworth! The French are here!'

I was immediately alert and sprang to my feet, taking command of the situation.

'The French? Where?' I asked, wondering if a group of spies could have penetrated our defences and even now be roaming the countryside.

'On the other side of the copse!' she said, gasping with a shortness of breath.

'How many?'

'A whole army of them.'

'An army?' I asked incredulously. 'Come, Miss Scott, how many did you see?'

'Well, just the one,' she admitted, 'but where one is, the rest cannot be far behind. Oh, Commander Wentworth, whatever shall we do?'

'Show me,' I said. 'But go cautiously.'

Flustered, she set off for the copse. I followed, and a trail of picnickers followed me.

'As soon as I saw him, I knew,' said Miss Scott, as she led the way through the copse and emerged on the other side.

The trees gave way to open fields and I scanned the area,

but saw nothing. My eye alighted on a high hedge with a man leaning over it, eating an apple. I was about to approach him and ask if he had seen anyone, when Miss Scott said, 'There he is, over there. He is over ten feet tall, just as it says in the newspapers, and a good thing I read them, for otherwise, I would not have known him for what he was.'

'Oh, Miss Scott . . .' said Anne, with quivering lip, as she came up behind me.

'Which newspaper have you been reading?' I asked her, as the 'Frenchman' continued to eat his apple, unaware of the alarm he had occasioned.

'The one my sister sends me, and I am glad she takes the trouble, otherwise I might have approached him unawares and been murdered ten minutes since.'

'I think such fears might be precipitate,' I remarked, leading the way to the far side of the hedge.

Miss Scott was astonished to see that, so far from being ten feet tall, he was no more than five feet six inches, and standing on a ladder.

'Good morning,' I called up to him.

'Morning,' he returned.

'And a fine morning it is.'

'Arrr,' he agreed.

I engaged him in lengthy conversation, and through his thick country burr I was able to discern that he was just finishing his lunch, prior to returning to his task of trimming the hedge. The rest of my party laughed, and gradually dispersed, and at last even Miss Scott's fears were soothed.

'Thought it is a mistake anyone could have made, I am sure,' she said, as she walked with Miss Anne and myself back to the picnic spot, 'for he certainly looked to be ten feet tall, and as everyone knows, the French are giants.'

'Rest assured, they are no taller than the English,' Miss Anne soothed her.

'Oh, my dear, you mean well, I am sure, but you have never been to France, so how can you possibly know?'

Miss Anne was dumbfounded by this logic, so I said to Miss Scott, 'You may rest assured, ma'am, that I have seen many Frenchmen, and I have yet to see one over six feet tall.'

She demurred; she doubted. But at last, saying, 'Well, if you say so, Commander, then perhaps it is so,' she relapsed into murmurs of relief.

On reaching the picnic spot, we settled down on our rugs once more.

Miss Elliot took no interest in the riddle game which resumed, professing herself bored. She, together with her father and Lady Russell, had not joined the trail of those eager to see the 'French', but had remained aloof. She yawned, and stood up, saying it was time to go home.

It was not difficult to see why she was dissatisfied, for there had been no sight of Mr Elliot, nor anyone unconnected with our party.

The day drew to a close. Disturbed by Miss Scott's alarms and Miss Elliot's remarks, the game lost its sparkle, and the Pooles and Shepherds began to speak of departure, too.

At last everything was gathered together, and nothing remained to show what an enjoyable day we had spent there, save a patch of shorter grass where the horses had grazed.

I handed Miss Anne into the carriage. Ignoring my brother's looks and the looks of Lady Russell, I rode beside her, entertaining her and being entertained by her in equal measure along the way.

We parted at last, when her carriage turned into Kellynch Hall, and I was left to reflect on one of the most enjoyable days I had experienced for a long time.

Saturday 9 August

'I see you ignored my advice yesterday, and singled out Miss Anne,' my brother said, when he had completed his parish duties. 'It is a good thing you are going to Harville's wedding next week, for at least that should keep you out of harm's way.'

I was annoyed by his interference, but I reminded myself that he had my best interests at heart, for I was conscious of having been the subject of one or two pairs of curious eyes, as well as those of Lady Russell, as I rode beside Miss Anne on the way home.

And now, as I sit here at my desk, looking out of the window over the fields surrounding my brother's house, I feel myself torn as I have never been in my life. A part of me wants to spend all my time with Miss Anne, and yet another part of me feels I should be more circumspect, for she will have to face her neighbours when I am safely back at sea.

And yet, although I am aware of a longing to feel the spray on my face, I am conscious of a growing reluctance to leave the neighbourhood, for Miss Anne is becoming increasingly important to me.

I never expected to find such a woman when I first came to Monkford, for who would expect such a jewel to be tucked away in the country? Or that I would be the man who could make her shine?

Monday 18 August

I accompanied my brother into Uppercross this morning, and as we walked past the Great House I saw Miss Anne, Lady Russell and Mr Charles Musgrove coming towards us.

There was something about Mr Musgrove's closeness to Miss Anne that I did not like, and I said to Edward, 'Here are three of our neighbours. I believe the Elliots and the Musgroves are family friends?'

'They have certainly been long acquainted,' my brother agreed.

There was a hint of ambiguity in his reply that I did not like, but I thought it better not to refine too much upon the matter. If I pursued it, I felt Edward would look at me askance. But I could not help noticing that Lady Russell did not look at Musgrove with the same jaundiced eye she turned on me.

I said as much to Edward.

'She likes him well enough in a general way, but if you are meaning that she approves of him as a suitor for Miss Anne, I think you are mistaken. Lady Russell is not eaten up with pride, like Sir Walter, but she knows the value of rank, and I believe she looks higher for her god-daughter. I do not believe she will encourage the match.'

'He is not a bad sort, I dare say,' I remarked, generous once I knew he was not a suitor. 'He is well enough looking, and the property of Uppercross is not negligible. He will probably suit Miss Welling.'

'You seem very anxious to find him a wife,' said Edward, amused.

'It is with Harville marrying. It has set my thoughts running on matrimony,' I returned.

Her party drew close and we exchanged greetings. My brother and I fell in with them, for we were all going to the high street, and we walked on together. I could see that Lady Russell was not pleased to have met with us, and she endeavoured to engage my attention, leaving Miss Anne to Charles Musgrove. But I was not to be deprived of Miss Anne's company. I asked her for her opinion on three occasions, and paid attention to her answers, and before anyone could stop us, we were deep in conversation, from which we did not emerge until our paths diverged.

Edward said nothing to me as we went on our way, but he looked at me, and I knew what was in his mind. Again, I had singled out Miss Anne, and again given her my wholehearted attention.

'How long will you be away for Harville's wedding?' he asked me.

'I go tomorrow, and will be back on Wednesday night.'

He seemed satisfied, for he knew as well as I did that it meant I could not talk to Miss Anne before Thursday.

Tuesday 19 August

I set out early, at a leisurely pace, blessing my horse, who made light work of the hills along the way. I arrived to find Harville in a nervous state, for though he welcomed me warmly, his conversation was punctuated by bouts of high spirits and equally frequent bouts of reflection.

'You are not regretting it?' I asked him.

He looked surprised, and I was reassured, for he could not cry off, even if he wanted to.

'Not at all,' he said. 'I am looking forward to it. Only, I am conscious of the fact that, after tomorrow, my life will never be the same again. It has made me unsettled. I cannot see the future—but I dare say it will become routine soon enough. I am surprised you do not follow my example and marry, Wentworth. A bachelor's life is a dry existence. You should find a good woman, someone you can love and esteem, someone to think about when you are away at sea, and someone to come home to when you are on shore leave.'

'Not I!' I replied, though not as heartily as I would have done a month go. 'I am far too young for such a step, and I have too much of the world still to see. And as for shore leave, I can stay with my brother when I am home.'

'Not as comfortable as staying with a wife,' he said.

'That is true, but a brother is not as hard to leave behind.'

His family were gathered about him, looking forward to the celebration. Benwick and Jenson were there, too, and I thought how quickly the time had gone since we had all met at the naval academy.

'It is about time you made an honest woman of Harriet,' said Harville's brother, laughing at him. 'You have been sighing over her for long enough!'

'It is a grave responsibility,' said his cousin, shaking his head.

'You speak as though Harville was going to be burdened with command of the Navy, instead of being given the duties of a husband to one pretty woman,' said Benwick.

'At least I have my friends to defend me!' said Harville.

But his peace was short lived. The rest of his family joined in and he was subjected to as many opinions on marriage as there were men in the room.

At last he cried, 'Enough!' and begged us all to talk of something else.

But as I retired for the night, I could not put his words from my mind. *Follow my example and marry, Wentworth.*

At last, feeling restless and knowing I would be unable to sleep, I slipped out of the house. It was a beautiful night, with a balmy breeze, and I made my way by moonlight along the road. As I did so, I thought of how I had felt, a few months ago, when Harville had told me he intended to marry. I had been incredulous, thinking him a fool, for the world was full of pretty young women, and why should he want to swap the smiles of so many for the smiles of one?

But as I stood at the crossroads, I understood.

Wednesday 20 August

Harville was up very early, and full of nerves. He found it impossible to tie his neck-cloth and I had to do it for him. Then he could not get into his coat, and Benwick and I had to assist him. He could not settle to anything, and although we tried to talk to him about his next ship, and his certainty of capturing more prizes as soon as he went back to sea, he did not listen to more than one word in ten.

It was far too early to go to the church, but he insisted we set out, with the result that we waited fifteen minutes at the altar. I thought he would wear his hands away with all the clasping and unclasping he did!

At last Harriet arrived, looking radiant in a satin gown. The service began, and as I watched Harville make his vows, I found that I no longer pitied him. I envied him.

As we emerged from the church, Harriet's mother was crying, and Harville's mother and sister were crying, but Harriet was beaming with joy.

We went back to Harriet's house for the wedding-breakfast. After we had all eaten and drunk our fill, toasted the happy couple and made our speeches, the Harvilles set out on their wedding-tour.

Jenson, Benwick and I lingered on, enjoying the hospitality of Harville's family. Benwick seemed very taken with Fanny, whilst Jenson talked to Harville's parents and I spent the afternoon talking to Harville's brother. We relived our battles and looked forward to the battles to come, hoping we might, at some time in the future, find ourselves on the same ship.

And then, at last, it was time for me to leave. I bade them all farewell, and thanked them for their kindness. They sent me off with their good wishes ringing in my ears, and I rode home at a steady pace. The weather remained fine, and I was treated to a magnificent sunset on the way. I reined in my horse and watched the spectacle, seeing the sky turn crimson before the sun sank below the horizon. Then I set off again, arriving shortly after dark. Edward was reading the newspaper, but as I entered the room he laid it aside and asked me how I had got on. I told him all my news and he asked me a number of questions about the service. I satisfied him as best I could, and he allowed it to have been well done.

Then he told me his own news, which was not so happy, for the curacy of Leigh Ings had been given elsewhere.

'Never mind, there is still the living of Trewithing,' I reminded him.

'There is, and it would suit me better to have a living, rather than another curacy. I must hope for better luck there.'

'Do you think it will fall to you?' I asked.

'Nothing is certain,' he said, 'but as I have friends in the neighbourhood, and as I do not think there is any particular interest in the living, I think it possible.'

'It would be a very good thing if it did.'

'Undoubtedly. I would have my own parish, a larger house, an increased stipend, and I would be better placed to hear of any other livings that might fall vacant.'

'The church is not an easy profession for a man with no one to speak for him, unlike the Navy, where a man may prove his worth,' I remarked.

'But it is still not impossible to rise in the world,' he said.

'With Sophia well married, and I a commander, I would like to see you become a bishop,' I said.

He only laughed, and said he did not have my ambition. Nevertheless, he expressed his intention of walking into town tomorrow in an effort to learn more.

We said our goodnights.

As I mounted the stairs, my thoughts returned to Harville, now married, and realized that a part of my life had changed. He and I had been as brothers, but now he had moved on to a new life, and I felt a restlessness inside me, a longing to move on to a new life of my own.

Thursday 21 August

Edward walked into town this afternoon to learn all he could about the living at Trewithing. Whilst he was out, a note was delivered from Kellynch Hall, and I had to contain my impatience until he returned, for it was addressed to him.

'Upon my soul!' he exclaimed as he opened it. 'We are invited to dine with Sir Walter Elliot at Kellynch Hall.'

'There must be some mistake,' I said.

'See for yourself.'

He threw the note to me. Sure enough, it was an invitation.

'I thought Sir Walter did not like me,' I said in surprise.

'My dear brother, not every invitation that arrives is a compliment to you. It is possible that he wishes to see me. If he has heard of my hopes—but no, he would be no more interested in the rector of a small parish than he is in the curate of an even smaller one. He is simply being neighbourly, that is all.'

'Either that, or he needs to make up his numbers.'

'You are not a very trusting man, Frederick.'

'I have found it better to err on the side of caution when going into battle,' I replied.

'Sir Walter is surely no match for a man of your abilities,' he mocked me.

No, I thought, *but Lady Russell is.*

I could not help wondering if she was behind the invitation. Did she want to see me, so that she might have an opportunity of getting to know me, and of observing my behaviour towards Miss Anne at close quarters? Did she, perhaps, think that a commander might not be a bad husband for her favourite, after all? Or did she want an opportunity to warn me away?

Friday 29 August

'You seem to have dressed with unusual care,' remarked Edward as I joined him in his sitting-room, prior to our setting out for Kellynch Hall.

'Not at all. I am always carefully of my appearance,' I said, adding, 'as long as it does not involve wearing veils.'

The weather being fine, we decided to walk to Kellynch Hall. When we arrived, I had my first full sight of it, for although I had glimpsed it when walking by the river, I had never seen it from the front. As we walked up the drive, I thought it a very fine house, and said so to my brother.

'Something similar would suit me when I have made my fortune,' I said.

'I do not doubt it, but you have to make your fortune first,' he returned.

As we drew closer, I thought of Kellynch, not as a house, but as Miss Anne's home. For her, every tree and every blade of grass was familiar, every brick and every stone. As I lifted my eyes to the attic, I thought of her as a child, looking out of the barred windows of the nursery on to the green lawns. I thought of her growing up there with a loving mother, and then losing her mother and going away to school, and then returning to the countryside she loved, the restful greens and browns of the park, with the blue sky above. I imagined her playing the piano in the drawing-room and looking out of the windows on to the same verdant expanse, or walking there through the changing seasons as the leaves turned from light green to dark green, and thence to orange and gold.

The drive was long, but at last we reached the house. We were admitted by a stately footman in splendid livery, and then shown into the drawing-room. It was large and well proportioned, with fine furniture and new curtains and rugs. Everything was of the first quality, and showed the refined tastes of Sir Walter and Miss Elliot. But there was something missing, for all its grandeur, and that thing was warmth.

Sir Walter and his eldest daughter turned superior glances on me, and Lady Russell looked at me as though I was a snake: something that would be safe if kept at a distance, but which could be poisonous if brought too close.

But a moment later I forgot Sir Walter, Miss Elliot and Lady Russell, as my eyes fell on Miss Anne. She smiled as she saw me, and the smile lit her face with a joy so bright it filled the room. She radiated happiness and good will. She came forward to greet me, and the two of us were immediately lost in conversation, only being recalled to our company when Lady Russell stepped forward to greet my brother and myself. Sir Walter and Miss Elliot did their duty and greeted us, too. Then Lady Russell began speaking to me, in an effort, I am sure, to separate me from Miss Anne.

'We have been fortunate to have you with us in Somersetshire for so long,' she said, in a way that made me feel she did not think it was fortunate at all. 'You have more than one connection to the area, I believe? Your brother lives here,' she said, glancing at him, 'and I believe your brother-in-law is from the county as well?'

'Yes, that is so.'

'You have only the one sister?' Sir Walter asked me, deigning to join in the conversation.

'Yes.'

'She has been married long?' he continued.

'For seven years.'

'Quite some time. And what kind of man is her husband?'

'He is captain of a frigate.'

'Ah, a sailor,' said Sir Walter, with an expression of distaste.

'A naval officer, and a good one,' I returned. 'He has served his country for many years and has helped to keep our shores safe.'

'Is he at sea now?' asked Miss Anne, with genuine interest.

I softened at the sound of her voice.

'He is.'

'Your sister must miss him,' she said. 'It cannot be pleasant for a woman to be separated from the man she loves.'

'No, indeed,' I said, regarding her tenderly, for I felt her words were for me. 'Nor for a man to be separated from the object of his affections.'

My brother cleared his throat noisily, then said in a jovial tone, 'Fortunately neither of them has to endure the pangs of separation, as my sister sails with her husband.'

'But how is that possible?' asked Miss Anne in surprise, turning towards him. 'I cannot imagine how she would survive, with only ship's biscuits to eat, and a hammock to sleep in. She must be very brave.'

I laughed at her idea of life on board ship.

'You may rest easy. She has a cabin to sleep in, and all the comforts any woman could want. She has good food to eat, and a servant to wait on her—'

'A servant?' she asked. 'Surely such a thing is not possible?'

'Of course it is. Naval officers are gentlemen'—here Sir Walter and Miss Elliot exchanged expressions of disbelief, but I ignored them—'and they are used to living well. They expect no less when they are at sea.'

'I am surprised there is room for a servant, for there are so many other calls on the space, but living on board must not be as cramped as I had imagined.'

'On a frigate there is not very much space, I grant you, but my brother-in-law will not rest easy until he is in command of a man-of-war, and he will end up an admiral, I have no doubt. On a man-of-war, you know, there could not be better accommodations, or anything more spacious—'

'—unless it is a fine house on land,' said Lady Russell, entering the conversation with the air of one who has remained silent long enough. "That has far better accommodation than a ship, for it has spacious rooms, large gardens and ample servants' quarters, everything to make life convenient and easy.'

'But a house has not such views,' I said.

'The prospects at Kellynch Hall are very fine,' said Sir Walter, not to be outdone.

'But they cannot compete with the ever-changing views at sea, or the splendours of Lisbon, Gibraltar or the Indies,' I returned.

'As to that, these foreign places are overrated. They are nothing compared to London or Bath,' said Sir Walter.

I saw Anne's expression change, and I asked, 'You do not like Bath?'

'No, I must confess I do not.'

'Only a fool would not like Bath,' said Miss Elliot.

Anne flushed, but I encouraged her to speak, saying, 'But it is an interesting place, is it not?'

'Perhaps. But I did not like it. I found it hard and glaring, unlike the countryside, with its colourful softness.'

She evidently did not want to talk of it, so I turned the conversation back to the sights to be seen from a ship, and Anne listened with rapt attention. My eyes were on her, so that I scarcely noticed Lady Russell, Sir Walter and Miss Elliot watching us disapprovingly, until my brother caught my eye.

I allowed him to turn the conversation to books. Here again, Miss Anne joined me in feeling, as we discovered new evidence that our tastes coincided in all important matters, and, once more, we could not stop talking. It was only, indeed, dinner that put an end to our conversation.

Over dinner Miss Anne and I continued to talk of books, whilst Sir Walter recited his lineage to my brother, listing every one of his ancestors and remarking on the high standing of a baronet, whilst Miss Elliot talked determinedly of Mr William Walter Elliot, and their expectation of seeing him at Kellynch before the summer was over.

Lady Russell said little, but whenever I looked up, I found her eyes upon me.

Dinner at last came to an end. I wanted to dance, and I suggested it, but the idea was dismissed and I had to content myself with looking at Miss Anne, instead of touching her. At last her attention was distracted by her father, and Lady Russell took me aside.

'You are very taken with Anne,' she said.

'I am indeed,' I said, as my eyes lingered on her.

'She is a very young girl, only nineteen, and as yet she has seen very little of the world . . .'

'Which is a great pity, for the world is a wonderful place,' I returned, 'and she deserves to see it. Her father and sister go to London each spring, I understand, but they do not see fit to take her. She ought to see it, and to have her share of the enjoyment. The museums, the theatres and the shops are all worth seeing. I have told her that she must demand to be taken to London when her father and sister next go.'

'I do not think it a good idea for her to make demands, and I beg you will not encourage her. It does not sit well with her character, for it is not in Anne's nature to be strident,' she returned, looking at me with an unfavourable eye.

However, I did not mean to let her browbeat me.

'Then, if she is not to make demands, someone must

make them on her behalf,' I said, looking at Lady Russell pointedly, 'or else she will still have seen very little of the world when she is five-and-twenty.'

Lady Russell did not like my reply, and I could tell that she was less than ever my friend.

She rallied herself, however, and, with the appearance of one coming to the point, she said, 'You are a man of the world, Commander, and so I will speak plainly, in the certainty that you will not misunderstand me. Anne is very young and inexperienced, and is easily swayed by those around her. I do not wish to see anyone taking advantage of her youth or inexperience. In time, she will meet a man of her own standing who can give her all the advantages she is used to, and more besides. I am sure you do not mean to harm her by yours attentions—'

'You may rest assured, Lady Russell, that I would never do anything to harm her,' I said sincerely.

'Ahhh,' she said, nodding. 'Then you relieve me of a great burden. I am glad we are of one mind in this matter, I felt it must be so. A man of your experience could not think otherwise. And now, we need say no more about it. You will be returning to sea soon, I believe?'

'Yes, as soon as a ship is available.'

'And you are looking forward to it?'

'I am eager for it,' I said, 'for then I can set about making my fortune. I mean to leave the Navy a wealthy man.'

'I wish you success in your ventures,' she said. 'You are young and strong, you have ambition, and I hope you may achieve your heart's desires. We are fortunate to have such a man protecting our shores.'

She gave a slight nod and then moved away. To begin with, I was pleased with our conversation, for I felt it had gone well, but as I thought back over it, I was left with the unsettling feeling that we had, perhaps, been at cross purposes. There had been something ambiguous in her speeches, and, although mine had been straightforward, I nevertheless felt she might have misconstrued them.

But then Miss Anne approached, and Lady Russell was forgotten. We did not mean to ignore the others, but our minds were so well attuned that we scarcely noticed them until it was time for me to leave.

I bade Miss Anne farewell, reluctantly, and took my leave of Sir Walter, Miss Elliot and Lady Russell, then Edward and I left Kellynch Hall.

He was quiet on the walk, but once indoors he said, 'Frederick, I must speak to you once again about your attentions to Miss Anne. You scarcely said a word to anyone else all evening. Your attentions are far too particular. It would be better if you left Monkford and visited some of your friends for the next few weeks.'

'I would like to oblige you, Edward, but it is beyond me,' I confessed. 'I cannot give her up.'

'What kind of talk is this? A man who has taken French ships cannot do without the company of a nineteen-year-old girl? You have simply to take yourself off and the thing is done.'

'You do not understand me. Not only *can* I not give her up, I *will* not give her up,' I said, acknowledging the feelings that had been growing in me ever since meeting her. 'I never thought I would meet a woman like her: her mind so superior, her taste so refined, her heart so open; her hair so soft, her eyes so bright, her skin so smooth, her countenance so beloved; her voice, her smile . . . In short, Edward, I am in love with her.'

He looked at me in concern.

'You have paid attention to many young women in your time, but I have never heard you say that you were in love before. It is serious, then?'

'It is. I cannot live without her, and I mean to ask her to marry me.'

He shook his head.

'I cannot like it. You have nothing to offer her.'

'I have my prize money.'

'You have spent it.'

'I will make more.'

'Do you never see a problem?'

'Never one I cannot solve.'

He sat down heavily.

'I cannot encourage you in this, Frederick. You will not have the blessing of her family, or Lady Russell. They want to see her marry a man of wealth and rank, and with good reason. Her entire future depends upon her choice.'

'You do no think I am a good match?' I asked him, surprised and a little wounded.

His answer was matter-of-fact.

'You have a long way to go in the world before you are a good match for a baronet's daughter. You will encounter a great deal of opposition if you go ahead with your plan. They will not give her to you willingly, and they may not give her to you at all.'

'Opposition is there to be swept aside.'

'We are not talking of the French Navy now. You cannot sail up the drive in a frigate, nor can you de-mast Kellynch Hall. Sir Walter will not be afraid of you, nor will he surrender. If he is set against you, he will withhold his consent.'

'Then I will marry her without it.'

'And would Miss Anne consent to such a marriage?'

I hesitated.

'You see, you do not only have yourself to think of.'

'You take too dim a view of things,' I told him, rallying. 'Sir Walter has not yet withheld his consent, and until he does, I see no use thinking about it.'

'And are you sure Miss Anne will have you, even with it?' he asked.

'I . . .'

I stopped. I had been about to say, *I am sure of it. She loves me*, but what if I was wrong? For the first time in my life I was hesitant, and I did not like the feeling. But I could not rid myself of the thought. What if she did not love me? I could not bear to think about it.

'I think she loves me, and tomorrow I will know for sure,' I said.

'Tomorrow? Do you really think you will have an opportunity to speak to her so soon?'

'A man of action makes his own opportunities, he does not wait for them to come calling,' I said.

I thought of her early morning walks by the river, and I made up my mind to meet her there, and ask her to be my wife.

Saturday 30 August

I had a terrible night, even worse than the restless sleep before a battle, for I was kept awake by a mixture of excitement and anticipation.

I rose at half past five, for I could toss and turn in bed no longer, and then I dressed carefully. Eschewing breakfast, I lifted the latch and went quietly outside. I turned my steps towards the river. As I did so, my spirits rose. The morning was one of soft air and a warm sun on the rise. The world was aglow with blue and green, and sparkling with the dew that clung to the grass. It was a perfect morning for a proposal—if Anne said yes.

Unused to feeling such uncertainty, I quickly banished it. I walked by the river and then stopped to skim stones, until I caught sight of a kingfisher. I paused to watch its turquoise plumage flash past, iridescent in the early-morning light, and I saw it dive into the water. I took it as a good omen: a halcyon bird had come upon me, giving me notice that my own halcyon days were about to begin. I saw the warm, calm summer stretching ahead of me, with Anne by my side, and I was joyful.

I walked on, and at last I was rewarded by the sight of her. It was still early, no more than half past six, and I was elated to think that she, too, had not been able to sleep. She saw me; hesitated; and then came on.

I walked towards her, quickening my step, until I was almost running. She sprang to meet me and then we stopped, inches apart, and looked at each other as though we could never get our fill.

She spoke.

I interrupted.

'I can be silent no longer,' I burst out. 'I have watched you these many weeks . . . I have talked to you . . . danced with you . . . been enraptured by you . . . I cannot go on without knowing . . . Anne, my dearest Anne . . . I am in love with you'—and here I took her hands—'please tell me, put me out of my misery, are you in love with me, too?'

She blushed, looked down, murmured something I could not hear, looked up, and pierced me with such a glance that my heart stopped beating. I stepped back the better to see her, then caught her hands and raised them to my lips, and thought that a happier man had never walked the earth.

'Anne,' I said, 'will you be my wife?'

She smiled. She blushed.

'Yes, Frederick,' she said.

Yes, Frederick! Never had two words sounded better to me. 'When I go to sea, will you come with me? Should you like that, Anne?'

'Yes, I think I should like it very much. You have told me so much about your life that I am longing to see it for myself.'

'The wonders I can show you!' I said, anticipating the pleasures she would experience; imagining the adventure, the excitement, and the newness of it for her, who had never been beyond her own shores. 'The ever-changing moods of the sea, its mountains and valleys, its smooth, glasslike plains. And the ports you will discover. The colours, Anne! The vibrant reds and blues and greens, not the dull colours of an English summer, beneath an English sky, but the brilliance of the Mediterranean and the clear light of the Indies.'

'I am longing to see it all,' she said with enthusiasm. 'I will be as well travelled as your sister before many more years have passed.'

'Indeed you will. The stories you will have to tell when you return!'

She was aglow with the sheer excitement of it, asking me how hot it was in the Indies, and whether it ever rained; whether she would understand the people, and whether they would understand her.

And then we embraced, and walked on . . . I scarcely know what we did . . . where we went . . . what we said . . . I was in a haze.

The sun climbed in the sky, but still we walked, now talking, now silent, with the world all before us, until at last our steps took us back to Kellynch Hall. The sight of it reminded me of the formality yet to be endured, the disdain of Sir Walter, his raised eyebrows, his cold glance, but they were all a small price to pay for winning Anne's hand.

'I must speak to your father,' I said. 'I will speak to him at once.'

She shook her head.

'You are too late. He has gone to visit a friend for a week, and,' glancing at the sun, which was now high in the sky, 'he will already have left.'

I was not to be disheartened.

'No matter, I will speak to him as soon as he returns.'

'Until then, we will have to be circumspect in company,' she reminded me.

I agreed. I longed to publish my prosperous love, but the matter could not be spoken of in company until Sir Walter had given his consent.

'But what does it matter?' I said to her. 'For we can meet every morning by the river, and we know, dear Anne, that we are engaged.'

We walked on together as the sun climbed towards midday and it became hot, in the joyous manner of an English summer, until at last she said, 'I must go in.'

'Stay awhile.'

'It will soon be time for luncheon, and Elizabeth will be wondering where I am. If I do not go now, she will send a maid to find me, and then she will ask me where I have been.'

Reluctantly I agreed.

She turned to go; I pulled her back; we embraced; she turned again. I let her go, but I looked forward to the day when we would never be parted.

I watched her as she walked back to the hall, her muslin gown fresh and pretty in the morning light, her shawl slipping from her shoulder and falling into the crook of her arm, her hair curling in the nape of her neck, and then she disappeared from view.

I stood watching the spot, and then I roused myself and returned to my brother's house, full of high spirits. I could say nothing of my love to the world at large, not yet, but I could tell my brother.

He was not at home, and did not return until half past twelve. By that time I was bursting with the news and poured it out almost as soon as he entered the house.

'I have asked Anne to marry me, and she has said yes!' I told him.

'You ought to let a man have his luncheon before springing that sort of thing on him,' he complained, going through into the parlour.

'Are you not going to congratulate me?' I asked him, though I was so happy I scarcely cared.

'Has her father approved?'

'Not yet.'

'Then I will defer my congratulations until he does. Have you eaten?'

'What care I for food?' I said.

'If you are going to see Sir Walter, you had better care for it. You cannot go to see him on an empty stomach.'

'As he is away until Friday, I scarcely think it matters. Food taken now will not last until then, so I will defer my meal awhile yet. Besides, I cannot eat. I am too happy!'

He sat down.

'At the very least sit down, you are making me nervous.'

I sat down. I stood up. I paced the room. I laughed. I sat down. I stood up again.

'Lovers!' said my brother, taking up his newspaper.

'Edward, she is wonderful!' I said. 'The most beautiful creature I have ever laid eyes on—'

'Her sister is far handsomer.'

'And her manners—'

'Are no better than those of any other gently raised female.'

'Her love of books, her musical taste, her knowledge of the world around her, and her thirst for more. Her intelligence would put a schoolmaster to shame—'

'An easy thing to do,' he declared, 'for they have not one ounce of sense between them.'

'And her taste . . . we think alike on everything,' I said, not to be dampened.

'Then I pity you,' he remarked drily, 'for you will never have anything to talk about.'

I laughed at him.

'Never anything to talk about? We never stop talking! Have

I not brought you the most wonderful creature for a sister-in-law?' I asked. 'The most beautiful, refined, elegant young woman, superior in every way? With such taste and discernment, such ability and sense?'

'You have not brought her to me yet,' he reminded me.

But I could tell he was pleased, for he shook his paper three times before turning each page, and that was a sure sign of happiness with him.

I was in high spirits all day, and in no mood to spend a quiet evening indoors. I went out for a ride, cursing the fact that I had not been invited to the dinner-party that was claiming Anne's evening, but consoling myself with the fact that I would see her tomorrow.

Sunday 31 August

I met Anne by the river this morning, and we spoke at length, our conversation ranging from our neighbours, to books, to our wedding-tour. I would have lingered there all morning, but, reluctantly, we had to part in order to dress for church.

As I sat in my pew, I could not help imagining the day, not too far distant, when she would stand beside me at the altar and become my wife. It was a very pleasant daydream, and it helped to pass the time during the long and tedious service.

Why my brother chose to lecture his flock at such length on such a beautiful day I do not know, for I was longing to be out of doors. I was sure the rest of the congregation shared my feelings, for I had never heard so much shuffling and coughing in all my life!

Edward ignored them and did not let us go until he had spoken for an hour. He ended with a stern warning against trespassing and the stealing of apples, no doubt with a view to making sure his own orchard would be safe this year.

I was able to speak to Anne outside the church, and after exchanging pleasantries we embarked on a more satisfying conversation. It was cut short by the appearance of Lady Russell, who greeted me coolly and spirited Anne away, but I knew it would not be long before we were acknowledged lovers and could talk to our hearts' content.

SEPTEMBER

Tuesday 2 September

I hoped to see Anne by the river this morning but, like yesterday, the weather was wet, and although it did not prevent me from walking there, she did not come.

I returned home to a hearty breakfast, over which my brother told me that he needed some gloves from Clark's. He complained that he was too busy to go and I offered to go for him, for I was restless and could settle to nothing. Besides, if the weather cleared, I thought that Anne might venture out for a walk and I might see her at Clark's.

I soon found myself entering the shop. When I went in, Miss Scott was at the counter, and was deep in a conversation about bolsters.

'It must be a large one,' she said to Mr Green, who stood ready to serve her. 'A very big one indeed.'

She was shown two, but she was undecided on which one to take, and, seeing me, she asked for my help, explaining, 'My sister has sent me such a dreadful report in the newspapers, I am beside myself with worry. The article is written by a man with impeccable information. It comes from the most reliable sources, and it says the French are only days away from invading our shores. They have a secret fleet of ships, and as soon as they set foot on English soil, it is their intention to murder us all in our beds. There is, however, a way to confound them. The newspaper recommends its readers put a bolster in their bed, topping it with a set of false curls, and then sleep elsewhere. I am going to sleep on the sofa, but I do not know what size bolster to buy. Would you advise me, Commander?'

I could not help but smile. Her agitation was genuine, however, and to relieve her spirits I took her to one side and spoke to her in a whisper.

'This is not generally known,' I said, 'but you are obviously the sort of woman who can keep a confidence, and so I will tell you. The Navy is working on a plan to confound the invaders even as we speak. I am on a secret mission to this part of the country, and as soon as Napoleon invades, I will be informed of it at once. I will make sure you are apprised of the fact without delay, and you will have time to flee before he arrives. Until such time you may walk freely about the neighbourhood, and sleep safely in your bed.'

'Oh, Commander, you take such a weight from my mind, but are you sure? Your information will not be delayed? You will not forget to inform me?'

'Not at all. You may rely upon the Navy, and you may rely upon me.'

She returned to the counter and told the assistant happily that she did not require a bolster after all. I was just about to step up to the counter when the door opened and, to my delight, Anne entered, accompanied by Miss Shepherd.

Before I could speak, Miss Scott, on her way out of the shop, greeted her with the words, 'Miss Elliot, you may rest easy, as we are not about to be murdered in our beds. Commander Wentworth is on a secret mission in this neighbourhood. He did not hesitate to confide in me, for he knows I am not one to gossip and that I would never breathe a word to a living soul, and so he assured me that he will inform me as soon as Napoleon invades. You must not say anything about it, however, for it is not generally known, and if he had not had complete faith in my discretion, he would not have told even me. I must enjoin you to secrecy, and I hope I may have your word not to mention it to anyone.'

'You may rest assured I will tell no one,' said Anne.

Miss Scott left the shop, and as Miss Shepherd approached the counter in search of some thread, I was able to speak to Anne alone.

We fell into conversation instantly, and I was heartened to hear that Anne had intended to join me yesterday, despite the weather being wet, but her sister had not been well, and had claimed her attention, making it impossible for her to stir out of doors. She had been prevented from walking by the river for the same reason this morning, but her sister's health having improved a little since then, she had been glad to take the opportunity of a walk.

We could not talk of our engagement for fear of being overheard, but we were able to talk of our future in a more discreet form. I talked of the fortune I would win, and asked Anne her opinion of what sort of estate I should buy, whether in the country or by the sea. She advised me to buy one with a stretch of coastline and a sandy cove so that I could walk by the sea every morning.

'A good idea,' I said. 'I like the water. I always value my walks by the river here.'

She blushed, and looked prettier than ever, and I counted myself the luckiest man alive. I imagined the two of us walking together on the beach of our future home, with our children playing around us. I would be Admiral Wentworth, and she my wife.

Miss Shepherd finished choosing her thread, and Anne and I had to part, but I consoled myself with the fact that Sir Walter would be returning in a few days and that I could then ask him for her hand.

I longed for a ball this evening, somewhere where I could dance with Anne, but I was engaged to play whist with my brother. I could not concentrate, but this, however, made me very popular, as it meant that I lost every game.

Wednesday 3 September

Anne and I had the luxury of an evening spent together at Mrs Grayshott's, where we were able to dance together. It was a joy to be able to touch her, and to spend much of the evening in conversation with her, and although I was tempted to overstep the boundaries of decorum by asking her to dance a third time, I managed to restrain myself, knowing that Sir Walter would soon be returning, and that then I would be able to dance every dance with Anne.

Friday 5 September

I went, as usual, to the river this morning, and I was rewarded by seeing Anne coming towards me. We strolled through the fields, her arm in mine, and I asked her when her father was likely to return.

'He will arrive in time for dinner,' she said.

'Then I will present myself tomorrow morning, though I resent every minute that keeps me from acknowledging you as my future wife. Little did I think, when I came into Somerset, that I would find such happiness.'

'Nor I. Your visit was spoken of, and I was curious to see you, but I did not expect a friendship to develop, let alone anything more. I thought you would be a rough-mannered and impatient man, a sailor who thought of nothing but battles and the sea. I did not expect you to be someone I could fall in love with.'

We walked on. I spoke of my impatience for her father's return, and I asked her if she had told Lady Russell of our engagement.

'No, not yet. I felt my father should know of it first. But as soon as he has given his consent, I will tell her.'

A shadow crossed her face.

'Do you doubt that he will give it?' I asked her.

'My father can be . . .' She paused. 'He is very proud of his heritage—our heritage. You do not know him very well—yet—but his favourite book is the *Baronetage*. He often takes it up to read it. He likes to read about the first baronet, and to remind himself that he comes from an illustrious line.'

'And you? Are you proud of your heritage?' I asked her.

'Proud of it, yes, but not blinded to the worth of everything beyond it. There are other things in life beyond the baronetcy, and other men of value beyond those listed there.'

'But you do not doubt he will give his consent?'

She hesitated, then said, 'No. No, I am sure he will give it. He might make matters uncomfortable for you, however.'

I laughed at the notion, for if I could withstand the might of the French Navy, I was sure I could withstand a cold look from Sir Walter. But I laughed inwardly, for I had no wish to wound Anne's feelings.

My brother was not so sanguine as I joined him for luncheon a few hours later.

'And have you thought that Sir Walter might say no?' he asked.

'Why should I?'

'Because that will probably be his answer.'

'It is a good thing my heart is not as faint as yours, for I am certain he will say yes,' I returned.

'You have no title, no fortune, no estate, nothing to offer his daughter beyond your youth and person.'

'So you said last week.'

'I am saying it again. It is as well to be prepared for whatever he might say.'

'There is something in that. But no, I will not think of it. He will give his consent, and Anne and I will be married. I am sure of it.'

Saturday 6 September

I could eat very little, and this morning I set off for Kellynch Hall. I was far too early, but I could wait no longer. I paced the lane until my watch told me I could proceed. I went up to the door. I asked to see Sir Walter. I was made to wait. I paced the hall. I was shown in. And there was Sir Walter, magnificently attired, with his hair arranged in the latest style, reading the *Baronetage.*

To begin with, he ignored me, as though he could not tear his eyes away from the book.

'Sir Walter,' I began.

He looked up slowly, but did not close the book.

It was not a propitious start.

'You wished to see me?' he asked.

'Yes, I did. I do. On a matter of importance. I would like your permission to marry your daughter, Anne.'

'Marry Anne?' he asked, in a tone of disbelief. 'You have not yet asked me if you might pay her your addresses. It is far too soon to be speaking of anything else.'

I was nonplussed, but came about.

'My affections have developed swiftly—'

'They have indeed. You have only been in Somerset a few months.'

'But that is long enough for me to know that I am in love with Anne. Although they have developed swiftly—'

'And will disappear as swiftly, no doubt,' he interrupted.

'That they will not,' I said. 'I know my own mind. I am in love with Anne, and I wish to make her my wife. She wishes it, too.'

He looked at me with haughty dislike.

'You have spoken to her already?'

'Yes, I have.'

'Without consulting me?'

I hesitated, then said, 'There would have been no point in my bothering you if Anne had made it clear to me she would not have me, and besides, I could not help myself.'

'Indeed,' he remarked. 'And are you always so rash?'

'Once my mind is made up, I act on it. I am a man of decision.'

'Is that what you call it?' he asked. 'I call it irresponsible and hotheaded.'

I smarted at his words, and was tempted to reply in kind, but I knew it would do my suit no good, and so I replied mildly.

'Do I have your permission, Sir?'

'You say that you have already asked Anne?'

'Yes, I have.'

'And she wishes to accept your offer?'

'She does,' I assured him, heartened by the memory.

'How very extraordinary. I cannot think why,' he said. 'She has been brought up to know her own place in the world, and to value it accordingly. Her name is in the *Baronetage*.' He took up his book and began to read it to me, in slow and measured stately tones. ' "Elliot of Kellynch Hall".' He paused dramatically. ' "Walter Elliot, born 1 March 1760, married 15 July 1784, Elizabeth, daughter of James Stevenson, Esq., of South Park, in the county of Gloucester; by which lady (who died 1800) he has issue Elizabeth, born 1 June 1785; Anne, born 9 August 1787 . . ." ' He broke off and turned the book towards me. 'Anne,' he said, pointing to her name. 'The daughter of a baronet. There she is, my daughter, surrounded by her illustrious family. Can you offer her a similar ancestry?'

'No, I cannot,' I said boldly, looking him in the eye, 'but Anne places love above rank, as I do.'

'Indeed?' he said.

'Well, sir, do I have your permission?' I asked him, wanting the matter closed.

He appeared to weigh the matter.

'Anne is not her sister,' he said. 'She does not have Elizabeth's style or manners, nor does she have Elizabeth's beauty. But still, she is Miss Anne Elliot, and can look higher than a sailor for a husband. The alliance would be degrading . . .'

I contained my temper with difficulty.

'. . . and if she disgraces her name by marrying so far beneath her, I will do nothing for her,' he went on. 'She will have no fortune. It would be better for you to give her up, for you will make nothing from your connection to her, not a penny.'

I was inwardly seething, but replied, 'I want nothing, only Anne.'

'And can you support her?' he enquired with disdain.

'I can.'

'You have a fortune, then?'

'Not yet, but I have been lucky in my profession, and I will soon be rich.'

'Indeed? You have a very sanguine view of the matter.'

'Am I to understand that you are refusing me permission?' I asked, in no mood for more of his insults.

He paused, then sighed, and said, 'Ah, well, if you had asked for Elizabeth, I would have sent you about your business, but as it is only Anne . . .'

I had to control my temper again. Only Anne, indeed! *Only* Anne.

'Yes, all right, very well, you may have my permission,' he said wearily. He rang the bell. 'Commander Wentworth is leaving,' he told the servant.

I was angry; but anger soon gave way before the happy prospect that stretched out before me, so I thanked him, and went to find Anne, to tell her that her father had given his consent.

I came upon her in the garden. She turned her face to mine anxiously, but as she saw my smile, her own face relaxed, and she ran towards me. I ran, too, and embraced her.

'Your father has agreed to the match! We need keep our feelings a secret no longer. I want to tell all the world of it! I am the happiest man alive.'

She smiled, and said, 'And I am the happiest woman. I am as eager to tell my friends as you are, but I ask only one thing: you must let me tell Lady Russell of it first. She has been like a mother to me for many years, and I want her to hear it from my own lips, before she hears of it from anyone else. We are dining with her on Tuesday evening at her house. It is to be a small party, only Lady Russell, my father, my sister and myself, and I will tell her then. Then we may tell the rest of our friends.'

'Very well. I have already told my brother—not of your father's consent, of course, but I told him I meant to ask you to marry me, and I told him that you had said yes. I am looking forward to telling him that our wedding can go ahead. I would like him to conduct the service. Should you have any objections?'

'None at all. I think it an excellent idea, if Mr Gossington does not object. I would like nothing better.'

'If Gossington conducted marriages as a general rule, he

might wish to perform the office himself, but since he customarily leaves such things to my brother, I see no reason why he should object on this occasion. I will write to my sister tomorrow. I would like her to attend the wedding, and, if she is on shore at the time, I know she and Benjamin will want to come.'

We talked more of the wedding, of Anne being attended by her sisters, and of my plans to ask Harville to stand up with me, and so engrossed were we that we lost all track of time, and Anne's maid had to come and warn her that it was time for her to dress.

We parted reluctantly, and I returned to my brother's house. I could not rest, however. I longed for Edward's company, so that I would have someone to talk to, but he had been called away to visit one of his elderly parishioners, and was not likely to return all night. The evening dragged on interminably, but tomorrow, everything will be different.

Wednesday 10 September

I cannot believe it. My heart is heavy as I write. Not long ago, Anne accepted my hand, her father gave his consent and we were the two happiest people alive. Yesterday evening, Anne told Lady Russell the news, and this morning Anne told me the marriage could not go ahead.

How can life change so suddenly? It does not seem real. Nothing has seemed real since I met her by the river this morning. The air was warm, the birds were in full voice—a perfect morning, with no hint of the thunderbolt that was about to smite me.

Then Anne appeared. I noticed at once that her step was slow, but I thought she was tired, or that she had not seen me. As she drew closer, however, I could see that her shoulders were bowed.

She looked up and saw me. Her expression was hesitant, and her step faltered.

'What is it?' I asked her, covering the last few yards between us in two strides. 'What is wrong?'

'Nothing, only . . . I have to speak to you.'

Then she said something I had never expected to hear: that she had reconsidered; that we were too young; that long engagements were never a good thing; that it would be unfair of her to burden me with an engagement when I still had my way to make in the world; that we must be grateful we had told no one of our engagement, for there would be no embarrassment in breaking it; and that it would be best if we forgot it had ever taken place.

I was dumbfounded. But I soon came about. Her objections were easy to do away with, and I reassured her that we were not too young, and that our engagement would not be a long one, for I would soon have enough for us to marry on.

'And then, Anne, our adventures will begin.'

She shook her head sadly.

'Ah, I see. You have changed your mind about going to sea,' I said, thinking this was what lay behind it. Although I was sorry, I was not downhearted. 'You have never been aboard ship, and, now that it comes to it, you are frightened,' I said gently, taking her hands. 'The thought of it is too much for you. I understand. But fear not. If you do not feel you can leave your home and family, your friends and neighbours, and above all, dry land, then I will not hold you to it. But that is no reason to break our engagement.'

She drew her hands from mine and said, 'No, Frederick, I cannot.'

'Cannot? Why not?' I asked, seeking to understand.

'Everyone around me is counselling me against it—'

'So that is it. They have bullied you into submission,' I said.

'No, they have not bullied me,' she said.

But, despite her loyalty to her family, it was clear that that was what had happened.

'I knew how it would be,' I said. 'Your father was condescending when I spoke to him yesterday, and he has told you I am not good enough for you, and you, Anne, my dear, gentle Anne, do not have the courage to stand up to him.' I was conscious of feeling disappointment as I said it, for I had thought she was stronger than that, but I quickly rallied. 'Take my strength, for I have strength enough for two.'

'It is not just my father,' she said in distress. 'Lady Russell thinks it would be a mistake, too. The anxieties of your profession, the inevitable delays. I am only nineteen—'

'That did not trouble you yesterday.'

'No. But I have seen so little of life . . . I must be guided by those who have seen more, and listen when they tell me it is impossible.'

'Impossible? To buy ourselves a snug little cottage as soon as I have captured another ship, and then, when I have enough prize money to buy something better, the estate we have talked about?'

'Lady Russell says it will never be. She says you will have other calls on your purse at this time of life.'

'I assure you I have a far greater knowledge of the calls on my purse than Lady Russell can have.'

'And you will be worrying about me whilst you are away. Lady Russell says—'

'Lady Russell!' I exclaimed impatiently. 'Always Lady Russell! Have you no heart and no mind of your own?'

She broke away from me, taking two steps back.

'She was my mother's best friend, and I am used to relying on her judgement, and she has always guided me well.'

I reassured her; she was resolute. I argued; she was firm. Back and forth we went, neither one of us giving ground.

'It will be to your ruin. I cannot marry you,' she said. 'I could not forgive myself if I stood in your way, and prevented you from advancing as your deserve. With a fiancée, you would be cautious. You would lack the reckless spirit a man needs to advance. You would not achieve your ambitions, held back by me.'

I could not believe what I was hearing. I refused to take it in, but as last I could argue with her no longer.

'You cannot mean to break faith with me?' I asked her, my courage faltering. 'Say it is not so?'

'Frederick . . .'

'I thought you loved me.'

The words were wrung out of me.

'I do,' she declared passionately. 'I love you, but—'

'But not enough,' I said.

I could not keep the grief out of my voice.

'It is not that.'

'It is exactly that. You do not love me enough to go against family and friends, to follow your heart wherever it leads, even if it leads to the ends of the earth.'

'Frederick—'

'Enough,' I said, hurt as I had never been before, not even when I had been injured in battle. 'You have made your feelings clear. You cannot marry me. Very well. I will not hold you to your promise. I will have no unwilling bride. Our engagement is at an end.'

I made her a bow and then I hastened away, for I could not bear it, to have happiness so close, and yet so far.

I left Elliot land, and walked back towards the village.

I was just turning into the lane when fate threw in my way the one person I did not wish to see, the very woman who had caused all my misery: Lady Russell.

She coloured when she saw me, and faltered, as well she might.

I was in no mood to mince my words.

'Ay, madam, well might you look so,' I said. 'You have done me a terrible disservice. You have taken from me the woman I love, and caused a great deal of unhappiness where there was nothing but happiness before. It is a bad day's work.'

'I have done nothing but give good counsel to Anne,' she replied, collecting herself. 'She has no mother, and it is up to me to guide her. Had I any scruples about the part I have played, I would have lost them when you spoke to me just now. I am not accustomed to being addressed in such a manner. You are a hotheaded young man, Commander Wentworth, with nothing to offer Anne but a long engagement followed by a lifetime of uncertainty and loneliness. I want something better for her. I want her to have the comforts she is accustomed to, and the company of a husband who does not spend half his life at sea.'

'I could soon have given her the comforts she needs. We are at war! There are plenty of opportunities for a resolute young man to make his fortune, for never was there a better friend to a penniless young captain of ability and ambition than Napoleon Bonaparte. I mean to rise in the world, and I would have taken Anne with me.'

'A baronet's daughter does not need a sailor to lift her,' she remarked in a superior tone.

'With my prize money I could have given her a better home than the one she has now. In a few years' time—'

'—you are likely to be as poor as you are now, for you spend your money as quickly as you win it.'

'With a wife to support, I would have changed my ways. I would not have wanted to spend my money rashly, for I would have had someone else to spend it on. I would have had a reason to invest in the funds, and watch my capital grow.'

'So says every young man, until he is married, but then it

is a different story. He finds the pleasures of youth hard to abandon, and the call of his friends too strong, and his wife is left to manage on whatever her husband chooses to give her.'

'And what this husband would have chosen to give her would have been his hand and his heart.' I saw a smile of derision on her lips. 'So, you would rather see Anne married to a man she does not love, than allow her to follow her heart?'

'Love! Young people always talk about love, but nine times out of ten it is nothing but a passing fancy. Anne is young. She will soon find someone else, and you will fall in love again the next time you are ashore.'

'You presume too much,' I said. 'You cannot know my feelings. You have no right to say that they will change, or that I am so fickle. I love Anne.'

'And are you the only one involved in matrimony? Is it enough for you to love her? Pray, consider, she must also love you.'

'And so she does.'

'But not enough to marry you.'

'No,' I said, bitterly. 'You talk of men's fickleness, but it is women's fickleness that is to blame, here, today: Anne's for not loving me enough to follow her feelings, and yours for persuading her to abandon me, in the hope of a better marriage in the future, to a man she will not care for. It is the curse of the Elliots, and all about them, to care more about money and status than affection and true worth.'

'Have a care, Commander,' she said warningly, 'for that statement smacks of bitterness.'

'You must forgive me, Lady Russell, but I am feeling bit-ter. When a man has lost everything he holds most dear, through the offices of others, he is prone to that particular emotion. Anne would never have rejected me if you had not interfered.'

She gave a tentative smile.

'Come, what is done is done,' she said, holding out her hand for me to shake. 'Let us part as friends.'

I would not take it.

'You are no friend of mine, and you are no friend of Anne's either, Lady Russell. I will bid you good day.'

And so saying, I hurried away.

Luckily, my brother was out when I returned, so I did not immediately have to tell him what had happened. I paced the room, but I could not bear to be indoors and I was soon out-side again, trying to ride off the worst of my despair.

To be loved, accepted, and then rejected. It was too much. I could not bear it.

In vain did I tell myself that it was better this way, that if she did not love me it was better to find out now rather than later, when the engagement had been spoken of, or, worse yet, when we were married.

I thought of Harville, and his prosperous love. His wife did not mind a little discomfort. She believed in Harville, and knew he would make his fortune. Lucky man. If I had such a woman beside me . . . But I did not want another woman. I wanted Anne. Try as I might, I could not drive her out of my mind. The way she looked at me, the way our tastes and thoughts and feelings coincided, the way she made me feel inside . . .

I could not root out those feelings. I had been rejected, and I wanted to feel them no more, but my heart was not under my command. I loved her still.

At last, weary in body as well as in spirit, I returned home.

I had some respite from my brother, as he was not at home, but at luncheon he returned.

'Well, brother, do not keep me in suspense. You went to see Sir Walter. What did he say? Did he welcome you with open arms, or did he tell you to come back when you had received a knighthood?' he asked.

I did not want to speak of it, but it could not be avoided.

'He gave his consent, but Anne has withdrawn hers,' I said shortly.

'Ah.' He said no more, but sat down at the table, then remarked, 'I told you she would have no taste for living at sea.'

'She was played upon by Lady Russell. She was happy to accept me on her own account, and would have braved her father's lack of warmth, but Lady Russell told her I was not good enough for her—told her that she would hold me back—and she did not have the courage to stand out against her.'

'I am not surprised. Lady Russell has been like a mother to her for the last five years.'

'So she told me.' I paused, as luncheon was brought in, and when we were alone again, I said, 'But there is a time when every young woman must follow her own inclination, and leave her mother behind.'

'It seems that, for Anne, that time has not yet come. You had better have something to eat,' he remarked as my food sat untouched on my plate.

'I am not hungry.'

'Come now, it is all for the best. A wife would have been an encumbrance. You would not have been so fearless in battle, knowing you had a wife to mourn you if you were killed, and perhaps children as well.'

'Hah! Why should I be killed?' I retorted, sweeping his remarks aside.

'And if you had been,' he went on, ignoring me, 'how would Anne have lived?'

I was uncomfortable with the thought of it, but I told my brother he should not dwell on such nonsense.

'Make your fortune, come back to Monkford, and ask the lady again,' was my brother's advice.

'That I shall never do. I cannot marry a woman who has no faith in me, and who has no constancy. A word, once given, should be kept. Faithfulness, courage and resolve, these are the things I value. These are the things Anne had, or I thought she had. But I was mistaken, for she had them not,' I said, still in pain.

'Then you are lucky to have escaped a match that would not have been to your tastes, for you must have found her out eventually,' was my brother's unsympathetic reply.

'Very true,' I said.

But I did not mean it.

I could not think it a good thing that Anne had rejected

me, and if she had come to me and told me that she had made a mistake, I would have welcomed her with open arms. To have her once again, to hold her . . . but she did not come.

I excused myself from Edward's whist club this evening.

'What, staying at home to brood?' he asked.

I denied it, saying that I was in no mood for company and would read a book instead, but I could not concentrate. I could not stop thinking about Anne. She would not have rejected me if she had truly loved me . . .

But it was folly to think of her, I told myself. She was shallow. Her heart was not as deep as mine, or she could not have told me to go. I would not regret her. I would learn my lesson. I would avoid the fairer sex. I would win such prizes from the Navy as would set me up for life, and I would have none but the sea as my mistress, for, even with all her moods, she was less capricious than a woman.

I would remain a bachelor for the rest of my days.

1814

JULY

Monday 25 July

And so, the *Laconia* has come into Plymouth at last. The war is over, my fortune is made, and my time at sea is at an end.

I can hardly believe it. The Navy has dominated my life for so many years that it is like a part of me, and I cannot imagine how I will feel when it has gone. No more living on board ship; no more sailing the oceans; no more coming into distant ports, with all the excitement it brings; no more hot, clear skies; no more foreign tongues around me; no more markets with strange and wonderful produce, or palm trees swaying beside white beaches.

And yet, although I am sad to see it go, I find I am looking forward to my new life on shore. I have been away from England for so long that it has all the novelty of a foreign port.

The soft, damp sir, the muted colours and the cooling breeze all have their charm, and I am glad to be home.

Tuesday 26 July

I went on shore for a few hours this afternoon, and I was greeted everywhere by cheers and thanks. Men shook me by the hand and children trailed after me, whilst women blessed me for saving them from the scourge of Napoleon. I tried to tell them that I had not won the war single-handedly, but they would have none of it, for they wanted someone to praise, and I was close at hand. And indeed, for the war to have ended at last, when it had been waging for so many years that the children who swarmed around me had never known a time of peace, was a great thing, after all.

Impromptu plays were being performed, with Napoleon—played by a variety of men of all sizes and girths—being defeated as the Allies went into Paris. There were many ribald comments, but it was all good-humoured, and there was the feel of a holiday in the air.

At last I returned to the ship.

'Admiral Croft is here to see you,' said my lieutenant, as I went on board, and there, sure enough, was Benjamin.

We clapped each other on the back, and congratulated each other on our service, and when we had talked of Sophia and Edward and all Benjamin's family, we settled down to talk of other things.

'I am just on my way back to Taunton,' he said. 'Sophy

and I are looking at some estates down there. We mean to rent one as soon as possible, for now the war is over, we need somewhere to live. You must come and stay with us when we are settled.'

'I would like nothing better.'

He told me he had just come from London, where he had been seeing to some business.

'I have never seen anything like it,' he said. 'The streets are thronged with people morning, noon and night. The fuss that was made of the Russians last month was enormous. The Tsar could scarcely appear without provoking spontaneous cheering. The crowd loved him, and they loved his sister, the Grand Duchess, too. A pretty young woman if ever there was one, though young to be a widow, poor lady.'

'The war has made many widows,' I said.

'Ay,' he said, thinking of some he had known. He roused himself. 'There was talk of her marrying again, to cement an alliance with England, but I heard the royal dukes were not to her taste. And then, of course, there were the usual arguments about the Princess of Wales, with the Whigs backing her efforts to attend the Royal Drawing-Room and the old Queen saying she could not be received. The public were on Princess Caroline's side, they booed the Regent when he passed in his carriage, and shouted out, "Love your wife!" but he, as always, took no notice.'

'And did you see any of the great military men?'

'It was impossible not to. Blücher was there. He was unable to move without people congratulating him, in fact, he was so surrounded by well-wishers in Hyde Park that he had to stand with his back against a tree! Wellington was there, too, but refused any pomp and circumstance, and rode round with a single groom. There were celebrations everywhere, and still are, with the Regent giving dinner-parties at Carlton House—a fairyland, by all accounts—and making plans for the Jubilee.'

'London seems awash with news!'

'It is. If you can get a leave of absence, you must go and see the Jubilee celebrations next week. They promise to be spectacular. There are coloured lanterns in St James's Park, and there is a Chinese bridge across the canal. There is to be a balloon ascent, and a re-enactment of the storm of Badajoz. And there is something that will interest you, as a naval man, for there is to be a mock Battle of the Nile on the Serpentine.'

'And how are they to manage that?' I asked, astonished at the idea of staging a battle in London!

'With ship's barges, fitted out with miniature cannon.'

'It is a good thing we had more than barges at our disposal, or we would never have won anything!' I remarked. 'But I will go if I can.'

He took his leave, and I found myself looking forward to the coming weeks: a trip to London, a sojourn with Sophia, and, at last, a chance to visit Edward and meet his new wife.

Friday 29 July

I saw Jenson this afternoon. His ship had just come in, and we exchanged news. He told me that Lencet had been killed in action in January, and he asked about Harville, whom he had not seen since we all served together in the year nine. I told him of Harville's wound two years ago, but that otherwise Harville, Harriet and their children were well. I told him, too, that Harville's sister, Fanny, was engaged to Benwick, and he was pleased to hear it.

We talked of our plans now that the war was over. Jenson told me he had decided to go into his family's business in the wine trade, and was planning to expand it by buying a fleet of ships, so that they could transport the wine as well as buying and selling it.

'And I suppose you will captain the flagship?' I asked.

'Of course!'

I told him about the celebrations in London and we decided to go there. He agreed to join me for breakfast, so that we may set out tomorrow together.

Saturday 30 July

Jenson and I were in the middle of breakfast, making the final plans for our trip to London, when a note arrived for me.

'I will take a turn on deck,' said he, preparing to rise.

'No need,' I said. 'It is from Harville. Stay. You will like to hear what he says.' I unfolded the letter and began to read it aloud. 'He is in Plymouth . . . is glad I am put in to shore . . . Oh, no!' I said, as I saw unhappy news, 'Oh, no!'

'What is it?' Jenson asked.

I shook my head in disbelief. I could barely bring myself to say the words.

'It is Fanny, Harville's sister. She is dead.'

'Dead?' he asked in horror.

I could do no more than nod my head.

'All the beauty . . . such a superior mind . . . this is terrible news,' he said. 'She had all her life before her.'

I read on, my eyes quickly scanning the page, and letting out a groan when I saw what Harville had asked of me.

'No! Oh, no, I cannot!' I cried aloud, shrinking from it. And yet, even as I did so, I knew it must be done, and that there was no one better than me to do it.

'What? What is it?' asked Jenson.

'Benwick,' I said. 'James. He does not know.'

Jenson's face fell.

'He has just come back from the Cape, and is under orders for Portsmouth. Harville cannot bring himself to break the news. He asks me to do it for him.'

'Frederick . . .' he said, with the deepest sympathy, for it was a task no man would envy.

And yet it could not be avoided. I folded the letter resolutely.

'I must do it at once. I must write for a leave of absence.'

'I will take the letter for you.'

'Thank you, Jenson, from the bottom of my heart. And I must hope it is granted, for I cannot wait for the answer.'

I wrote my letter and then stood up.

'I must go at once. Poor Benwick. How will he bear it? To

lose her just when his hopes were to be realized, when his long engagement was to come to an end, and when he was to take Fanny to wife. He has waited for this moment for years, and now for it to be snatched away from him, and in such a way. It is too cruel.'

He nodded in mute agreement.

And then I left the ship, and set out on my dreadful errand.

AUGUST

Monday 1 August

A terrible day. A terrible, terrible day.

I arrived in Portsmouth in the early hours, having travelled night and day from Plymouth, and rowed out to the *Grappler*. Benwick was delighted to see me. He was all smiles as he congratulated me on my success, telling me it could not have happened to a more deserving fellow, then demanded my congratulations on his promotion and on his wealth. He was so full of good spirits that he did not notice my dejection, and he broke my heart by saying, 'At last I will see Fanny. I cannot wait! That was the hardest part of being at sea, Wentworth, having to leave her behind. I have kept her waiting for two years whilst I made my fortune and earned my promotion, but now our engagement can come to an end and we will be married as soon as the banns can be read.'

I could have wept. I did not know how to tell him, I could not find the words. But at last my mood communicated itself to him and he looked at me uncertainly. I told him I had bad news and bade him lead me down below. Once in his cabin, I told him, and he crumpled. I have never seen a man brought so low. He sank down, for his legs would no longer support him, and he was like a man stunned. He neither moved nor spoke. And then, at last, it washed over him, in waves of despair, and I thought he would go mad. I never left his side, but sat with him all day and all night, and as I did so, I hoped I never had to live through such a terrible day, ever again.

Thursday 11 August

At last, Benwick is over the worst. He no longer raves, though I find his quietness sad almost beyond bearing. He is like a hollow man.

I cannot help thinking of him as he was at twelve years old, walking hesitantly into the Academy, looking around him nervously, a small lad for his age, but soon impressing us with his intelligence and his courage. I can see his confident step when he graduated from the Academy, and his interest when he first noticed Fanny at Harville's wedding. I can remember him smiling when he told me that she had accepted his hand; his regret that he could not marry her until

he had won his promotion; and his determination to suc-
ceed, for her sake.

And now the life has gone out of him, as though his heart
died with Fanny.

Friday 12 August

I had a letter from Sophia this morning, but I hardly had time to
glance at it before Harville arrived. I put it away as soon as I
saw him, for I was glad of his company, and delighted to see
that he had brought Harriet with him. Benwick's spirits lifted a
little as he saw them, and talking to them gave his heart some
ease. They spoke of Fanny for hours, and then Harville said that
Benwick must go and live with them. Benwick protested at first,
saying they did not have room, but Harriet added her entreaties
to Harville's, and at last he agreed. It was a relief to me, for I
would not like to think of him being by himself at such a time.

Harville and I had a chance for some conversation alone,
as Harriet continued to talk to Benwick. He told me he means
to look for a bigger house, one that will afford them more
room, and spoke of his hopes to find something by the sea. I
wished him luck, and he promised to write to me, to give me
his direction, as soon as he was settled.

They set out together this afternoon, a sad party, and I
watched them go with a heavy heart. They should have been
going to arrange Benwick's wedding, if fate had been kinder.
Instead, they were going to share their grief.

It is my only consolation to know that, with such loving

people around him, he will be well looked after, though I fear he is wounded too deep for a full recovery. Fanny Harville was a very superior young woman. He is unlikely to meet her equal, and without another such attachment, what will there be to restore him to life?

Monday 15 August

And so, I find myself in London, almost three weeks later than I expected. I met up with Jenson and told him how Benwick had taken the news. We were neither of us in the mood for company or celebration after that, and we had a quiet dinner at Fladong's before arranging to meet tomorrow.

Tuesday 16 August

I dined with Jenson again this evening, and our talk naturally turned to Benwick.

'The only mercy is that he might, in a year or two, recover his spirits,' said Jenson. 'If he does, he will still be young enough to look about him and find a wife.'

'It will be hard for Harville if he does,' I remarked.

'But harder for Benwick if he does not.'

I agreed, and then we turned our attention, deliberately, to more cheerful things, for we did not want to dwell on something that could not be changed. Even so, our spirits were low for the rest of the evening, and we parted early, arranging, however, to meet again tomorrow.

Wednesday 17 August

When I arrived in London a few days ago, I was not in a mood for the celebrations that were going on in the city, but today I began to take more interest in them. Jenson and I walked out this morning, and the bustle lifted our spirits. Everywhere around us we saw smiling faces. There was a festival air, and an atmosphere of goodwill. After so many years at war, London was celebrating peace in style.

I turned my thoughts away from the past and thought of the future.

I must buy an estate, and find a woman I can respect, and set about making myself a life.

Saturday 20 August

I had a letter from Sophia this morning, and I was able to give it more attention than her last one, which still lay, half read, in my pocket. I was pleased to learn that she and Benjamin had found an estate to rent, and that they were delighted with it. I read all through her description of elegant furnishings, a fine park and splendid vistas . . . and then her final line confounded me, for she told me its name, and I learnt that the estate she and Benjamin had fixed on was Kellynch Hall.

The name took me back. It reminded me of the summer of the year six, Sir Walter and Miss Elliot, and Anne . . . Anne dancing with me; Anne walking by the river; Anne and I, talking of everything and nothing, lost in each other's company . . .

Anne being persuaded to abandon me, and no doubt being married by now, to a baronet or higher, someone with the rank to satisfy her father's pride and the fortune to satisfy Lady Russell's avarice.

I am determined not to regret her, for I am sure she does not regret me. I put her behind me long ago, and her fate no longer concerns me. Apart from some natural curiosity, I have no desire to see her again. As the Elliots are to remove to Bath, it is unlikely that I will come across her, and if we do by any chance meet, it will be as strangers.

Her power with me is gone.

SEPTEMBER

Thursday 29 September

Today was the day fixed upon for my sister to move into Kellynch Hall, and though I was still busy dealing with the affairs that had occupied me for the last few weeks, I spared a thought for her and Benjamin.

OCTOBER

Monday 3 October

I had a letter from Sophia this morning, telling me that she
and Benjamin had settled into their new home, and inviting
me to stay. I wrote back to accept her invitation, telling her I
would be with her next week.

Saturday 8 October

I had a good journey into Somersetshire, but as I drew near
the neighbourhood of Uppercross I could not prevent memories from intruding. The last time I was in this town I was buying a new pair of gloves for a ball, I thought . . . the last time I
passed that tree, I was going on a picnic . . . the last time I saw
that road, I was full of bitterness and grief . . . and then I saw

Kellynch Hall, and I remembered when Edward and I had been invited to dinner, and I had spent the whole evening talking to Anne.

And then the carriage was pulling up in front of the door, and I was being shown in, and there was no more time for memories. Sophia rose to greet me. She was brown from all her travels, and was looking very well. She was pleased with her new home, for the house, the grounds and the gardens were all to her liking.

Benjamin and I greeted each other warmly, and tea was brought in.

'You should find somewhere soon yourself, Frederick,' said Benjamin. 'And when you do, make sure you get a good man of business to handle everything for you. We were lucky in Mr Shepherd, for he was competent, and the details were concluded with all expediency. Did you meet him when you were last here?'

'I believe I may have done,' I said, unwilling to talk of that time.

'He seems to take care of Sir Walter,' Benjamin went on, with a smile and a shake of his head. 'Just as well, for the man seems to need someone to take care of him.'

'Hush, Benjamin!' said my sister, as the tea was brought in. 'You will give Frederick the wrong impression. Sir Walter is an elegant man of great refinement.'

'But very little common sense. Wanted to live the life of the first man in the neighbourhood, but did not have the wherewithal to do it, and so he mortgaged his lands, with the result that he incurred debts, and eventually had to rent out his home.'

'Better than carrying on in the same manner and ruining himself, or refusing to pay his debts and ruining those to whom he was indebted,' said Sophia. 'I dare say he will soon come about. He can live much more cheaply in Bath than here, and the income he gains from letting the house will help him to clear his encumbrances.'

I felt a perverse satisfaction in knowing that our fortunes had been reversed, and that the man who had looked down on me as a suitor was now a poor man, whilst I was rich.

'Miss Elliot is a very handsome woman,' said Sophia. 'I was surprised she was not married.'

I felt a jolt. Was she speaking of Miss Elizabeth Elliot, or had Elizabeth married, in which case Anne would be Miss Elliot . . . but no, Anne would have married, of course. Perhaps the youngest daughter, Mary, was now Miss Elliot. However, I wanted to be sure.

'Which Miss Elliot do you mean?' I asked casually.

'The eldest daughter, Elizabeth.'

So. She had not married. Mr Elliot had not come up to scratch.

'Perhaps she found no one to suit. She has inherited all her father's pride, and I dare say will not be easy to please,' said Benjamin. 'Her sister has married, though, and married quite well.'

And there it was, the news that I had expected, and yet which confounded me nonetheless, for although I knew Anne must have married in all that time, it was still a shock to hear of it.

'She has married Mr Charles Musgrove, one of our new neighbours,' Sophia went on. 'They live at Uppercross Cottage and have two little boys. Mr Charles Musgrove is the son of Mr and Mrs Musgrove, who live at the Great House.'

Then she had married Charles Musgrove after all.

'I am sure I hope she is very happy,' I said coldly.

'The Musgroves have been very attentive,' said Benjamin. 'Mr Musgrove senior paid us a call almost as soon as we arrived and welcomed us to the neighbourhood. It was very good of him to visit us with such alacrity, and his son, Mr Charles Musgrove, was hardly any less attentive, for he and his wife called soon afterwards. We returned the call, and although we did not find Mr Charles Musgrove at home, his wife was there with her sister.'

Her sister. Miss Mary Elliot, who had been at school when I last visited the neighbourhood.

'Did you meet Mrs Charles Musgrove when you stayed in the area before?' asked Sophia.

'I believe so,' I replied shortly, unwilling to talk of the past.

The brevity of my answer went unnoticed in the midst of the general conversation.

'She does not have the pride of her sister, but then she does not have her sister's beauty, either,' said Sophia.

'I always thought her . . .' *far more beautiful*, I had been going to say, but stopped myself in time, adding, '. . . a pretty girl.'

'Pretty? I cannot agree with you there, but perhaps she has lost some of her bloom. The two little boys wear her out, I think, and she is inclined to be sickly,' said Sophia.

'Or fancy herself so,' said Benjamin.

She had changed very much indeed, then, I thought, if she was worn out and fancied herself sickly. But it was eight years since I had seen her, and eight years can change a lot of things.

'The Musgrove girls, though, Mr Charles Musgrove's sisters, now there are two pretty young ladies, if you please,' Benjamin went on. 'Lively manners, and full of fun. You could do worse than pick one of them.'

'Benjamin,' said Sophia reprovingly.

'What?' he enquired. 'It is time Frederick was married, and one girl is as good as another, in the end.'

'Frederick has only just arrived. Do not plague him.' She turned to me. 'If you have finished your tea, perhaps you would like to see the park?' she asked.

I had no desire to see it, and to be reminded of former times, but I could not refuse and so I expressed my readiness to see it at her convenience. Before long, I found myself once again walking through the fields and by the river so familiar to me, and it was a good thing my sister had plenty to say, for I fear my recollections would have made me an indifferent conversationalist if she had fallen silent.

We dined alone, just the three of us, and after a quiet evening playing cards, I retired for the night.

I found my room to be large and spacious, at the front of

the house, overlooking the drive, and I wondered whose room it had been when the Elliots were in residence?

Had it been Miss Elliot's? Or Anne's?

Monday 10 October

As we were walking through the park this morning, Benjamin, Sophia and I swapped stories of the Navy. After a while, Benjamin asked me about Harville, and I told him the sad news about Fanny, adding that Harville had taken Benwick to live with him. Benjamin asked where they lived, and I told him that Harville had not yet settled, as he needed a bigger house, but said that Harville had promised to write to me as soon as he was established, and that I, in return, had promised to visit him.

'I hope you will also be going to see Edward. He is longing to show you his wife,' Sophia said.

'As soon as I can find time to go into Shropshire, I will be pleased to meet her. Is she as amiable as Edward says?'

'Yes, and very pretty.'

'A beauty,' said Benjamin.

I am looking forward to meeting her, and to renewing my friendship with my brother.

Tuesday 11 October

On my way through the village this morning I found myself being hailed by a number of people who remembered me from my previous visit, and from them I learned all the neighbourhood news. Mr Shepherd's daughter, Miss Shepherd, married Mr Clay, had two children by him, lost him, and returned to live with her father, only to then be taken up by Miss Elliot, who invited her to Bath.

'A very lucky thing for her,' said Mrs Layne. 'Only think, she is staying with the Elliots and goes with them everywhere. What a chance for her to have some entertainment, for I do not believe her marriage was a happy one, and who knows? Perhaps she might meet an eligible gentleman and contract a more prosperous marriage.'

'Kitty,' said her husband reprovingly. 'Captain Wentworth does not want to hear all the tattle.'

'Why is it that men call information about their neighbours—people they know, and are therefore interested in—*tattle*, but call information about people they do not know, have never met, and never will meet *news*, and put it in the papers for everyone to read?'

'There is someone I would like to hear news of,' I said to her. 'Miss Scott. Is she happy now that peace has been declared?'

'Yes, indeed. She went to live with her sister, you know. As soon as peace was declared she decided to move. I have no idea why. When she lived here, she was in constant fear of invasion, being so close to the sea, but as soon as all threat had passed, she moved into the heart of the country!'

'I am sorry not to see her.'

'I will send her your regrets the next time I write.'

By the time I returned for luncheon, I had learnt the fate of most of my brother's parishioners, and I had also met his replacement, a studious young man who seemed to be much liked in the parish, and who invited me to dine with him.

Wednesday 12 October

Mr Musgrove senior called this morning to pay his respects, and to invite Sophia, Benjamin and me to dine with him and his family at the end of next week. He tried to press for an earlier date, but Benjamin had urgent business to attend to, so that we could accept nothing sooner.

Thursday 13 October

I returned Mr Musgrove's civility by returning his call today, and found Mr Musgrove at home with his wife and his two daughters.

Miss Musgrove, a young lady of some twenty summers, positively sprang out of her chair when I was announced and dropped me a deep curtsey whilst looking me up and down with admiring eyes. Her sister, Miss Louisa, was no less pretty and no less admiring. They reminded me of playful puppies, full of life and eager to please. My spirits soared, and I thought, *Here is just the sort of lighthearted company I need to rid myself of the lingering griefs of the summer.*

I was invited to sit down, and treated with so much cordiality that I was soon feeling at home.

'And how do you find Uppercross, sir?' asked Mr Musgrove, when we had all taken a seat.

'I find it a very pleasant place to be. The air is pure, the countryside varied, and the people'—with a bow to him—'most agreeable.'

He was pleased with my answer, and laughed and rubbed his hands together, and said he was pleased to find such good neighbours in Sir Walter's tenants. He did not appear to remember me from eight years ago, and, as I had no desire to awaken old memories, I did not remind him.

'Ah, yes, Uppercross is a fine place,' said Mrs Musgrove. 'My family has always lived in the neighbourhood,' she went on, speaking to me. 'My sister is married to a gentleman, Mr Hayter, who lives not far away, at Winthrop. You might have seen it? It lies on the other side of the hill.'

I said I had not yet had that pleasure.

'Uppercross is all very well, though I wish we could go to London, or Bath,' said Miss Musgrove.

'What! Go to London or Bath, and miss all the fun at home?' said her mother. 'I will remind you of that, the next time we get up a dance.' She turned to me. 'We are very fond of dancing in the Great House, Captain.'

'You must come to our next ball, Captain Wentworth,' said Miss Musgrove.

I was delighted with the idea, for I was tempted by her wide smile and her bright eyes.

'Promise!' said Miss Musgrove. 'We must have you dance with us, must we not, Mama?' she said, turning to her mother.

'Indeed we must. You will be very welcome, Captain Wentworth, whenever you can spare us the time.'

'Do say you will come,' pleaded Miss Louisa. 'We would so like to have you here.'

'Please?' said her sister.

'How can I refuse?' I answered with a laugh, for it was a long time since I had been so pleased!

'Now let the good captain alone,' said Mr Musgrove, 'before you worry him half to death. I declare, Captain, it is a troublesome thing to be the father of two such noisy girls,' but he said it with great affection, and it was obvious he loved them dearly. 'You will stay to dinner?' he asked me, as I accepted his invitation to sit down.

It was with real regret that I could not accept his kind invitation, for the atmosphere in the house was a happy one, and everywhere I looked there was good cheer, but I had promised Sophia I would bear her company.

'Then you will come tomorrow?' he said.

'Oh, yes, Captain, do say you will,' Mrs Musgrove entreated me.

I could hold out against their entreaties no longer and declared myself very happy to accept.

The rest of the visit passed very agreeably, with the two girls asking me about my battles and telling me of the neighbourhood dances, and, in short, flattering me with such attention that I was sorry to leave.

The time for parting came, however, and I returned to Kellynch Hall in excellent spirits.

Sophia and I dined alone, for Benjamin's business had taken him away from home, and we had so much to say to each other after the years spent apart that it was very late when we went to bed.

Friday 14 October

It was a fine day, the sort of crisp autumn weather that makes exercise an invigorating delight. I set out for an early morning ride, with the mist clearing to reveal a beautiful day. When I returned home for breakfast, I had a hearty appetite.

The day was spent in writing letters and seeing to business in town, then this evening I set out for the Great House. I was conscious of some curiosity and not a little apprehension as I walked up the drive, for I knew that Mr and Mrs Charles Musgrove were to dine with us. How would Anne look? Would she remember me? Or would she have forgotten me? Yes, most probably, I thought, my pride suffusing me. Well, let her. I had forgotten her, carried on with my life, earned my promotion and won my fortune. I was not going to pine for a girl with no resolution, one who married another man just a few years after agreeing to marry me.

I went in, and as I found that Mr and Mrs Charles Musgrove were not there, I felt my spirits lift. I was made much of by the two Miss Musgroves and I was hardly given any less warm a greeting by their parents. It was the sort of welcome to make me feel, once again, immediately at home.

Hardly had I sat down, however, when the mood changed

and Mr Musgrove, looking more serious, said, 'It is lucky you could not dine with us yesterday, after all, Captain, for we would not have been good company. We had a calamity in the family.'

'Oh, it was awful! We were all in a terrible state,' said Mrs Musgrove, wafting her fan vigorously in front of her, for the heat from the fire was intense. 'My heart was in my mouth when I heard the news, for, of course, one always thinks the worst. All sorts of ideas flashed through my mind, each one worse than the last. I do not know how we got through the day.'

'Let us not keep the captain in suspense,' said Mr Musgrove. 'We were very much dismayed because our grandson had a nasty fall.'

'Ay, very nasty, very nasty indeed,' said his wife.

'I am very sorry to hear it. It was not serious, I hope?' I asked, concerned for the little fellow.

'We feared so at the time, and called Mr Robinson, the apothecary, straight away.'

'It was Anne who sent for him,' said Mrs Musgrove. 'Anne has always been very sensible and she took charge at once, so that little Charles was given the best attention right away. She sent for him even before she sent word to us.'

'Very sensible of her,' said Mr Musgrove.

'Well, Robinson examined him and said he had a dislocated collar-bone. Robinson replaced it—'

'Oh, that was nasty, and very painful for him, poor little man,' said Mrs Musgrove.

'You may imagine that we were all vastly relieved when he had done, and said that he believed, with plenty of rest, all would be well,' said Mr Musgrove. 'It gave us hope, and we were able to come home again.'

'Though I do not believe I ate a mouthful of dinner for worrying about him,' Mrs Musgrove said.

'However, he had a good night and seems to be going on well,' said Miss Musgrove briskly, as though anxious to be done with little Charles and the talk of his fall.

'Ay, Mr Robinson does not believe there will be any lasting damage, for which we are all very grateful,' said Mrs Musgrove. 'We thought my son and his wife would have to cry off tonight, but they are so pleased with little Charles's progress that they feel they can leave him for a few hours. Had things been different, they would have had to stay at home, which would have been a grave disappointment to them, for they are very desirous of seeing you,' she said politely, with a bow in my direction.

At that moment, Mr and Mrs Charles Musgrove were announced. As I heard the names I felt myself tense, despite my belief that I had put the past behind me. I did not immediately look round. Mr Charles Musgrove came into the room with a quick step and I recognized in him the same man I had seen in the year six, the man Anne had described as a family friend. As my eyes ran over him, I was surprised she had married him, for he was nothing out of the ordinary, and was even less well favoured than I remembered him. He was certainly not the catch Lady Russell had wanted for Anne, and it gave some solace to my pride to know that her schemes had come to nothing, after all.

'Here you are, just in time to meet Captain Wentworth,' said Mr Musgrove. 'Captain Wentworth, might I introduce my son, Mr Charles Musgrove—'

I greeted him, and was then forced to turn my head to include his wife in my vision, and to my astonishment I saw that it was not Anne, in fact it was a woman I had never seen before in my life.

'—and my daughter-in-law, Mrs Charles Musgrove, who was Miss Mary Elliot before she married,' Mr Musgrove finished.

So it was Anne's sister who had married Charles Musgrove! I was elated, though I did not know why, and then amused, and then I felt foolish and not a little angry with myself as I realized how much time I had wasted thinking about the meeting.

Mr and Mrs Charles Musgrove greeted me warmly and were evidently very much interested in their new neighbour.

'Are you sure it is all right for you to leave little Charles?' asked Mrs Musgrove, when the greetings were over. 'I am not easy about him. I know Mr Robinson is hopeful, but I am worried that he might have a setback.'

'You may be perfectly easy, Mama,' said Charles.

'Oh, yes, perfectly easy, for we did not leave him alone. Anne is with him,' said his wife. 'Anne is my sister,' she explained to me.

'Well, if Anne is with him, I am sure he will be all right,' said Mrs Musgrove.

'Of course he will. Anne is the very person to look after him. She does not have a mother's sensibilities, and besides, she can make him do anything. He always attends her more than he attends me. I do not have any fears for him, you know, for he is going on so well that I feel quite at ease. Anne can always send word if anything should happen, and we are only half a mile away.'

We all sat down, and I smiled to find that Miss Musgrove and Miss Louisa managed to seat themselves one on either side of me, both vying for my attention.

'I believe you met Anne when you were here before,' said Charles, as he settled himself on a sofa next to his mother.

'Yes, we were acquainted,' I said.

'Really?' asked Mary.

'You were away at school at the time, but Anne was at home,' said Charles. 'It must have been in the year five, or thereabouts?'

'The year six,' I said.

'Ah, yes, you are probably right. Your brother was the curate at Monkford, was he not?'

'Yes, he was.'

'I hope he is well?'

'Yes, thank you, very well. He is married now.'

'A good thing, marriage,' said Mrs Musgrove comfortably. 'Every man should marry.'

'And every woman,' said Mr Musgrove, looking at his two girls benignly.

I longed to ask whether Anne was married, but my pride would not let me.

'You will see Anne before long, I dare say, for she is staying with us at present,' said Charles. 'Her family has gone to Bath, but my wife was not well and needed her sister so Anne stayed behind.'

'Indeed, I could not have done without Anne,' said Mary.

We went into dinner. Mr Musgrove escorted Mary, Charles escorted his mother, and I was left to take in the Miss Musgroves, one on each arm.

I was delighted with them. They were full of questions about my life at sea and they made playful remarks that set us all laughing, bringing good cheer to the table, and, after dinner, they entertained us by playing on the pianoforte and the harp.

'Such musical girls,' said Mrs Musgrove happily. 'They are so clever, I do not know which of them plays better. What is your opinion, Captain Wentworth?'

'They are both very accomplished,' I said, admiring them as much as their mother could have wished, for their faces were full of life, and their posture enchanting–though I believe they did not play very well! It was hardly surprising. They were far too boisterous to endure many hours spent practising their instruments, and I was sure they abandoned the task in favour of walks or shopping or gossip as often as they could.

'And so they are, very good girls, both of them. I like to hear them both, and I never know which I like more, the piano or the harp. Mr Musgrove and I are spoilt for choice. Let us have some singing,' she said then to the girls.

They were eager to do as she asked and I went over to the pianoforte and joined in with their songs. They smiled up at me most agreeably, and it was difficult to know which of them I liked best, Miss Musgrove with her glossy curls, or Miss Louisa with her bold manner and her dimples.

At last the singing came to an end and we resumed our conversation. It was not long before Charles Musgrove invited me to go shooting with him on the morrow.

'We will meet at the Cottage for breakfast and then take our guns out afterwards,' he said.

'I would not like to be in Mrs Musgrove's way, with a sick child in the house,' I replied, though really my objection was because I felt a strange reluctance to see Anne.

I was honoured for my concern, there was some discussion back and forth, and the upshot of it was that we should breakfast at the Great House, and then to go out with Charles Musgrove afterwards.

All too soon it was time for me to take my leave. Buoyed up by an evening spent in the uncomplicated company of such pretty, spirited girls and their convivial family, I returned to Kellynch Hall.

As I walked up the drive, I found my thoughts straying to Anne once again, and thinking how strange it was that my brother-in-law should have rented Kellynch Hall. Of all the houses in Somersetshire, why did he have to rent that one? A place that held so many memories? And a place that would bring me into company with Anne? It was only by chance that I had not already met her for, if not for the child's fall, she would have been at the Great House and I would have passed the evening in her company.

As I remembered the past, I felt a spark of anger for her vacillating character, and an ache of bruised pride at the way she had treated me. And then I calmed myself. I knew I would have to accustom myself to seeing her, for we would often be together, and it would not do for me to let any trace of resentment show. I made up my mind not to mention the past and I decided that I would treat her with perfect good humour, simply as a woman I once knew.

But even so, I could not help my thoughts dwelling on her as I went inside. *Anne Elliot*, I thought, *after so many years*. *Anne Elliot.*

Saturday 15 October

I joined the Musgroves early for breakfast. The Miss Musgroves were as pretty a pair of breakfast companions as any man had a right to expect, and were just as animated as they had been yesterday. They talked constantly during breakfast and kept trying to delay Charles and me, until Charles could bear the delays no longer and stood up, saying it was time for us to set out. The girls could not bear to part with us—let me confess it, with me! for what interest has a brother to his own sisters?—and declared their intention of coming with us as far as the Cottage. Their excuse was a desire to call on their nephew and see how he went on, though they had not mentioned him all morning.

I was content to have their company, for what man could resist the attentions of two such pretty girls? But again I felt a reluctance to see Anne. It could not be avoided, however, and so I thought it better to give her notice of it. Why I was anxious to spare her a sudden shock I did not know, but so it was.

We reached the Cottage and I could not help smiling at its name, for it was in fact an extended farmhouse, very spacious, with French windows looking over neatly trimmed gardens and a pretty veranda.

The girls giggled and chattered by my side as we went in. I saw Mrs Musgrove at once and looked around for Anne, but I saw no one except a dull, faded creature of hesitant manner who was that moment attending to a little boy. I thought she was a nursery governess until she turned towards me and, with a start, I realized it was Anne.

'You might remember my sister, Miss Anne Elliot,' said Mary.

So. She had not married, and it was hardly surprising, for her beauty had gone. The bloom of her cheek; the brightness of her eye; all had disappeared. Her figure was bowed; and she was, in fact, so careworn, that I would not have believed it possible she could have changed so much in only eight years.

'Miss Elliot,' I said.

'Captain Wentworth.'

Our eyes half met. I bowed, she curtseyed. And all the time I kept thinking: *Once, we would have had eyes for no one but each other.*

I continued to move and speak, though without any idea of what I was saying. And then, mercifully, Charles appeared at the window, having collected the dogs, and we were away.

In a few brief minutes, all my memories of Anne's beauty and grace had been demolished, and I was left with nothing but anger and bitterness, for if she had only had a little more resolution then it could all have been otherwise.

'What do you think of Anne?' asked Miss Musgrove, as we reached the end of the village.

'She is so altered I would not have known her again,' I said.

As I spoke, I remembered her as I had seen her on that first morning, walking by the river, with the sun shining on her hair. I remembered the light catching the ripples on the water; and I remembered her eyes being even brighter than the ripples as she laughed at me.

But that Anne had gone forever. She had let me down, deserted me, disappointed me, and shown a feebleness of temper that I could not understand or forgive. She had given me up to please others, and I could still feel the pain of it, but now it was a dull ache and nothing more. Fate had thrown us together again, but her power over me had gone.

The Miss Musgroves walked with us to the end of the village. Their bright spirits formed a marked contrast to the scene we had just left, but even their butterfly minds could not lift me out of my dark thoughts. It was only after a morning's strenuous exercise that I was able to feel myself again.

I parted from Charles at last, thanking him for the morning's activity, and then I returned home and sat with Sophia. She told me about her morning, and about her plans to buy a one-horse chaise so that she and Benjamin could drive around the country. Then, after listening to my account of my morning, she asked me, 'And what do you think of the Musgrove girls?'

'They are pretty, lively creatures,' I said.

'And do you think that you could marry either of them? You ought to be thinking of settling down, you know.'

'I dare say I have a heart for either of them, if they could catch it,' I returned lightly. 'I would have any pleasing young woman who came in my way.'

Except Anne Elliot, I thought.

She smiled at my levity, then said, 'I think either of them would make an agreeable wife. Have you no preference?'

'None at all. I am quite ready to make a foolish match. A little beauty, and a few smiles, and a few compliments to the Navy, and I am a lost man. Should not this be enough for a sailor, who has had no society among women to make him nice?'

She laughed at me, knowing I spoke in jest, and said I was the most fastidious man she had ever known.

'Do you not have any virtues in mind?' she asked. 'Any tastes or desires that would help you choose one of the Miss Musgroves over the other?'

'A strong mind, with sweetness of manner,' I said. 'That is all I ask. Something a little inferior I shall of course put up with, but it must not be much. If I am a fool, I shall be a fool indeed, for I have thought on the subject more than most men.'

'Then you have thought about it quite enough, and it is now time for action. I would like to see you settled, Frederick, and I am sure you will find your strong, but sweet, young lady soon. Who knows, but she may be residing at the Great House this very minute!'

We took luncheon together, then I set out for my afternoon ride.

A strong mind, I thought, that is my essential requirement. I will have no weak woman who will change her mind to please others. I will not marry until I find someone with strength of character and a mind of her own.

Thursday 20 October

Benjamin returned home today, and it was charming to see with what warmth my sister welcomed him. Theirs has been a happy marriage indeed.

Friday 21 October

Sophia, Benjamin and I dined with the Musgroves this evening, and we were quite a large party. Mr and Mrs Charles Musgrove were there. So, too, were some cousins of the Musgroves, the

Hayters, who lived nearby. And, as little Charles was much recovered, Anne also dined with us.

As I walked into the room, I remembered that there was a time, long ago, when we had opened our hearts to each other, but, although we spoke once or twice this evening our remarks never went beyond the commonplace, indeed, she said very little altogether. I did not know what to make of her silence, whether it was a general thing with her to be silent; or whether she was embarrassed, remembering past times; or whether, indeed, she had grown as proud as her family, and thought me beneath her notice.

It was a relief, then, to find that the Miss Hayters were just as noisy as the Miss Musgroves, for their chatter hid any awkward pauses, and the girls entertained us all with their nonsense.

They were fascinated by my life at sea and, gradually their questions brought me out of my introspection and drew me into the present. Their ignorance of seafaring matters was profound, and Miss Musgrove was astonished to find that we had food on board ship.

'But how did you suppose we lived, if we had no food?' I asked her. 'We would starve to death!'

'I suppose I thought you ate when you reached land,' she said.

'And how often would that be?'

'I do not know, I am sure,' she remarked. 'Once a week, perhaps?'

I laughed, and she continued, saying, 'Then, if you have

regular meals, you must have shops on board? How wonderful! I would dearly love to see them.'

'The very idea! Shops on board, indeed! Where would we put them?' Benjamin asked her.

'On deck,' she supplied.

'What! On deck? Do you think there is room amongst the cannons? Our ships are spacious, I grant you, but they are not as large as London!'

'Well, then, below deck,' she said, laughing. 'I am sure you must have room, for I cannot think what else you would put there. Besides, you must have shops, else how would you buy your food? You cannot have it delivered?'

Sophia and Benjamin smiled and I took pity on her, saying, 'We take it with us.'

'And how do you eat it?' asked Miss Musgrove. 'You cannot have a table and chairs, so I suppose you sit on deck and balance a plate on your knees?'

'And I suppose you think we eat with our fingers?' Benjamin asked, laughing even more.

'You cannot mean you have cutlery?'

'That is exactly what I mean.'

'I should not like to eat at sea, all the same,' said Miss Louisa. 'I would hate my meat raw.'

'Raw?' demanded Benjamin.

'I would not thank you for raw meat either,' said Sophia. 'We have a cook to dress the food, and a servant to wait on us.'

I saw Anne smiling, and I was taken back to the time when she had been as ignorant of the habits on board ship as the Musgrove girls now were. I remembered the delight I had taken in educating her, for I had felt the glow of her intelligence, and I had been heartened by the pleasure she had taken in learning about everything connected with me.

I resolutely turned my attention back to the Miss Musgroves. They would not be satisfied until I had explained to them everything about living on a ship: the food, the work, the hours, the daily routine.

Miss Musgrove then brought out the Navy List and the two sisters pored over it in an attempt to find out the ships I had commanded.

'Your first was the *Asp*, I remember; we will look for the *Asp*,' she said.

I remembered the *Asp* fondly, as every man remembers his first command. I thought of the happy times I had had with her but I would not admit it, teasing them by saying she had been a worn-out and broken-up old vessel.

'The Admiralty entertain themselves now and then with sending a few hundred men to sea in a ship not fit to be employed,' I said. 'But they have a great many to provide for; and among the thousands that may just as well go to the bottom as not, it is impossible for them to distinguish the very set who may be least missed.'

The two girls did not know what to make of this speech, but Benjamin laughed and said that never was there a better sloop than the *Asp* in her day.

'You were a lucky fellow to get her!' he said, turning to the ladies and saying, 'He knows there must have been twenty better men than himself applying for her at the same time. Lucky fellow to get anything so soon, with no more interest than his.'

'I felt my luck, Admiral, I assure you,' I replied. 'It was a great object with me at that time: to be at sea, a very great object; I wanted to be doing something.'

I felt my mood darken again as I recalled the reasons for it. I had been eager to escape because I had been rejected, and I had wanted something to take my mind off my troubles, for I had not wanted to spend the rest of my life brooding about Anne.

Benjamin luckily knew nothing of this.

'To be sure you did,' he replied. 'What should a young fellow like you do ashore for half a year together? If a man has not a wife, he soon wants to be afloat again.'

'I am sure you should have been given a better ship, whatever you say,' Miss Louisa remarked, 'for I am sure you deserved it.'

'Did you have any great adventures on the *Asp*?" asked Miss Musgrove.

'Many,' I said.

I regaled them with tales of my time with the *Asp*, the privateers I had taken, and the French frigate I had secured.

'I brought her into Plymouth,' I said, as they hung on my every word. 'We had not been six hours in the Sound, when a gale came on, which lasted four days and nights, and which would have done for poor old *Asp* in half the time, our touch with the Great Nation not having much improved our condition. Four-and-twenty hours later, and I should only have been a gallant Captain Wentworth, in a small paragraph at one corner of the newspapers; and being lost in only a sloop, nobody would have thought about me.'

I thought I saw Anne shuddering, and I felt as though the years had rolled away, leaving us close once more. But then I saw her pull her shawl higher and I realized she had done nothing more than shiver with the cold.

My attention was soon drawn back to the Miss Musgroves, who were full of exclamations of pity and horror. Then, having dispensed with the *Asp*, the girls began to look for the *Laconia*, and I took the List out of their hands to save them the trouble. I read aloud the statement of her name and rate, and present noncommissioned class.

'She, too, was one of the best friends man ever had,' I said. 'Ah! those were pleasant days! How fast I made money in the *Laconia*! A friend of mine and I had such a lovely cruise together off the Western Islands. Poor Harville, sister! You know how much he wanted money: worse than myself. He had a wife,' I said, thinking of Harriet, and the day on which I had stood up with him at his wedding. 'Excellent fellow! I shall never forget his happiness. He felt it all so much for her sake. I wished for him again the next summer, when I had still the same luck in the Mediterranean.'

Mrs Musgrove spoke, in a low voice, and took me by surprise by saying something about it being a lucky day for them when I was made captain of that ship. I did not understand her and I did not know how to reply.

'My brother,' whispered Miss Musgrove. 'Mama is thinking of poor Richard, who died.'

I was none the wiser and waited expectantly for more to follow, and follow it did. It seemed that Richard Musgrove had been, for a time, under my command. I searched my memory and remembered him eventually, a troublesome youth, with little aptitude for the sea.

'Poor dear fellow!' continued Mrs Musgrove, 'he was grown so steady, and such an excellent correspondent, while he was under your care! Ah! it would have been a happy thing if he had never left you. I assure you, Captain Wentworth, we are very sorry he ever left you.'

I remembered the difficulty I had had in making him write even one letter to his family; that is, one letter that was not begging for money, and I could not echo her sentiment, but I did not say so, for I saw that she was suffering. Instead, I joined her on the sofa, and entered into conversation with her about her son. I did everything in my power, by sympathy and a listening ear, to soothe her pain.

By and by, she calmed herself, until she was ready to join in the general conversation once more.

'What a great traveller you must have been, ma'am!' she said to my sister.

My sister told her of her travels, saying, 'But I never went beyond the Straits, and never was in the West Indies. We do not call Bermuda or Bahama, you know, the West Indies.'

Mrs Musgrove did not disagree, indeed I would have been surprised if she could accuse herself of having ever called them anything in the whole course of her life!

As Sophia spoke of her life at sea, I was pleased to see that Mrs Musgrove's tears had dried, and that she was absorbed in the conversation.

'But were you not frightened at sea?' asked Mrs Musgrove.

'Not a bit of it. When I was separated from Benjamin, I lived in perpetual fright, not knowing when I should hear from him next; but as long as we could be together, nothing ever ailed me,' she said.

Mrs Musgrove heartily agreed with this sentiment, saying, 'Yes, indeed, oh yes! I am quite of your opinion, Mrs Croft, there is nothing so bad as a separation, for Mr Musgrove always attends the assizes, and I am so glad when they are over, and he is safe back again.'

I caught Anne smiling at this, and I was reminded of the way our minds had always run together. It seemed as though they still did, on occasion, for we were both amused at the idea of Mr Musgrove being in as much danger when attending the assizes as Admiral Croft when he was sailing the North Sea!

'Mama, let us have some dancing,' said Miss Musgrove, growing tired of a conversation in which she had no part, and, still in high spirits, being eager for some exercise.

'Oh, yes, we must!' said Miss Hayter.

'I was just about to suggest it myself,' said Miss Louisa.

'What an excellent idea,' said Mrs Musgrove. 'And, see, we have Anne to play for us, and no one ever plays better, for I am sure her fingers fly over the keys!'

I was taken aback at this, for Anne had been relegated to the pianoforte without a by-your-leave.

'Does Miss Elliot never dance?' I asked Miss Louisa, troubled, as she claimed me for her partner.

'Oh, no! never; she has quite given up dancing. She had rather play. She is never tired of playing,' came the quick reply.

I did not believe it, for Anne had always loved to dance, and I was torn between a desire to defend her and to say she must have her share of the dancing, and exasperation that in all this time she had not learnt how to defend herself. Overlooked when her father and sister had gone to London without her; overlooked now, when her friends danced; but if she had had a little more spirit, a little more strength of character, she, too, could have had her share of the entertainments.

I danced twice with each of the Musgrove girls, and twice with each of the Hayter girls, and it was impossible not to be cheered by their enjoyment, though somehow it was not as cheering as it should have been, for I was ever conscious of Anne at the pianoforte.

At last the dancing came to an end. Anne left her seat and went over to the sofa to join Mrs Musgrove, and I went over to the instrument and tried to pick out an air for Miss Musgrove. I had got no further than the first line, however, when

Anne returned, and saying, 'I beg your pardon, madam, this is your seat,' I relinquished it.

I hoped to see some spark of the former Anne, some light in her eye, but there was nothing.

'No, not at all,' she said, drawing back.

And that was all I said to her. But although I continued to talk to the Miss Musgroves and the Miss Hayters, now and then sharing a word with Charles Musgrove or Charles Hayter, all the time I was conscious only of Anne: Anne talking low to Mr Musgrove, Anne moving over to the table, Anne taking a seat next to Miss Hayter.

Anne, always Anne.

Wednesday 26 October

I had been at home so little this week that Benjamin feigned astonishment to find me in the drawing-room just before dinner.

'What, not going to Uppercross?' he asked.

'I am not there every day, you know!' I replied.

'As near as makes no difference! I cannot say I blame you. The Musgrove girls are very pretty, and the Miss Hayters are almost as well-looking. And none of them is averse to being wooed by a captain home from the sea. Or do you go there for the pleasure of Mr and Mrs Musgrove's company?' he asked.

'But of course! They are most agreeable people.'

Sophia smiled, then said, 'And when are you going into Shropshire? The Musgroves are not the only agreeable people in England, you know. Your brother is very agreeable, too. He is longing to introduce you to his new wife.'

'A country parson cannot hope to compete with the joys of a house full of young women, even if he has a wife!' said Benjamin jovially. 'Frederick has been spoiled by the flattery of those girls.'

I cried out against it, but he is right, I am very fond of their society. They never tire of hearing about the naval battles I have passed through, or my life on board ship, or my promotion, or the ports I have visited. And in return, they never tire of telling me about their friends, their family, their neighbours, their gowns and bonnets. And when all has been said, there is dancing and music to occupy us in a most enjoyable way.

'Come, Frederick, tell us, have you still not decided between them?' asked Benjamin teasingly.

'I am in no hurry,' I said.

'Miss Musgrove is the prettiest,' said Benjamin, 'and I like the eldest Miss Hayter, but I think I like Miss Louisa more. She is as spirited a girl as I ever hope to meet.'

'When you have finished finding Frederick a wife, perhaps you would turn your attention to encouraging him to visit his brother. You should not neglect Edward,' said Sophia to me. 'He wants you to meet his wife, you know, for she is a very fine young lady, and you promised him a visit.'

'Never fear, I will go and see him before very long, but for now, I will have to take her virtues on credit.'

'He wants to show you the house, too,' said Benjamin. 'You are not the only one who has been lucky in your advancement.'

'No, indeed, he has been fortunate to achieve his own living, particularly such a good one,' said Sophia.

'Ay, it is not easy to find preferment in the church,' I said, 'far less easy than in the Navy, where a man's battles will speak for him. Even with some interest it is difficult. I was speaking to Charles Hayter about it only yesterday. You know Charles Hayter? He is brother to the Miss Hayters, and cousin to the Miss Musgroves. He lives with his family at Winthrop, just over the hill from Uppercross.'

'Yes, we have met him,' said Sophia.

'He has a curacy, but it is six miles distant. Fortunately, residency is not required, so he lives with his father at Winthrop. There was talk last night of his getting the curacy of Uppercross, a very good thing, for it would mean only a two mile journey to attend to his duties instead of his current six-mile trip.'

'You must talk to Edward about it when you visit him,' said Sophia. 'I will be writing to him tomorrow. Shall I give him notice of your arrival?'

'Tell him, if it is convenient for him, I will call in a fortnight,' I said.

She was pleased, and we went into dinner.

Thursday 27 October

This morning when I went to visit the Miss Musgroves I found them from home. Mrs Musgrove assured me they had gone to the Cottage to see their nephew so I followed them, but when I was shown into the drawing-room I was taken aback to find Anne there instead. She was quite alone, apart from the little invalid Charles, who was lying on the sofa.

'I thought the Miss Musgroves would be here,' I said, walking over to the window to rid myself of my sudden agitation. 'Mrs Musgrove told me I should find them here.'

'They are upstairs with my sister. They will be down in a few moments, I dare say,' she replied.

She did not seem comfortable; no more was I; but fortunately the child called to her and we were able to escape our embarrassment, she by kneeling down by the sofa to tend to Charles, and I by remaining at the window.

I did not know what to say. Were we destined to treat each other coldly, because of what had passed between us? Could we not put it behind us and be civil, at least? I almost suggested it, but such a tide of feeling rose within me at the thought of mentioning the past, or even alluding to it, that I remained silent.

A fourth person then arrived, but not one to make matters easier, for it was Charles Hayter. He did not seem pleased to see me, and I wondered whether he and Anne were friends, or more than friends, for if they were, then it would explain his attitude towards me. I glanced towards Anne, but there was no sudden smile on her lips, no joyous welcome, and I dismissed such notions. Anne invited him to sit down and wait for the others, and accordingly, he took a seat.

I wanted to make up to him for my coolness on his arrival and so I went over to him, preparing to make a remark about the weather, but he was apparently not disposed for conversation, because he took up the newspaper and buried his head behind it.

And so we sat, not talking, until there was a distraction in the way of a very small boy, who ran into the room.

'Ah, Walter,' said Hayter, glancing up once from his newspaper before burying his face once again.

Walter, a stout young man of some two years old, ran over to his brother. As he was of an age to tease his brother rather than to be of any help, however, Anne endeavoured to keep him away, but he was in the mood for attention, and as soon as her back was turned, he made a nuisance of himself by climbing onto it. As she was busy with Charles, she could not rid herself of him, but could only tell him to get down.

Her orders to him were in vain.

She contrived to push him away, but the boy had the greater pleasure in climbing onto her back again.

Hayter looked up from his paper and said, 'Walter! Leave your aunt in peace,' but Walter paid him no heed.

Seeing a need for action, I lifted the boy from her back and carried him away to the other side of the room, where I entertained him so that he could not return to plague her.

I received no thanks from her; indeed I looked for none, but I felt a mixture of emotions at having rendered her a service.

I should be angry with her for betraying me. I *was* angry with her. And yet I felt a bittersweet pleasure at being able to help her when she needed it.

The atmosphere was strained, and it remained so until Mary and the two Musgrove girls found us. Anne immediately quit the room. Then there was the exchange of civilities, after which Hayter and I escorted the young ladies back to the Great House.

The atmosphere on our walk was not a happy one. Miss Musgrove seemed out of spirits and Hayter seemed to be angry, so I declined their invitation to go in.

Once back at Kellynch Hall my steps turned towards the river and I strode along, lost in thought. Why had Anne ignored me? And why had she left the room as soon as she had been able to relinquish her care of little Charles to his mother? Did she really dislike me so much? If *I* had been the one who had wronged *her*, I could have understood her manner, but *she* had wronged *me*. Could it be that she had resented me for speaking so harshly to Lady Russell?

I pondered the subject until I caught sight of Sophia's chaise bowling along the drive, and I returned to the Hall in a dissatisfied state of mind. I could not understand Anne's behaviour. But perhaps it had nothing to do with me. Perhaps she had been late for a visit, delayed by the need to look after Charles, and had had to hurry out as soon as she could leave the boy.

That seemed more likely, for she had spoken barely two words to me since I returned, and she probably never thought of me at all.

NOVEMBER

Tuesday 1 November

Sophia had a letter from Edward this morning, saying he would be away next week, but inviting me to visit him on the 19th. I wrote back and confirmed the arrangement. I am looking forward to meeting his wife and to seeing him again.

Saturday 5 November

Charles Musgrove and I had arranged to spend the morning together and I set out for Uppercross Cottage in good spirits, for it was a beautiful morning with the copper leaves shining in the autumn sunshine. As I drew near the Cottage, however, my steps began to drag, for I did not want to find myself in another embarrassing situation. I need not have worried because

I found Musgrove out of doors, ready and waiting for me. Our sport was good for the first half hour, but no sooner had we really begun to enjoy ourselves than we had to return, for the young dog with us was not fully trained and had spoiled our sport.

When we returned to the Cottage, we found that the Miss Musgroves were about to set out on a long walk, accompanied by Mary.

'Come with us!' Louisa pleaded.

'We do not want to spoil your exercise,' I said.

She laughed at the idea, and cajoled and entreated, until Charles and I gave in, and we all set out together. I walked ahead, with Henrietta on one arm and Louisa on the other, and Anne fell behind with Mary and Charles.

We soon came to a stile and, as it was rather high, Charles helped both Anne and Mary down. It was left to me to help Henrietta, and then Louisa. As she was the smallest of the party, she had to jump, and I caught her round the waist to assist her when she landed. She found the experience so delightful that she climbed back onto the stile and then did it again. We all laughed, and when we reached the next stile, nothing would do for her but that I should jump her down again.

We spoke of generalities and then I mentioned that my sister and her husband had gone on a long drive. As we walked on together, I told Louisa about their habit of overturning, saying, 'But my sister indulges her husband, and does not mind.'

'I should do just the same in her place,' said Louisa gaily. 'If I loved a man as she loves the admiral, I would always be with him, nothing should ever separate us, and I would rather be overturned by him than driven safely by anybody else.'

'Really?' I said with a laugh, catching her tone. 'I honour you!'

But as we fell silent to negotiate a steep hill, I thought over what she had said, that she would not let anything part her and her husband. She was a resolute young woman, one with plenty of strength, and the more I thought about it, the more I was convinced that she would not let anyone tell her what to do. I glanced at Anne and then looked away, though why I should still feel so strongly about something that happened eight years ago I could not imagine.

We reached the top of the hill and below us we could see the Winthrop estate. As we were so near, Charles Musgrove professed his intention of calling at the farm and paying his respects to his aunt. Mary declared she could not walk so far and, after some conferring, it was at last arranged that Miss Musgrove should go with him whilst the rest of us would stay behind.

We sat down to wait. Mary was fractious, and Louisa soon asked me if I would help her glean some nuts. I agreed. We made a good beginning, for there were plenty of nuts to be had. We went up and down the hedgerows and, as we did so, I learned that there was an understanding between Henrietta and Charles Hayter.

At once I understood why he had been annoyed to find

me at Uppercross Cottage, and why he had not spoken to me: he had seen in me a rival for his lady's affections. It seemed that my presence had made an estrangement between them, and that Henrietta had intended to call upon him to set things to rights, but had almost changed her mind when Mary had declared herself too tired to go.

'What! Would I be turned back from doing a thing that I had determined to do, and that I knew to be right, by the airs and interference of such a person, or of any person, I may say?' she asked. 'No, I have no idea of being so easily persuaded. When I have made up my mind, I have made it. And Henrietta seemed entirely to have made up hers to call at Winthrop today; and yet, she was as near giving it up out of nonsensical complaisance!'

'She would have turned back, then, but for you?'

'She would, indeed. I am almost ashamed to say it.'

'Happy for her, to have such a mind as yours at hand! Your sister is an amiable creature; but *yours* is the character of decision and firmness, I see. Let those who would be happy be firm. If Louisa Musgrove would be beautiful and happy in her November of life, she will cherish all her present powers of mind.'

I realized, when I had finished, how strange my words must have sounded to her, for they reflected on much of my life that had gone before. She was, indeed, silent for a while, but at last she spoke again, turning the conversation. She could not have hit upon a theme closer to my heart.

'Mary is good-natured enough in many respects, but she

does sometimes provoke me excessively by her nonsense and her pride—the Elliot pride. She has a great deal too much of the Elliot pride.'

I silently agreed.

'We do so wish that Charles had married Anne instead.'

I was dumbfounded. Charles had wanted to marry Anne? I had never suspected it.

'I suppose you know he wanted to marry Anne?' asked Louisa.

I could not command myself immediately, but at last I said, to be quite clear, 'Do you mean that he proposed to her and she refused him?'

'Oh! yes; certainly.'

'When did that happen?'

'I do not exactly know, for Henrietta and I were at school at the time; but I believe it was about a year before he married Mary. I wish she had accepted him. We should all have liked her a great deal better; and Papa and Mama always think it was her great friend Lady Russell's doing, that she did not. They think Charles might not be learned and bookish enough to please Lady Russell, and that, therefore, she persuaded Anne to refuse him.'

Could it be true? Could Lady Russell once again have persuaded Anne to refuse another suitor?

'When were Mary and Charles married?' I asked nonchalantly.

'Four years ago, in 1810,' said Louisa.

I was left with much food for thought. Had Lady Russell

persuaded Anne to turn down another suitor, or could there be some other explanation? A part of me felt there must be, for I did not believe Lady Russell would be set against Charles Musgrove. He had a respectable home, good prospects, and she had appeared to like him when I saw her with him in the year six.

Could it be that Anne had turned him down on her own account?

I stole another glance at her, trying to read the answer in her face, and I was still trying to solve the riddle when I was startled by the sight of Sophia and Benjamin in their one-horse chaise. They pulled up beside us and asked if any of the ladies would like to be driven home.

'There is room for one more, and, as we are going through Uppercross, it will cut a mile off the journey,' said Benjamin.

The ladies declined, but as we crossed the lane I noticed that Anne looked fatigued. I spoke in an aside to my sister, and she said, 'Miss Elliot, I am sure *you* are tired. Do let us have the pleasure of taking you home. Here is excellent room for three, I assure you. If we were all like you, I believe we might sit four. You must, indeed, you must.'

Benjamin added his voice to his wife's, and I assisted Anne into the carriage. As I touched her hand, I felt all the power of my previous emotions. I recalled the times I had touched her before, dancing with her, walking with her, embracing her, and I could not understand how we had grown so estranged.

Had I been wrong to leave in the year six? Had I been wrong not to go back? Had I been a fool not to write to her, as I had almost done, in the year eight, when I found myself with a few thousand pounds? Pride had held me back, and the fear of being rejected again. But if I had conquered my pride and routed my fear of another rejection, then might the last six years have been different?

I watched her as she drove off, still puzzling over what I had heard. She had had a chance to marry respectably, and yet she had declined it. Why? What did it mean? Did it mean that he did not match up to another love?

But no, such thoughts were folly. She had shown neither interest nor enjoyment in my company since my arrival in the neighbourhood; indeed, she had done everything in her power to avoid me and to make any intimate conversation impossible. She had made her feelings clear.

Monday 7 November

I was unsettled to learn that Anne and I were to be thrust into closer acquaintance, for over breakfast my sister informed me that Anne would shortly be leaving her sister's house and staying at Kellynch Lodge with Lady Russell.

'The news is all around Uppercross. Lady Russell will soon be returning from an engagement that has kept her absent for several weeks,' said Sophia. 'I hear very good things of her. An intelligent, sensible woman, by all accounts. Did you meet her when you were here before?'

'I believe so.'

'And was she as amiable as the reports would have her be?'

'I saw very little of her,' was all I would say.

'It will be good to see some new faces about the place, at church and so forth,' said Benjamin. 'Lady Russell and Miss Elliot will add variety to our evening gatherings. Living in our neighbourhood as they will be, we must have them to dine with us.'

I was not sure whether I liked the idea or not. To see Anne again, to be with her, was a strange kind of torment. Why did she turn down Charles Musgrove? Was it for me? The thought plagued me. Yes, she was cold with me. Yes, she avoided me, but could that not be through awkwardness? I wished I knew.

A letter was brought in and I seized it, eager to distract my thoughts from the unanswerable problem of Anne. As I began to read, I found it to be from Harville.

'Capital!' I said, as my eyes went down the page.

Sophia looked at me enquiringly.

'At last, Harville has found a bigger house, in Lyme. He and Harriet are to stay there for the winter. This is a stroke of luck, for it is not twenty miles away! I will ride over there today.'

'Splendid,' said Benjamin. 'You can see how that poor fellow—what was his name?'

'Benwick.'

'That's it, Benwick, you can see how he goes on. Poor man, to return home, only to find his fiancée dead. It is not the way a man expects it to happen. That he might not return he knows, but that the ones on shore should die is a sad blow.'

'It was a bad business,' said Sophia.

'If I can render him or Harville any assistance, I will be happy to do so, for you know that Harville is now lame, wounded badly two years ago. A visit will give me a good opportunity to learn all their news.'

'You might have some news of your own to give him before long,' said Sophia.

'Ay, it is about time,' said Benjamin. 'You are lagging behind. Harville unfurled his sails years ago and has outraced you, Frederick. He has three children now, has he not?'

'He has, fine children all of them.'

But whilst he continued to tease me, I refused to be drawn. I set out soon afterwards and rode to Lyme. As I saw the sea, I reined in my horse and feasted my eyes upon it. I let my gaze wander over the pleasant little bay and the line of cliffs stretching out beyond it. I let my eyes drop to the Cobb and thought how useful it was, for it formed an excellent sea wall and provided a place for fishing boats to be tied up.

At last I rode on, going down into the town. I followed the main street as it went down to the sea, until I came to Harville's house. It was small and dilapidated but it had a splendid location, for it was in a sheltered spot near the foot of the pier and had an unrivalled view of the sea.

I was made very welcome, with Harville and his wife greeting me warmly and the children running round my feet.

They had grown since last I saw them, the baby most of all, for he was not a baby anymore, rather a fine lad of three years old who ran along behind the older children, eager for his share of the fun.

'Well, what do you think of our new home?' asked Harville.

'It is almost like being on a ship,' I said appreciatively.

'We chose it for that reason,' he said.

We went in and I saw Benwick sitting by the fire. He welcomed me cordially, but his spirits were low. They brightened a little as the three of us reminisced about out experiences on the *Laconia*, however.

'That was a fine ship,' said Benwick.

'And with three of the Navy's finest officers aboard!' I said.

But as Harville and I relived one adventure after another, Benwick became quiet, and he retired early. Harville and I sat up talking and, as we did so, Benwick's past became a subject for us.

'I am forever grateful to you for breaking the news to him,' said Harville. 'Nobody else could have saved poor James. I am only thankful you stayed aboard with him for a week, helping him over the worst of it.'

'I was glad to do it, though it was little enough.'

I fell silent, thinking of Harville's sister, the girl I had met back in the year six, and Harville's hints that he would like us to marry. A pretty girl, with a superior mind, the sort of girl that is not met with every day. I thought sorrowfully of her early death.

'Do you mean to keep Benwick with you?' I asked at last.

'Yes. He has no family, and his health being poor it is difficult for him to set up a home by himself. Besides, Fanny's memory unites us.'

Tuesday 8 November

The children woke us early and we were soon out of doors, for the morning was fine and the winter sunshine beckoned. We walked down to the Cobb.

'It is much busier in the summer months,' said Harville, as the gulls cried above us. 'The town is full of visitors, and the boarding houses are full. The assembly rooms are open, and there is plenty to do. It is rather quiet over winter, but it suits us.'

I looked at the bathing machines drawn up on the beach and imagined them full of people in the summer.

We reached the Cobb and the two eldest children pleaded to be allowed to go on to the high part.

'Please, Papa, there is no wind today to blow us off.'

'Very well,' said their father. 'But you must take my hands.'

They did as they were bid. Harriet held little Thomas's hand, and we all went up together. The air was still and the sun warmed our faces. Benwick quoted poetry, and I thought how much Anne would have enjoyed walking along the

Cobb, with such a view, quoting Byron. I thought of the house we had planned to have by the sea, and I was angry with her again for rejecting me. We could have been happy, as Harville and Harriet were happy.

We came to the end of the Cobb and turned back. A breeze sprang up and I could see why Harville would not let the children walk there without holding his hand, for a sudden gust of wind could have blown them over. We reached the end of the Cobb and went down the steps, then returned to Harville's house in time for an early luncheon.

I set out soon afterwards, for I had a long ride ahead of me, and I wanted to be home before dark. This I almost achieved, and I found that I was ready for my meal.

Sophia and Benjamin were eager to hear about my day, and I, in turn, was eager to hear about theirs. They had spent it exploring the countryside to the north, and Sophia was delighted that they had taken only one tumble!

Wednesday 9 November

I went to Uppercross this morning and I found that I had been missed. The Musgroves complained that I had not been to see them for two whole days, and Louisa teased me about it, saying I no longer cared for them. I explained why I had not been able to call, and I was honoured for my attention to my friend.

'I have never been to Lyme. What is it like?' she asked.

'The countryside is very grand. There is a long hill leading into the town and the main street is steeper still. The bay is small but pleasant, and there are cliffs stretching out to the east of the town. In the summer there is plenty to do, with sea-bathing and assemblies, though everything by the way of amusement is shut up now for the winter.'

'I am longing to see it,' she said. 'We should all go.'

Her suggestion met with an enthusiastic reception, and before long the visit was being planned. The first idea was to go in the morning and return at night, but this was thought to be too arduous for the horses, and when the matter was considered fully, it was apparent that there would not be enough daylight to see the town at this time of year if travelling had to take place in the same day as well. In the end, it was decided we would travel there tomorrow, stay overnight, and return on Friday.

I left the party in high good humour, for they were all looking forward to it.

Thursday 10 November

We met at the Great House for an early breakfast, and then set out. Mary, Henrietta, Louisa and Anne took the coach, whilst Charles and I went in the curricle. The journey was long, and by the time we arrived it was well past noon. We made straight for an inn, at which we secured accommodation and bespoke our dinner, and then we walked down to the sea. Although the public rooms were shut up, there was enough in the grandeur of the landscape and the splendour of the sea to interest the ladies. As we walked, I told them of the neighbouring areas: Charmouth, with its high grounds and its small bay backed by dark cliffs; the village of Up Lyme; and Pinny, with its green chasms and dramatic rocks.

We lingered on the seashore, looking at the ocean, and then I went to call on Harville whilst the others walked on to the Cobb.

Harville was delighted to see me again, and when I told him of my party, nothing would do for him and his wife, and Benwick as well, but that they should come out and meet my friends.

Harville pressed us to dine with him, and Harriet added her entreaties. Only the fact that we had already bespoken dinner at the inn made them accept, reluctantly, that we could not join them. They consoled themselves by inviting us back to their house at once, and we were happy to accept.

It was a time of good cheer and, my gaze being drawn to Anne, as so often happened, I saw something of her former animation, for she was engaged in lively conversation with Harville. Her eyes were bright, and I discovered that the tone of her mind had not changed, for every word she uttered was a word I could have uttered myself.

I found myself once again torn between frustration with her for rejecting me, anger with myself for not writing to her in the year eight, and hope that she might yet be in love with me.

When we left, Louisa was in raptures.

'How friendly they all were, and how industrious,' she

said. 'Did you see the toys Captain Harville had made for his children? We never had finer toys ourselves. It seems to me that sailors are the only people who know how to live. They have given us so much, they should be respected and loved by every one of us.'

Her speech was unaffected, but, after Anne's conversation, it seemed to belong in the schoolroom.

To Anne herself I said little, for I did not know what to say. I could not speak to her intimately in such surroundings, amongst so many people, and yet I could scarcely bear not to speak to her.

All through dinner I was aware of her, and I stole glances at her whenever I could. What was she thinking? What was she feeling? I was longing to speak to her after dinner, but we had a surprise visit from Harville and Benwick, so it was out of the question.

Harville and I gave in to the entreaties of the Miss Musgroves and entertained them with stories of our adventures aboard the *Laconia*, but again and again I found my glance wandering to Anne. She had gone to sit by Benwick, who had retreated to a quiet corner, for his spirits were still low and would not easily stand such a noisy gathering.

It was like her kind and generous spirit to bear him company, and from what little I heard of their conversation, I could tell they were talking of poetry. I wished that I was the one sitting in the corner with her, talking to her in such a free and open way, instead of being forced to entertain the other ladies.

Harville and Benwick left at last, and once again I hoped I might have a chance to speak to Anne, but the ladies retired straight away.

As I followed them some half an hour later, I felt myself growing increasingly frustrated at the insipidity of the general conversation and wanting something more; something I had always found with Anne.

Friday 11 November

I rose early and I was eager to be out of doors, for it was a fine morning, with the tide rushing in before a south-easterly breeze. I hoped to meet Anne in the parlour, but, on going downstairs, I discovered that she had already gone out. Louisa was there, however, and, breakfast not being ready, she suggested that we might go for a walk upon the Cobb. We went out and walked down to the sea. It was grey, flecked with white, and overhead wheeled the squawking gulls.

We had not been out of doors for very long when we saw Anne and Henrietta. Anne was blooming. The fresh wind had lent colour to her cheeks and a brightness to her eye, and she looked as she had looked eight years ago, when I first knew her. The day faded into nothingness, and I stood in a cloud of silence, seeing nothing, hearing nothing, nothing except Anne. She was laughing, for the wind was whipping her hair across her face, and, as I watched her, she raised her hand and pushed it back from her cheek, tucking it behind her ear. Then her eyes met mine. How long we stood thus I do not know, but however long it was, it was not long enough. I drank her in, her mild dark eyes, her laughing countenance, and her soft brown hair; all held me entranced.

And then a sudden gust of wind blew against us, and Louisa clutched at my arm, bringing me back to the present. I tried to reclaim the moment, but Anne had turned away, and it was gone beyond recall.

'You are out early,' said Henrietta.

I said nothing, for the vision of Anne, restored to loveliness, had rendered me speechless.

'But not as early as you,' said Louisa. 'I thought Captain Wentworth and I were the only two people awake.'

'We have been out a full half hour, have we not, Anne?' said Henrietta.

Anne seemed to be having as much difficulty as I in replying. The silence was covered by Louisa saying that there was something she wanted at the shop, and she invited us all to go back into town with her. We declared ourselves willing to accompany her and walked back across the beach.

As we came to the steps leading upwards, we saw a gentleman at the top, preparing to come down. He drew back and gave way so that the ladies could pass. Anne and Henrietta ascended first, and as they reached the top, I saw the gentleman looking at Anne, and then looking again. I was hit by a wave of jealousy, for he had no right to look at her in that way. I contained myself, and we walked on to the shops in peace.

Once Louisa had made her purchases we returned to the inn, where we found breakfast waiting for us. Mary and

Charles were there and, when we had rid ourselves of our outdoor clothes, we joined them.

We had nearly finished when we heard the sound of a curricle outside. Charles jumped up to see if it was as fine as his own and we all collected at the window to look. The owner of the curricle came out, and I perceived him to be the same gentleman who had passed us on the steps up from the beach.

I saw Anne smile, and once again I felt a hot rush of jealousy, this time worse than before. Why had she smiled on him, and not on me?

On a sudden impulse, I asked the waiter, 'Pray, can you tell us the name of the gentleman who is just gone away?'

'Yes, sir, a Mr Elliot.'

'*Elliot?*' I asked in astonishment, whilst there was a general murmur all around me.

'A gentleman of large fortune, came in last night from Sidmouth,' the waiter went on. 'Dare say you heard the carriage, sir, while you were at dinner; and going on now for Crewkherne, on his way to Bath and London.'

'Bless me!' cried Mary. 'It must be our cousin.'

So *this* was Mr Elliot, the man Miss Elliot had assiduously pursued, and lost, all those years ago, the man she had deemed worthy of her hand—and who was now evidently in mourning, for he wore crêpe around his hat. I wondered who had died and, making discreet enquiries of Charles, I discovered that Mr Elliot had married some years before, but that he had recently been widowed. There were no children, he told me, but Sir Walter had not made overtures to him again, on account of some slighting remarks he had made about his relatives, which had reached Sir Walter's ears.

But what a man for Anne to meet, here, now! I thought in dismay.

'What a pity that we should not have been introduced to each other!' went on Mary. 'Do you think he had the Elliot countenance? I hardly looked at him, I was looking at the horses; but I think he had something of the Elliot countenance. I wonder the arms on the carriage did not strike me!'

Charles remarked that the greatcoat had been hanging over the panel, and Mary exclaimed that, if the servant had not been in mourning, she should have known him by the livery.

I, on the other hand, was vastly relieved that we had not known his identity sooner, for then introductions must have been made, and Anne would have come to know him further.

'Putting all these very extraordinary circumstances together,' I said, trying to hide my agitation, 'we must consider it to be the arrangement of Providence that you should not be introduced to your cousin.'

I looked at Anne, hoping she would see it as such. To my relief, she seemed to have no wish to pursue the acquaintance, for she said that their father and Mr Elliot had not spoken for many years, and that an introduction was not desirable.

I was heartened but, without knowing her mind, I could not know her full reasons for not wanting to pursue the acquaintance. Was it because of her father, as she said, or was it . . . could it be . . . that her feelings were already engaged– by me?

I tried to read the answer in her face, but I could detect nothing. I wished I knew why she had refused Charles Musgrove; I wished I knew if she was indifferent to me, or whether she was merely reserved; if she had ever missed me; and if she regretted her decision to reject me.

We were soon joined by the Harvilles and Benwick, for we had arranged to take a last walk with them before departing. Harriet gave it as her opinion that her husband would have had quite enough walking by the time he reached home, and so we determined to accompany the Harvilles to their door, and then set off home ourselves.

We parted from the Harvilles as planned, and were about to return to the inn when some of the party expressed a wish to take one final walk along the Cobb. Louisa was so determined to have this last pleasure that we gave in to her, and Benwick came with us.

There was too much wind on the high part to make the walk enjoyable so we decided to go down the steps to the lower part. Louisa insisted on being jumped down them by me, as she had often been jumped down from stiles.

I tried to discourage her, saying the pavement was too hard for her feet, but she insisted. I gave in to her demands but, as I did so, I began to think that a determined character was not so very desirable after all. If it was firm in its pursuit of right, then it was estimable, but if it was firm in pursuit of its own desires, it was simply wilful.

I had done the damage, however, and must, for the time being, abide by it. I jumped her down the steps with no harm done, and there it should have ended, but she ran up the steps to be jumped down again.

Again, I tried to persuade her to abandon the idea, but I spoke in vain.

'I am determined I will,' she said.

She jumped with no further warning. I put out my hands; I was half a second too late; she fell on the pavement on the Lower Cobb . . . and I looked at her in horror, for she was dead.

A thousand thoughts went through my mind, tormenting me for my folly: I should not have made so much of her; I should never have jumped her down from a stile; I should not have encouraged her to think that being headstrong was a virtue; I should not have brought her to Lyme. A thousand thoughts, whirling round as I caught her up, my body reacting to the crisis as it had reacted to countless crises at sea, taking charge, doing what was necessary, looking for a wound, for blood, for bruising . . . but there was nothing. Yet her eyes were closed, she breathed not, and her face was like death.

'She is dead! She is dead!' screamed Mary, catching hold of her husband.

Henrietta fainted, and would have fallen on the steps, but for Benwick and Anne, who caught and supported her between them.

'Is there no one to help me?' I cried, borne down by a weight of guilt and despair, and feeling my strength gone.

'Go to him, go to him, for heaven's sake go to him.'

It was Anne's voice; Anne, who could be relied upon in a

crisis; Anne rousing Charles and Benwick, who were at my side in a moment, supporting Louisa. As they took her from me, I stood up, but, underestimating the effect the shock had had on me, I staggered, and once more catching sight of her pale face, I cried, 'Oh God! her father and mother!'

I could not bear to think of them at Uppercross, imagining us happy, and trusting me to bring their daughter safely home again.

'A surgeon!' said Anne.

Her common sense restored me to sanity.

'True, true, a surgeon this instant,' I said, and I was about to go and fetch one when Anne said that Benwick would know better where one was to be found.

Again, her cool, calm common sense prevailed. Benwick gave Louisa into Charles's care and was off for the town with the utmost rapidity.

'Anne, what is to be done next?' cried Charles, and I realized that everyone was looking to her in their extremity.

'Had not she better be carried to the inn? Yes, I am sure: carry her gently to the inn,' said Anne.

Her words roused me once again and, eager to be doing something, I took Louisa up myself. Her eyes fluttered, and I felt a moment of wild, surging hope as they opened and I knew her to be alive! What joy! What rapture!

'She lives!' I cried.

There was a cry of relief from all around. But then her eyes closed, and she gave no more sign of consciousness.

We had not even left the Cobb when Harville met us, for

he had been alerted by Benwick on his way for the surgeon, and had run out to meet us. He told us we must avail ourselves of his house, and before long we were all beneath his roof. Louisa, under Harriet's direction, was conveyed upstairs, and we all breathed again.

The surgeon was with us almost before it had seemed possible, and to our great relief he declared that the case was not hopeless. The head had received a severe contusion, but he had seen greater injuries recovered from.

'Thank God!' I said. 'Thank God!'

My cry was echoed by her sisters and brother, and I saw Anne silently giving thanks. But my thanks were the most heartfelt of all. I had not killed her, I who had encouraged her recklessness and taught her not to listen to others. But I had injured her. It was burden enough. I sank down into a chair and slumped across the table, my head sunk on my arms, unable to forgive myself.

By and by I roused myself. I could not leave the arrangements to Anne—Anne, who had done so much, who had kept her head, and proved herself superior to all others in every way.

It was quickly arranged that Benwick would give up his room so that a member of our party could stay, giving Louisa the comfort of a familiar face in the house with her, and Harriet, an experienced nurse, took it upon herself to nurse her.

'And Ellen, my nursery-maid, is as experienced as I am. Together we will look after her, day and night,' she said.

I tried to thank her, but she would not take thanks, saying

that she was glad to repay me for my kindness in breaking the news of Fanny's death to Benwick. Then she returned to the upstairs room, where Anne was sitting with Louisa.

I was glad that Anne was with Louisa. It was always Anne people turned to in a time of crisis. It was Anne who had managed matters when her nephew had dislocated his collar-bone; it was Anne who had directed us when Louisa had taken a fall. Anne, always Anne who, without any fuss, showed the strength of her mind by her ability to know what was best, and to see it brought about in a quiet, calm manner. I had tried to forget her, but it had proved impossible, for she was superior to any other woman I had ever met.

'This is a bad business,' said Charles.

His face was white with worry.

'My poor father and mother. How is the news to be broken to them?' said Henrietta.

There was a silence, for no one could bear to think of it. But it must be done.

'Musgrove, either you or I must go,' I said.

Charles agreed, but he would not leave his sister in such a state.

'Then I will do it,' I said.

He thanked me heartily, and said I must take Henrietta with me, for she was overcome by the shock.

'No, I will not leave Louisa,' Henrietta said.

'But think of Mama and Papa. They must have someone to comfort them when they hear the news,' said Charles.

Her heart was touched, and she consented to go home. It

was a relief to all of us, for at home she would be well taken care of, and we would not have to worry about her as well as her sister.

'Then it is settled, Musgrove, that you stay, and that I take care of escorting your sister home,' I said. 'But as to the rest, your wife will, of course, wish to get back to her children; but if Anne will stay, no one so proper, so capable as Anne.'

It was at that moment that Anne appeared. Anne, collected and calm. Anne, the sight of whom filled me with strength and courage.

'You will stay, I am sure; you will stay and nurse her,' I said gently, longing to take her hands in mine as I had done once before, marvelling how I could fold both of them in my own. Such small hands, and yet so capable.

She coloured deeply. I wanted to speak to her, to ascertain her feelings, and to tell her mine, but now was not the time, so I made her a bow and moved away.

She turned to Charles, saying that she was happy to remain.

Everything was settled, and I hastened to the inn to hire a chaise, so that we could travel more quickly. The horses were put to, and then I had nothing to do but wait for Henrietta to join me. At last she came, but, to my surprise, Anne was with her. The reason was soon made clear to me. Being jealous of Anne, Mary had demanded to be the one to stay and help with the nursing, and had said that Anne should return to Uppercross.

I was angry at the arrangement, but it could not be helped,

and so I handed the ladies into the chaise. I looked at Anne, but she avoided my eyes, and then, I, too, climbed into the chaise, and we were away.

We spoke little on the journey, for our spirits were low, and I had plenty of time to think about how I should tell Louisa's parents.

When we reached the neighbourhood of Uppercross, I said to Anne, 'I think you had better remain in the carriage with Henrietta, while I go in and break the news to her parents. Do you think this a good plan?'

She did, and I was satisfied.

I left the chaise at the door and went into the house. I was welcomed warmly, though with some anxiety, for Mr and Mrs Musgrove had become worried owing to the lateness of the hour. I felt a moment of sick apprehension as I was reminded of the nightmare of breaking the news of Fanny's death to Benwick, but this news was not so bad. This news had hope. I took courage from the thought, and I began to speak.

There was alarm. How could there not be? But though I did not seek to lessen the seriousness of the situation, I told them, many times, that the surgeon did not despair, and that he had seen worse injuries recovered from. Mr Musgrove, after the first shock, comforted his wife, and when she was sufficiently calm, I escorted Henrietta and Anne indoors.

As soon as they were as comfortable as possible, I returned to Lyme, so that I would be on hand in case I should be of any assistance.

And now here I am at the inn once more, in my own

room, but unable to sleep. As I sit here, I can think of nothing but Anne: our meeting, our courtship, our separation, and our meeting again.

I have acknowledged at last, what I believe I have known all along, that I am still in love with her. I have never stopped loving her. In eight years I have never seen her equal because she has no equal.

As soon as Louisa is out of danger, I must tell Anne how I feel and ask her, once again, to be my wife.

Saturday 12 November

Louisa passed a good night, and, to my enormous relief, there had not been any turn for the worse. The surgeon called again and pronounced himself satisfied, saying that a speedy cure must not be looked for, but that everything was progressing well, and that if she was not moved or excited, he had hopes of a full recovery.

My relief was profound. If only she could be restored to full health and spirits, I would be a grateful man.

As soon as the surgeon left us, Charles went to Uppercross to give his parents an account of Louisa's progress. He promised to return, however, and at last he did so, bringing with him the Musgroves's nursery-maid. She, having seen the last of the children off to school, spent her days in the deserted nursery, patching any scrape she could come near, and she was only too pleased to visit Lyme and nurse her beloved Miss Louisa.

And so, twenty-four hours after the accident, I find that things are as well as can be expected. Louisa is being nursed by her own Sarah; Mr and Mrs Musgrove have been relieved of the worst of their fears; and, if all goes well, I will soon be with Anne again.

Monday 14 November

Louisa regained consciousness several times today, and when she was conscious, she knew those about her. We were all heartened by this, so much so that Harville and I took a walk this afternoon. We went outside, turning our steps away from the Cobb, for neither of us could bear to visit it, and headed into town.

'I cannot tell you what I have felt for you over these last few days,' said Harville. 'I have been so sorry, Frederick, knowing what agonies you must be suffering. It was terrible to see James lose his fiancée last year; I could not bear to see you lose yours, too.'

I was horrified, for it was clear that Harville believed Louisa to be my fiancée. I was about to put him right when I remembered my conduct towards her, recalling the way I had accepted, even encouraged, her attentions. I felt myself grow cold. I had thought no harm in it, for both she and her sister had flirted with me, but as soon as Henrietta had made her preference for Charles Hayter plain, I should have taken less notice of Louisa. I should have called at Uppercross less, gradually withdrawing my attentions so that no slight should have been perceived. But instead I had proceeded on the same course of conduct, out of . . . what? Love? No, for I had never loved her. I saw that clearly. Out of what, then? Pride? Yes, angry pride. I was ashamed to own it, even to myself, but so it was. *I do not regret you*, I had been saying to Anne. *Your rejection did not hurt me. See, I am happy with another.*

I felt all the wrongness of it, and wished it undone, but the wish was a vain one. I had paid Louisa too much attention; Harville had mistaken her for my fiancée; and I could not now ruin her reputation by saying that there had never been an engagement between us. I was bound to her, if she wanted me, as surely as if I had asked her to be my wife.

'You are downcast,' said Harville, noticing my change in mood, and ascribing it to the wrong cause. 'Stay hopeful. The surgeon does not despair of the case. He believes she will make a full recovery. She is welcome to stay with us for as long as necessary, and so are you. Perhaps it would do you good to see her?'

'No!' I said.

He was taken aback by my vehemence.

'That is, the sight of me might excite her, and she needs to rest,' I said. 'I had better not go near her, for the sake of her health. I must not do anything to jeopardize her chances of recovery.'

He honoured me for it, and, to my relief, said no more.

We returned to the house but, as I sat in the parlour, my heart was heavy. I had learnt, gradually, over the last few months, that Anne was the only woman I could ever love, and at the very moment when I had hoped to declare myself, the chance had been snatched away from me. If Louisa recovered, I might soon find myself married to a woman I did not love. And if she did not . . . it was too terrible to think of.

I occupied myself with Harville's children, and found that their chatter lifted my spirits out of their black mood.

As for the future, I could do nothing to change it, so I made an effort to put it out of my mind.

Tuesday 15 November

A welcome surprise occurred this morning. The Musgrove family arrived at the inn, where they quickly established themselves before going to see Louisa. Mr and Mrs Musgrove were eager to see their daughter, and were greatly relieved when she regained consciousness for a few minutes and recognized them. They thanked the Harvilles over and over again, and were particularly grateful for the fact that Harriet was an experienced nurse, which made her the best person to tend the invalid. They took it upon themselves to help her in any way they could.

'As soon as Louisa is well enough to be moved, we mean to take her to the inn, where we can care for her entirely,' said Mrs Musgrove to me, 'but until such time we are grateful to your friends for taking her in.'

It was another anxious day, but as there was no relapse, and as Louisa continued to gain strength, it passed as well as could be expected.

Wednesday 16 November

Mrs Musgrove asked me this morning if I would like to go in and see Louisa, but I replied in the way I had replied to Harville, saying that I was afraid the shock of seeing me might be injurious to her, and that it might produce a setback. Mrs Musgrove said no more about it, and I was relieved, for I had decided that I would do everything consistent with honour to disentangle myself from Louisa. I would not desert her if she felt herself engaged to me, but neither would I encourage any tender feelings in her if they did not already exist.

Thursday 17 November

I returned to Kellynch Hall today, to let Sophia know how Miss Louisa went on, and to give her all the details of the accident that she did not already know. She was very distressed, as was Benjamin, that such an accident should have befallen such a well-loved young girl.

I could not stay long, for I had promised to return to Lyme, and I wanted to drive as far as possible in daylight, but I gladly stayed for luncheon and, hungry from exhaustion of body and spirits, I made a hearty meal.

Afterwards, I enquired after Anne.

'If not for Miss Elliot, we would all have found it much harder to bear,' I said. 'She is none the worse for her exertions, I hope?'

Sophia assured me that she was calm and composed.

'You relieve my mind,' I said, and my words were heart-felt, 'for her exertions were great. It was she who kept her head and lent assistance, when the other ladies were over-come; indeed, when I myself was overset. I cannot praise her too highly.'

And indeed I could not.

After writing to Edward to tell him I would not be able to visit him I left Sophia and set out once more. On my way past Lady Russell's house I left a note for Anne, telling her that Louisa was as well as could be expected, for Anne had started her visit to her godmother. Then, having left her the note, I returned to Lyme.

Friday 18 November

Louisa's recovery continues slowly but steadily. Her periods of consciousness are longer and more frequent. God willing, she will continue to improve.

Monday 21 November

Louisa has continued to improve over the weekend, and she sat up for the first time today, a source of great joy to all of us.

There seems hope, real hope, that she will make a full re-covery, and I think, at last, everyone in the house is beginning to believe it.

Tuesday 22 November

Life has returned to something resembling normal. Mary spent the morning at the library, and this evening she quarrelled with Harriet about precedence at supper. Charles Musgrove suggested an outing to Charmouth and his idea was met with approval.

I took advantage of the opportunity to say that I, too, thought of going away for a few days. As they had all accepted the idea that I did not want to see Louisa because I did not want to excite her, no one saw anything strange in my suggestion and I said I would go next week.

Thursday 24 November

Louisa sat up again today and had a conversation with her mother. Her lucidity delighted them both. Mrs Musgrove was all smiles as she told us about it, and her other children were greatly relieved, for it sent them off on their visit to Charmouth in good spirits. I remained behind, but made my plans for my trip to Plymouth, and declared my intention of leaving on Tuesday.

Friday 25 November

The younger Mr and Mrs Musgrove returned to Uppercross, satisfied that Louisa was making good progress, but the elder

Musgroves are still here as they are reluctant to leave their daughter. They hope she will soon be able to make the journey to Uppercross and are looking forward to having her at home, but I doubt if she will be able to return before Christmas, and it could indeed be some weeks more before she is ready to make such a long journey.

Tuesday 29 November

I took my leave of the Musgroves this morning. First I said good-bye to Mr and Mrs Musgrove so that, if they were displeased by my actions and demanded to know my intentions towards their daughter, I could reassure them and, if necessary, stay. However, they showed no displeasure, but instead they thanked me for all I had done. I then took my leave of all the rest. It was a melancholy affair, but once done I felt a sense of release. I must consider myself bound to Louisa if she has attached herself to me, but if my absence can lessen that attachment I will rejoice to be free.

DECEMBER

Monday 5 December

I wrote to Harville, as I had promised to do, giving him my direction. He promised to keep me informed as to Louisa's condition.

Tuesday 6 December

I saw Jenson by chance this morning and we fell into conversation. He invited me to dine with him and I agreed readily enough, for I was afraid of the thoughts that tormented me whenever I was alone.

He was in high spirits as he told me all about his progress in the wine trade, after which the conversation naturally turned to the battles we had seen. He mentioned our triumphs of the year eight, when, for the first time, we found ourselves with several thousand pounds, and as he talked, my thoughts drifted back to that time. I had been on shore after my early success, and I had been tempted to write to Anne and tell her of my good fortune, and to offer her my hand once more. I had gone as far as taking up my pen, but pain and doubt had assailed me, and I had let them have their sway. Pride, wounded dignity, fear that she had forgotten me, fear that I would make myself ridiculous, fear of rejection—all these had held me back. But if I had mastered my fears, if I had written, as I wanted to do, then what would she have said? Would she have said yes?

'. . . must come and see the ship tomorrow. What do you say?' asked Jenson.

His words brought me back to the present.

'The shipyard is not far from here. You can see the hull, and I can show you the plans,' said Jenson.

I realized that he had invited me to see his new ship, which was in the process of being built, and I gave my consent to the idea. But as he talked on, telling me of the ship's design, my thoughts returned again to the year eight. If I had asked Anne to marry me then, what would she have said?

Wednesday 7 December

An interesting day. Jenson showed me his ship and she was a beauty. It was good to hear his cheerful conversation, and his high spirits raised my own, so that I was able to pay attention to everything he said. I dined with his family this evening, and found them to be sensible and agreeable people. They have invited me to dine again next week, and I have decided to extend my stay so that I may accept.

Friday 9 December

I wrote to Edward, apologizing for not keeping to our earlier arrangement but telling him I would like to see him, for I was now free to travel. I suggested I should visit him for Christmas, if he found it convenient, and gave him Jenson's direction.

Saturday 10 December

A letter came from Harville this morning, telling me that Louisa continued to make good progress, and that they were now quite a cheerful party. He mentioned that Benwick entertained Louisa by reading her poetry when she was well enough, and I was glad to think of them both finding pleasure in each other's company.

Tuesday 13 December

I had a letter from Edward, saying he was delighted with the idea of my spending Christmas with him and his wife, and so it has been settled, I am to go to him.

Wednesday 14 December

I dined with Jenson's family again this evening, and after dinner, he and his father suggested that I might go and work for them as a captain of one of their vessels. I thanked them, but told them that my seafaring days were over, unless my country had need of me. They took no offence and wished me well, but as I returned to the inn, I found myself thinking that, if Louisa did not imagine herself engaged to me, and if Anne no longer loved me, then I might change my mind and accept Jenson's offer.

But if she no longer loved me, then why had she never married?

Thursday 22 December

And so, at last, I am in Shropshire. It was a relief to my spirits to be with Edward again, indeed, I did not know the full extent of their oppression until I arrived. I was delighted to meet Edward's wife, a lovely young woman, full of gentle humour and sense, with engaging manners and personal elegance. Her spirits are just those to suit him: lively enough to make her an attractive companion, but quiet enough to enable her to help him in his work; and I believe they are very happy. And why should they not be? They have each other, their house is a gentleman's residence of ample proportions, and the living is prosperous.

They made me very welcome, and set an excellent dinner

before me. We spoke of their marriage and my time at sea; of their neighbourhood and neighbours; of Sophia and Benjamin; and then of generalities.

Once dinner was over, Eleanor withdrew, leaving us to our port. I congratulated Edward on his wife, and he smiled and told me he was a lucky man.

'I have a beautiful wife, and I have done well in the church,' he said expansively. 'Not as well as you hoped—I have not become a bishop!—but I like the life I have.' Then he turned astute eyes on me and said, 'But all is not well with you, it seems. You must have sustained a shock when you found that Sophia had taken Kellynch Hall.'

I said nothing, for I was afraid his sympathy might unman me.

'Come, there is no need to hide it from me. It is eight years since Anne rejected you, and in all that time you have never spoken of another woman. You still think of her.'

'Yes,' I admitted. 'I do. And you are right in supposing I was shocked when Sophia and Benjamin took Kellynch Hall. Of all the houses in Somersetshire, for them to settle on that one.'

'And how is Anne? She remained in the neighbourhood when her family went to Bath, I understand?'

'Yes.' And then, before I knew what I was doing, I was telling him everything. It was a relief to my spirits to be able to speak at last, for I had never mentioned my short-lived engagement to another living soul, kept silent by a desire to protect Anne's reputation as well as my own pride. Edward was the only person in the world I could talk to, and now that I found myself in his company again, out it all poured: my meeting with Anne, the Musgroves, our trip to Lyme, and Louisa.

'Well,' he said, when at last I had done. 'You always liked action, Frederick, and it seems you have managed to find it here as well as at sea.'

I shook my head.

'That poor girl,' I said.

'You cannot blame yourself. She wanted to jump, you tried to dissuade her, but she would not listen. It is not your fault. Besides, in ninety-nine cases out of a hundred it would not have led to any great ill. You would have caught her anyway; or she would have fallen and sprained her ankle, and nothing more. It was unfortunate she hurt herself so badly, but it was not something you could have foreseen.'

'No,' I admitted, feeling much better than I had done for a long while, for although Edward had always been quick to deflate me when I was full of conceit, now that I needed solace he gave it in full measure.

'Still, I cannot acquit myself of ungentlemanly behaviour,' I said.

'You were wrong to encourage the attentions of the young ladies, certainly, and it was even worse of you to encourage them through pride, but you did not wilfully mislead them, for you did not understand your own feelings at the time. You will have to abide by the consequences, and may yet have to pay for your folly, but do not despair; everything may turn out for the best. Louisa is only nineteen. She is at an age when her feelings are changing rapidly. She may not have regarded herself as engaged to you, and even if she did, she may yet see a man she likes better. You look surprised!' he said mockingly. 'Yet you are not the only man in the world. There are others younger, richer, handsomer, more courteous and more gentlemanly—there is no need to look at me so. I love you very well, and I think any woman would be sensible who did likewise, but you are not the embodiment of every virtue.'

I was forced to smile, and say ruefully, 'True enough.'

'Now, enough of Louisa. Tell me about Anne. Is she much altered?'

'She looks the same as she ever did,' I said, as I recalled the brightness of her eye and the freshness of her complexion on the Cobb.

And then my spirits fell, and I told him of her coldness, and of how she avoided me. And then they rose as I told him that she had turned down Charles Musgrove, at which point he said, 'Ah,' thoughtfully. And then I told him how I had admitted to myself that she was the only woman I could ever wish to marry.

'Brooding will not help matters. You must fill your time here, so that you do not have time to think. We will keep you busy with visits and parties. Never fear, you will come about.'

The opportunity to unburden myself had done me good, and his common sense had further heartened me, so that it was with tolerable spirits that I left the table with him and joined Eleanor in the drawing-room. She played the harp and sang to us, and the evening was more enjoyable than I had any right to expect.

Sunday 25 December

It was a bright, sunny morning, and every one of Edward's parishioners turned out for church. The sermon was affecting and the singing was uplifting. Afterwards, I had a chance to talk to Edward's neighbours, and then we went home to a hearty meal.

I wondered how Anne was spending her Christmas, and whether she was happy.

Wednesday 28 December

Edward had a letter from Sophia this morning. He gave it to me to read. She talked of their Christmas celebrations, and of Benjamin's bad toe, which she hopes will soon be better, but fears may be gout. She mentioned that they might go to Bath for the waters, and said that Lady Russell and Anne were already there.

I frowned.

'You are reading the part about Lady Russell,' said Edward, reading my frown correctly. 'You still have not forgiven her for the part she played in separating you and Anne?'

'No, I have not. It was a bad day's work. I am surprised that Sophia likes her,' I remarked.

'But I am not. They are both of them sensible women.'

'Hah!' I replied. 'Poor Anne! To be once more with her father and sister, who will slight her as much as ever, and in Bath, a place she has never liked. If only I was free, I could go to her,' I said.

'Perhaps her father and sister treat her better now,' said my brother, taking the letter back from me when I had done.

'Perhaps. But I do not believe it. I am sure they are just as bad as they ever were.'

A letter from Harville told me that Louisa was now so much better that she was able to rise every day, and that, although she was quiet, for her nerves were still delicate, she was almost fully recovered, and would soon be returning home to Uppercross.

The time is soon approaching, then, when my fate will be decided forever.

1815

JANUARY

Sunday 1 January

And so, it is here, the New Year, but whether it will be a year of good or ill, who can say?

Wednesday 4 January

I went round the parish with my brother today. It is a pretty place, and his parishioners are good people. It is no wonder he is so happy. A refined couple by the name of Darnley told us they were making up a party to go for a drive next week, and asked us to join them. We agreed with pleasure. The weather is mild for the time of year, and it is pleasant to be out of doors.

Tuesday 10 January

'You seem very cheerful today,' remarked Edward, as we rode out with the Darnleys' party.

'Perhaps,' I said cautiously.

We had fallen a little way behind the others, and were free to talk, though I did not know whether it was a good thing or a bad.

'Well,' he said. 'Are you going to tell me about it?'

'I have had another letter from Harville,' I said. 'He writes to me from time to time.'

'He is well?'

'Yes, he and his family are thriving.'

'And?'

'And, after he had spoken of his family, he mentioned that Louisa and Benwick seem much taken with each other, and that they spend all day reading poetry together. He made some veiled comments about men protecting their treasures lest they should be stolen, and then he asked me when I would be returning to Lyme.'

'Ah, I see. He thinks you might be displaced in Louisa's affections.'

'Yes.'

'No wonder you are so cheerful.'

'And yet I cannot believe it,' I said, shaking my head. 'Benwick lost his fiancée less than a year ago, and she was a very superior young woman.'

'A man does not always want a superior young woman for

a wife. Sometimes he wants a sweet disposition and an affectionate nature.'

'Very true.'

'And will you be going to Lyme?'

'No. I have written to Harville and told him that I will not be able to return. I remarked that I was delighted that Louisa was making such good progress, and I was also delighted that Benwick was more cheerful. I went so far as to say it sounded as though they were doing each other good, and that this must surely be something that would please all their friends.'

'That seems very plain.'

'As plain as I dared make it, at any rate.'

One of our party turning round and calling to us that moment, we put our horses into a trot and rejoined the main group.

The visit was very enjoyable. The house was fine, the gardens better, and the weather was kind. We have arranged to take another outing in two weeks' time, and I find I am looking forward to it. It seems that I might soon be free of my restraints and able to live again.

Tuesday 31 January

Sophia and Benjamin have determined to go to Bath, for it is almost certain that he is gouty.

'I told him he should not drink so much port, but he would not listen,' said Edward.

'I would like to see Bath,' said Eleanor. 'I have never been.'

'Then we will go later in the year,' Edward promised her.

We whiled away the rest of the evening by talking of the gaieties to be had in Bath, and the society to be met with. Edward and I recalled everything we could from our rare visits there, and we entertained Eleanor with talk of the baths, the concerts and the assembly rooms until it was time to retire.

FEBRUARY

Monday 13 February

A smile broke out on my face this morning as I read my letters.

'What happiness!' I said. 'Louisa is to marry Captain Benwick! They fell in love during her convalescence. It is all here, in this letter from Harville. Splendid fellow! He wrote to me as soon as he heard the news.'

'Captain Benwick is a friend of yours, I collect?' said Eleanor.

'Yes, he is indeed.'

'And Louisa? Was she not the girl who had the accident at Lyme?'

'Yes, she was.'

'Then it is a very happy outcome to a sad event,' said Eleanor approvingly.

'And so it is!' I cried.

I was glad that I had ordered my horse before opening my letters, for within half an hour I was able to leave the house and ride out in the frosty morning, with my breath clouding the air in front of me. When I had ridden far enough, and was out of sight and sound of any house, I reined in my horse and shouted, 'Free!' at the top of my voice. 'Free! I am free!'

I laughed with the joy of it. After all these weeks of anguish, I was free at last to go to Bath! Free to find Anne! Free to marry her, if she would have me.

Doubts assailed me. I patted my horse's neck and rode on, trying not to listen to them, but they would not be denied. She might not have me. She might refuse me. But despite my fears, there was room for hope. She had turned down at least one man of better pretensions than myself, when she refused Charles Musgrove, and over and over I had asked myself, *Was it for me?* I knew there was only one way to be sure. I must go to Bath at once and then I would know, once and for all.

Over luncheon, I told Eleanor and Edward of my intentions. Eleanor was not surprised, assuming I was going to see Sophia, but Edward guessed my true reason. He spoke to me about it after dinner when Eleanor had withdrawn.

'You are going to see Anne?' he asked.

'I am.'

'Then I wish you luck.'

'Thank you. I will need it. I scarcely dare see her, for in her looks, her words, will be comprised my future happiness.'

'You have never lacked courage, Frederick. You will bear it, whatever the answer is, but I hope for your sake it is a happy one,' he said.

I thanked him for his good wishes, and told him that I meant to set out first thing tomorrow morning.

I spent the rest of the day thinking of what I would say to her when I saw her again.

Wednesday 15 February

And so here I am, in Bath, ready to face the future.

Thursday 16 February

I called on Sophia and Benjamin this morning. They were surprised to see me, but made me very welcome, and insisted I remove from the inn where I had taken a room, saying I must stay with them. I could not stand out against such kindness and I did as they suggested. I was pleased to find that their house was comfortable, and in a good part of town.

After giving them Edward's compliments, I asked them, casually, if they had seen the Elliots.

'No, we have not yet found out where they are living, but as soon as we discover their address we mean to call on them,' said Sophia.

I could not rest, and making business my excuse, I left the

house soon afterwards with the intention of discovering where Anne was living for myself. I had not gone far before I fell in with another party of my acquaintance just before Milsom Street. They suggested we should walk on together and I agreed.

'My brother is renting the estate of Sir Walter Elliot,' I said. 'He is in Bath at present. Do you happen to know him?'

'Yes, we have been introduced. He is here with his daughter, Miss Elliot,' said Mr Lytham.

'His other daughter is here as well. She has newly joined them. A Miss Anne Elliot,' remarked Mrs Lytham.

I asked if they knew where Sir Walter was living, and, as we turned into Milsom Street, Mrs Lytham informed me that the Elliots were renting a house in Camden Place.

It began to rain, and I was glad of the umbrella I had purchased. I was about to open it to shelter the ladies when Mrs Lytham remarked that she would like to buy some ribbon. We agreed to go to the shop together, in an effort to avoid the rain. We had only just entered when I saw . . . Anne, right there in front of me!

I started, and felt the colour flood my face. After rehearsing our first meeting so many times, I had never imagined it like this, for I had not foreseen an unexpected encounter. All my practised speeches went out of my head and I could do nothing but stand and stare at her, as a range of emotions flooded over me: surprise on seeing her, relief that I had found her, pleasure on seeing her and chagrin that she was not alone.

She, on the other hand, seemed perfectly composed. Was

I nothing to her, then, that she could see me unexpectedly with such equanimity? Had she forgotten me, and forgotten what we once were to each other? Had those feelings died in her breast? Had she come to regard me as nothing more than an old acquaintance?

I had thought . . . hoped . . . that her rejection of Charles Musgrove meant that there was a chance for me, but what if it meant only that she did not like him, or that she did not think him good enough, or that, as Miss Musgrove suspected, Lady Russell had not liked him?

'Miss Anne,' I said, embarrassed, and suddenly tongue-tied. 'It is an honour and a pleasure to see you again.'

She smiled and made me a curtsey.

The smile gave me hope that my presence was not entirely unwelcome, and I wanted to say more, but as one of my party happened to speak to me at that moment, I had to go to the counter. As soon as I was free, however, I approached Anne and spoke again, scarcely knowing what I said, but determined to say something. I asked her about her father, I believe, and spoke about the weather, but I was not comfortable, I was not easy, I could not assume that manner which we had had before, of perfect understanding, because there was not a perfect understanding between us.

I saw her sister; her sister saw me; I was ready to speak; but Miss Elliot turned away. So different from Anne!

'Where is the carriage?' Miss Elliot asked. 'Lady Dalrymple's carriage should be here by now. Mrs Clay, go to the window and see if you can see it.'

I recognized in Mrs Clay, the daughter of Mr Shepherd, now married and widowed, as I had heard. She went over to the window as commanded, and I was seized with a fear that Anne was about to leave. I turned to speak to her, eager to make the most of my opportunity, but I was too late! Lady Dalrymple's carriage was announced. Miss Elliot and Mrs Clay immediately made for the door, and I took what opportunity I could, by offering my arm to Anne. I hoped that we might be able to continue our conversation as I escorted her to the carriage.

'I am much obliged to you, but I am not going with them,' she said. 'The carriage would not accommodate so many. I walk: I prefer walking.'

'But it rains,' I said.

'Oh! very little. Nothing that I regard,' she returned.

An inspiration hit me, and I offered her my umbrella. Then I thought of a better suggestion, and begged to be allowed to get her a chair.

'I am very much obliged to you, but the rain will come to nothing, I am sure,' she said.

I was about to offer her my arm as well as my umbrella and walk her home, thanking Providence for the opportunity that had been thrown in my way, when she dashed my hopes by saying that she was waiting for her cousin, Mr Elliot, who had just gone on an errand and would be returning at any minute.

So Elliot was in Bath, and she preferred walking with him to walking with me. I was downcast. What had he been saying to her whilst they had been in Bath? Had he been making love to her? Winning her affections?

At that moment, I saw him walking down the street, and I felt my spirits sink. He would not have any difficulty in winning her family's approval, if he wanted her for his wife. Her sister might be jealous, it was true, and this might distress Anne for a while. But other than that, in age, appearance, birth and fortune he was an excellent match.

Was that how she would see it? I asked myself, glancing at her profile. I could not believe it. No, not Anne, who had a heart as deep as mine, and who would not marry without love, I was sure.

But perhaps she loved him. Perhaps she could see in him everything she had seen in me eight years before.

At that moment, Elliot walked in. I recollected him perfectly. There was no difference between him and the man who had stood on the steps at Lyme, admiring Anne as she passed, except in his air, because, whereas before he had looked at her as an admiring stranger, now he looked at her in the manner of a privileged friend. He appeared to see and think only of her, apologized for his stay, and was grieved to have kept her waiting. He was anxious to get her away without further loss of time, and before the rain increased; and in another moment they walked off together, her arm under his, saying only a 'Good morning to you!' before they left.

As soon as they were out of sight, the ladies in my own party began talking of them, saying that Mr Elliot appeared to like Miss Anne very much. Mrs Lytham said that her friend

Mrs Veer had told her that Mr Elliot was always with her family, and that it was easy to see how it would end.

I was devastated. To lose Anne to a man like Elliot, when I had been so close to speaking to her myself!

'She is pretty, I think, Anne Elliot; very pretty when one comes to look at her. It is not the fashion to say so, but I confess I admire her more than her sister,' said Mrs Lytham.

'Oh! so do I,' replied Miss Stanhope.

'And so do I,' replied another. 'No comparison. But the men are all wild after Miss Elliot. Anne is too delicate for them. What do you think, Captain Wentworth? Do you not think her the handsomer of the two?'

I was about to reply truthfully, and to say that indeed I did, when I recollected my manners and said that I thought both ladies extremely beautiful.

'Very politic!' said Lytham with a laugh.

'Ay,' said Mr Runcorne. 'Never be drawn on the relative beauty of ladies, for you may be sure it will come to their ears, and though you will have the smiles of one for ever more, you will have the other's frowns.'

The men laughed heartily, and the women continued to talk of Anne.

'A pretty woman, and not as proud as her father and sister,' said Miss Stanhope. 'She has an old school friend, a Mrs Smith, you know, who lives in poverty in Westgate Buildings. Many people would drop such an acquaintance, for it is not a nice neighbourhood, but Miss Anne visits her friend assiduously.'

CAPTAIN WENTWORTH'S DIARY

'Are you sure?' asked Mrs Lytham.

'I am, for I have seen her there myself as my carriage was driving through the neighbourhood.'

'Then that is another thing in her favour. Mr Elliot will be getting a good, as well as a pretty, wife,' said Lytham.

'A spring wedding, I think,' said Mrs Lytham.

A spring wedding! I could not bear to think of it! To lose Anne, so soon, to another man?

'Impossible!' I broke out.

The whole party looked at me, startled, and I felt myself redden with embarrassment. I sought around for an explanation for my outburst, and luckily, one was to hand.

'He was wearing crêpe around his hat. He is in mourning,' I said.

'Ah, yes, very true. A summer wedding, then,' said Mrs Lytham.

'He might not care to marry again,' I said, more to convince myself than Mrs Lytham.

'He does not seem to be inconsolable,' she remarked. 'Quite the reverse. He seems very interested in Miss Anne. What kind of woman was his wife?'

'Not a woman of any birth, but intelligent, accomplished and an heiress, by all accounts,' said Miss Stanhope.

'Ah.'

'She fell in love with him—'

'I am not surprised, for he is a fine-looking man.'

'—and she was determined to have him.'

'Really? I heard it was he who pursued her,' said Lytham.

'Not a bit of it. He was destined for Miss Elliot,' said Miss Stanhope.

'Then Miss Elliot should have fixed him when she had the chance,' said Mrs Lytham.

'She tried, on more than one occasion. She and her father sought him out in London some ten years ago. They made much of him, and invited him back to Kellynch Hall, but he was a young man at the time, I might even say a very young man, and country relatives were not to his taste, so that he slipped the net.'

'My dear, where did you hear all this?'

'At the Pump Rooms, where else?' said Miss Stanhope.

'Ah, of course.'

'And, now that he is a widower, it appears he prefers Miss Anne,' Miss Stanhope finished.

'She will be the future Lady Elliot, then, and mistress of Kellynch,' said Mrs Lytham. 'That will be hard for her sister to bear. But I am glad of it. I like her. She will fill the role very well.' She turned to me. 'Your brother has rented the Elliot's house, I believe, Captain Wentworth?'

'That is so. He took it at Michaelmas.'

'A good time of year for a remove. Does he mean to stay there?'

'For the time being, yes.'

'Then he had better hope that Sir Walter does not meet with an accident, or Sir Walter's heir will be wanting it back again!'

'Is his fortune very large?' asked Lytham.

'Certainly,' said Mrs Runcorne. 'He is now a man of means, and lives with liberality—my cousin was acquainted with him in town.'

They began to ask me about Kellynch Hall. I did not want to speak of it; it held too many memories; but the ladies would not be satisfied without a minute description of the principal rooms.

To my relief, that seemed to satisfy them, for the conversation then turned away from Anne and moved on to their other acquaintance.

I dreaded the topic returning, however, for I could not trust myself to be silent if Mr Elliot was mentioned again, and so I took my leave.

I was engaged to dine with Sophia and Benjamin, but I found it difficult to keep my mind on the conversation at dinner. I found myself trying to decide what I would say to Anne when I saw her, but I could think of nothing that satisfied me. I decided to rely on the genius of the moment, and I only hope my wits do not desert me.

Friday 17 February

I set out for Camden Place but, as was the case yesterday, I saw Anne quite by chance, this time whilst walking down Pulteney Street. To my dismay, I saw that Lady Russell was with her. To my further dismay, I saw that, as soon as Anne saw me, she looked immediately at her companion.

Is she, then, still swayed by Lady Russell? I asked myself.

I did not know, but if she was, I feared my hopes would soon be dashed, for I had no reason to suppose that Lady Russell liked me any more than she had done eight years before. I might have made my fortune but Lady Russell, once she had made up her mind, was unlikely to change it.

Lady Russell looked in my direction but our eyes did not meet. I tried to catch Anne's eye, but she had cast her gaze down, and would not look at me. I wanted to cross the road and speak to her, but the presence of Lady Russell, and Anne's own downcast gaze, deterred me. I strengthened my resolve . . . but the moment had passed.

I cursed myself inwardly, wondering when and where I had become such a coward. I had never been frightened when taking a ship into battle; but talking to Anne, finding out whether or not she still loved me . . . that terrified me.

Saturday 18 February

I was persuaded to go to the theatre tonight by a party of friends. The play was very good but I did not enjoy it because Anne was not there, and if Anne was not there, I could see no reason for being there myself.

I was invited to a concert on Tuesday evening and, unable to think of any reason to refuse, I was forced to accept.

I hope I will have an opportunity to speak to Anne before then. I might see her at church tomorrow, or I might see her in the Pump Rooms. If not, I will have to call in Camden Place, welcome or not, and pay my respects to Sir Walter.

Sunday 19 February

I hoped I might see Anne at church this morning, but she and her family must frequent a different church, for I saw nothing of her.

Tuesday 21 February

I spent a fruitless day hoping to see Anne in the public buildings, and returned to my sister's for an early dinner.

'Have you called on Sir Walter yet?' I asked her.

'No, not yet,' came the reply.

'I think I will call tomorrow. I feel I should pay my respects.'

'A good idea. I will go with you,' she said, 'and I will persuade Benjamin to come, too.'

Having arranged matters to my satisfaction, I felt more able to relax, and, after dinner, I went out to the concert in a happier mood. I arrived early, and decided to wait for the rest of my party inside. I went into the Octagon Room . . . and I was astonished to see Anne. She was with her father, sister and Mrs Clay. I received a cold look from her father, and so I made up my mind to bow and pass on, hoping to speak to Anne later in the evening when her father and sister were not nearby. But Anne stepped forward and said, 'How do you do?'

With those simple words my spirits lifted, for she had made an effort to speak to me, and perhaps all was not lost.

I stopped next to her, and enquired after her health, and the health of her family and friends. I heard a whispering between her father and sister, and then, to my surprise, Sir Walter acknowledged me. More slowly, and more grudgingly, Miss Elliot did the same. I made them a slight bow in return—slight, because their own acknowledgement had been slight—and then gave my attention back to Anne.

'You did not get wet, I hope, the other day when you walked home in the rain?' I asked her.

'No, not at all.'

There was a silence and I felt I should move on, but I could not do so.

'Perhaps I was a little wet,' she said.

'It must have been uncomfortable for you.'

'Oh, no, not really.'

We fell silent again, and I searched my mind desperately for something else to say, for I did not want to leave her, nor did she seem to want to leave me.

'Are you enjoying your visit to Bath?' I asked.

'Yes, it is most agreeable, thank you.'

I had so much I wanted to say to her I hardly knew where to begin, but I could not say anything of importance in the Octagon Rooms, in full view of her father and sister, with other people liable to enter at any moment. I wished I was at

Kellynch Hall, walking by the river, with Anne by my side, so that I could say everything that was in my heart. But instead, I had to content myself with trivialities.

'The Rooms are very fine,' I said.

'Indeed they are,' she said, greeting my words with more warmth than they deserved.

I took courage from it, for she was not disgusted by my banalities. However, I could not think of anything else to say. I cursed myself inwardly for my stupidity.

'The fire is hot,' she said, rescuing us both from silence.

'You are standing too near,' I said, immediately solicitous. 'Pray let us move aside.'

'No, I am not too hot at all, it is just . . . the fire is a little warm,' she ended lamely.

We fell silent again. She would not meet my eye but looked past my shoulder, and I could not complain for, having managed one glance at her, I found myself looking at the ceiling.

What did it mean? I asked myself. She was embarrassed, that much I could tell, but why? Was she longing to open her heart to me and tell me that she had missed me? It seemed too much to hope for. Perhaps she was ashamed of her father and sister for not taking proper notice of me, and wanted to make it up to me by taking notice of me herself. Or perhaps she was ashamed of Lady Russell, who had walked past me in the street without saying a word. Perhaps she was trying to smooth over our past differences, so that we could meet in the future without embarrassment. Or perhaps . . . my spirits quailed . . . perhaps she was trying to find the words to let me know that she and Mr Elliot were betrothed.

I knew I must give her an opening to speak, and I thought I could do so by raising the subject of Lyme, for it was at Lyme she had first seen Mr Elliot.

'I have hardly seen you since our day at Lyme,' I said. 'I am afraid you must have suffered from the shock, and the more so from its not overpowering you at the time.'

'No, I assure you, I was not overcome. I was only glad to be of service to Louisa and Henrietta.'

'It was a frightful hour,' I said, remembering it in all its detail: Louisa's fall, my guilt and remorse, the fear I had felt when I thought she was dead. But things had turned out far better than I had, at one time, thought possible, and, smiling again, I said, 'The day has produced some effects, however; has had some consequences which must be considered as the very reverse of frightful. When you had the presence of mind to suggest that Benwick would be the properest person to fetch a surgeon, you could have little idea of his being eventually one of those most concerned in her recovery.'

She agreed, but said she thought it would be a happy match, for they both had good principles and good temper.

'With all my soul I wish them happy, and rejoice over every circumstance in favour of it,' I said, and my words were heartfelt.

But as I spoke of the Musgroves, and their true parental hearts that were anxious to promote their daughter's comfort, I found myself gradually losing sight of Louisa and James, and thinking more of myself and Anne, for Anne had had no such parental goodwill.

I stopped as I realized where my words were tending. I glanced towards Anne and saw that her thoughts had been following mine, for she was blushing. Moreover, she had fixed her eyes on the ground and would not look at me. I remembered how it had been for us: many difficulties to contend with, opposition, caprice—everything Benwick would not have to endure.

Searching around for another subject I found I could no longer bear idle talk, I had to give her an intimation of my thoughts. I had to let her know they were unchanged, for perhaps—perhaps, if she was not irrevocably settled on Mr Elliot—she could still love me. I cleared my throat and went on, although I spoke haltingly, not sure what to say, afraid of saying too little, or too much.

'I confess that I do think there is a disparity, too great a disparity, and in a point no less essential than mind,' I said. 'I regard Louisa Musgrove as a very amiable, sweet-tempered girl, and not deficient in understanding, but Benwick is something more. Had it been the effect of gratitude, had he learnt to love her because he believed her to be preferring him, it would have been another thing. But I have no reason to suppose it so. It seems, on the contrary, to have been a perfectly spontaneous, untaught feeling on his side, and this surprises me. A man like him, in his situation! With a heart pierced, wounded, almost broken! Fanny Harville was a very superior creature,' I said, looking at Anne, and hoping to convey with my eyes that I found her a very superior creature, 'and his attachment to her was indeed attachment.' Again, I looked at Anne, and sought to convey that my attachment to her was indeed attachment. 'A man does not recover from such a devotion of the heart to such a woman!' I said. 'He ought not; he does not,' I finished.

If ever a man could speak of love with his eyes, I spoke of my love then. I waited breathlessly for Anne's reply, but she said nothing. I wondered if I had gone too far, and said too much? And then I wondered if she had understood me, or if she had really thought I was speaking of Benwick, and Benwick alone. She did not seem to know what to think, or what to say.

At last she spoke.

'I should very much like to see Lyme again.'

I was astonished.

'Indeed! I should not have supposed that you could have found anything in Lyme to inspire such a feeling. The horror and distress you were involved in, the stretch of mind, the wear of spirits! I should have thought your last impressions of Lyme must have been strong disgust.'

'The last few hours were certainly very painful,' she admitted, 'but when pain is over, the remembrance of it often becomes a pleasure. One does not love a place the less for having suffered in it, unless it has been all suffering, nothing but suffering, which was by no means the case at Lyme. We were only in anxiety and distress during the last two hours, and previously there had been a great deal of enjoyment. So much novelty and beauty! I have travelled so little, that every fresh place would be interesting to me; but there is real beauty at Lyme; and in short,' she blushed slightly, 'altogether my impressions of the place are very agreeable.'

I felt my emotions pulled in two directions. Were her recollections of it agreeable because of me? If so, what happiness! Or were they agreeable because of her seeing Mr Elliot for the first time there? If so, what misery!

I longed to ask, to find out, but at that moment there was a stir in the room. It had become fuller and fuller whilst I had been speaking to Anne, and it was now energized by the entrance of Lady Dalrymple. Anne moved away to greet her, and I was left alone, to wonder whether Anne's eagerness to greet her was caused by the fact that she was attended by Mr Elliot.

They formed a happy group: Lady Dalrymple enjoyed the fawning of all about her; Sir Walter and Miss Elliot basked in the honour of her acquaintance; Mr Elliot was much taken with Anne; and Anne . . . Anne seemed to welcome him. My heart ached and, unable to bear it, I left the room.

When I was at last sensible of my surroundings again, I found myself in the Concert Room. Mrs Lytham soon found me and began talking about the music that was to come. I was incapable of rational speech, but fortunately she was very fond of music, and talked enough for both of us.

'Lady Dalrymple is here, I see,' said Mrs Lytham.

I looked round—I could hardly help it, as Lady Dalrymple's party entered with a bustle that was designed to catch every eye. I turned away, but not before I had seen Anne—radiant Anne, whose eyes were bright and whose cheeks were glowing with a light that came from within—sit on one of the foremost benches, next to Mr Elliot.

I took myself off to the farthest side of the room, so that I would not have to see them together, but I could not take my eyes away from her. I kept glimpsing her through the sea of feathered headdresses, her face close to Mr Elliot's, and in the interval succeeding an Italian song, I had the mortification of seeing her speak to him in a low voice, intimately, to the exclusion of all others, with their heads almost touching.

There was a break in the performance, and I was hailed by Cranfield. He and a group of other men were discussing music and politics, and I was forced to join in. I could barely keep my mind on the conversation, however, and my gaze kept returning to Anne. She was still with Mr Elliot; still talking to him; still enjoying his company.

I heard my name, and realized that Sir Walter and Lady Dalrymple were speaking of me. I could not hear their conversation, but I imagined Sir Walter saying, *Captain Wentworth once had pretensions of winning my daughter, but, as you can see, she has made a better choice, and means to marry the next baronet.* He had never liked me, and he must rejoice in my total rout.

The room began to fill again in preparation for the second act, and I noticed that Mr Elliot did not return to his place by Anne. Despite my fears, I made the most of my opportunity and stepped forward with a view to sitting next to her, but others were quicker, and her bench soon filled up. I watched it; I could not help myself; and to my great good fortune, they soon tired of the music and left the room. There was a space next to Anne. I hesitated, tormented by doubt once more. Should I go to her, and discover once and forever that she regarded me as nothing more than an acquaintance from the past? Or to do nothing, and perhaps miss my opportunity with her?

I took my courage in both hands and went over to her.

'I hope you are enjoying the concert. I expected to like it more,' I said, thinking that, if Mr Elliot had not been present, I should certainly have been better pleased.

'The singing is not of the first quality, it is true, but there are some fine voices, and the orchestra is good,' she said.

I was heartened by the fact that she was disposed to talk to me, and that she did not appear to look round for Mr Elliot whilst we spoke. I was just beginning to enjoy our conversation, and was about to take my seat in the vacant space next to her, when Mr Elliot tapped her on the shoulder.

'I beg your pardon, but your assistance is needed,' he said to Anne. 'Miss Carteret is very anxious to have a general idea of what is next to be sung, and she desires you to translate the Italian.'

There was something so intimate in his gesture of touching her, and something so confiding in his manner of speech, that all the joy drained out of me. I could not sit there and listen to song after song of the agonizingly beautiful music, with its romantic Italian lyrics, whilst Mr Elliot was behind us, ready to touch her shoulder again at any moment with the air of an acknowledged lover, and to bend his head close to hers, and talk to her in a low voice, their thoughts as one. I could not bear it. I knew I had to leave before the second act began, before I found myself trapped in the acutest misery. I excused myself hurriedly, saying, 'I must wish you good night; I am going.'

'Is not this song worth staying for?' she asked in surprise.

'No! there is nothing worth my staying for,' I said bitterly. And with this, I hurried out of the room.

I arrived back at Sophia's house in time for supper, but I could not pay attention to her. Declaring myself exhausted, I retired to my room, where I thought of nothing but Anne and Mr Elliot, Mr Elliot and Anne.

Wednesday 22 February

I awoke to find the winter sun shining through my curtains, but the brightness, which would usually have cheered me, could not restore me to happiness, for the memory of the concert was too clearly etched on my mind.

Friday 24 February

I went out for a walk after breakfast and, to my surprise the first person I met when I set foot out of the door was Charles Musgrove! There was a start on both sides, and then a smile of recognition, which was quickly followed by a moment of awkwardness on Charles's part. I could tell that he was thinking of

Louisa, and wondering if I had been wounded by the news of her engagement. I hastened to put his mind at ease.

'I am delighted to see you, Musgrove,' I greeted him warmly. 'We have not seen each other since Lyme. Who would have thought that the incidents there would have had such a welcome outcome? I was so pleased to hear of your sister's engagement. Such a beautiful and courageous young woman deserves every happiness in life, and I believe Benwick is just the man to give it to her. He is an excellent fellow, with a steady character, and I am heartily glad for them both.'

'It is good of you to say so, Wentworth,' he said, shaking me warmly by the hand, as a look of relief spread across his face. 'I thought . . . but there now, that is all in the past, and I know my sister will be pleased to learn that you wish her well.'

'I do, with all my heart,' I assured him.

Having established matters satisfactorily between us in this respect, we fell into step, and I asked him what he was doing in Bath.

'I am here with my family. My mother is here, and Mary of course, and the Harvilles are with us. I do not know if you are aware of the fact, but my mother invited the Harvilles to Uppercross when Louisa was well enough to come home. My mother wanted to thank them for all they had done for Louisa. I believe I may say they have enjoyed their visit, and their children have enjoyed playing with my younger brothers and sisters. It was Harville who gave us the idea of visiting Bath, for he needed to come on business, and I decided to come with him, for the country is very dull at this time of year.

Then Mary decided she could not bear to be left behind, and my mother declared that she would like to visit some friends here, and Henrietta thought it an excellent opportunity to buy her wedding clothes. So here we are, all six of us, ready to enjoy ourselves in our various ways.'

'A splendid idea. I am glad that Henrietta and Hayter have decided not to wait before getting married. Long delays are an evil, in my opinion. If two people love each other, they should formalize their affections straight away.'

As I spoke, I thought of myself and Anne. If only we had had a chance to formalize our affections in the year six!

'I suppose so, though I do not believe they would have gone ahead if not for a great piece of luck,' said Musgrove. 'What do you think, Wentworth? Hayter has acquired a living.'

'Indeed? I am very happy for him. Where is it?'

'Only five-and-twenty miles from Uppercross, in Dorsetshire. It is not his forever; he holds it for a youth who is at present too young to take it up; but it will be his for many years, and by the time the boy is old enough, Hayter is sure to have found something else.'

'It seems eminently suitable.'

'Yes, I am happy for them.' Then, turning to matters nearer to hand, he said, 'I have just secured a box at the theatre for tomorrow night. I hope you will join us?'

I expressed myself delighted.

Harville joined us at this point, having undertaken a commission for one of the ladies, and we went on, all three of us together.

'You will come and pay your respects to my mother?' asked Musgrove, as we approached the White Hart.

'With the greatest of pleasure.'

We went into the inn. As we did so, Musgrove went on ahead, and I was left to walk behind with Harville. It seemed a long time since we had been in the Navy together. Life at sea had its problems, but I found myself thinking that it was a great deal more straightforward than life on land.

'Tell me about Louisa Musgrove,' I said. 'Has she completely recovered?'

'She is well, but not as lively as formerly, or so I understand,' he said. 'Of course, I did not know her before the accident, but her family has often mentioned that she was always singing or dancing or running about.'

'Yes, she was,' I said.

'Whether her languor will pass, I do not know. Perhaps, as she continues to improve, her vigour will return.'

'It was good of you and Harriet to look after her.'

'We were only too happy to do it. Any friend of yours, Wentworth . . . I did think, at one time, that you intended to marry her. It appears I was wrong.'

'I was a friend of the family, but nothing more,' I said. 'I am pleased that she and Benwick are happy.'

He was silent.

'You do not like the engagement?' I asked.

He hesitated.

'I do, of course. James is a good man, and she seems a delightful girl. Only . . . it is selfish of me, I know, but I do not like the idea of him forgetting Fanny. They were engaged for years, Wentworth, and she has only been dead for seven months.'

'She was a wonderful girl, superior in every way,' I said gently.

'Yes, she was. I am partial, of course, because she was my sister, but I truly think she was special. And James thought so, too. But now . . . I miss Fanny,' he said with a sigh.

I spoke of her beauty and her good nature, recalling the times we had all three spent together, and Harville was cheered.

'You are right, of course. James has a right to happiness, and I am pleased he has found it. It just seemed too soon . . . but better too soon than too late. I am glad for him. Yes, I am.'

We went up to Mrs Musgrove's rooms, and as soon as I walked in, I saw Anne!

I was taken aback, and yet I should have expected it, for this arrival of the Musgroves would inevitably bring us together at some point. She was connected with them, being their friend, and so was I. Nevertheless, I could not trust myself to do more than greet her politely. She looked as though she would like me to draw close and I wondered, fleetingly, if I could be mistaken in thinking there was something between her and Mr Elliot, after all.

My hopes were dashed before they had time to take root, however, for Mary, standing at the window, called our attention to a gentleman standing below.

'Anne, there is Mrs Clay, I am sure, standing under the

colonnade, and a gentleman with her. I saw them turn the corner from Bath Street just now. They seem deep in talk. Who is it? Come, and tell me. Good heavens! I recollect. It is Mr Elliot himself.'

'No, it cannot be Mr Elliot, I assure you. He was to leave Bath at nine this morning, and does not come back till tomorrow,' said Anne.

So she was aware of all his comings and goings! I thought, turning my eyes towards her.

'I am certain it is him,' said Mary, adding, affronted, 'I am sure I may be expected to know my own cousin. He has the family features; he is the same man we saw in Lyme. Only come to the window, Anne, and take a look!'

Anne appeared embarrassed, and I was not surprised, for all eyes had turned to her, but as she said nothing, the room fell silent.

It was an uncomfortable pause.

'Do come, Anne,' urged Mary, 'come and look yourself. You will be too late if you do not make haste. They are parting; they are shaking hands. He is turning away. Not know Mr. Elliot, indeed! You seem to have forgot all about Lyme.'

At last, Anne moved to the window. What did her hesitation mean? That she did not want to see him? Or that she did not want to appear to be eager to see him? I wished I could read her thoughts.

'Yes, it is Mr. Elliot, certainly,' said Anne calmly. 'He has changed his hour of going, I suppose, that is all, or I may have been mistaken.'

This spelled hope. If she was mistaken, then she could not have been attending to him when he told her of his plans.

What torture it was to examine every sentence, to see if it proved a love affair between them, or the reverse!

'Well, Mother,' said Musgrove, when Mrs Clay and Mr Elliot had disappeared from view, 'I have done something for you that you will like. I have been to the theatre, and secured a box for tomorrow night. I know you love a play, and there is room for us all. It holds nine. I have engaged Captain Wentworth. Anne will not be sorry to join us, I am sure. We all like a play.'

'A play! The very thing,' said Mrs Musgrove. 'As long as Henrietta likes the idea—'

'Good heavens! Charles, how can you think of such a thing?' broke in Mary. 'Have you forgot that we are engaged to go to Camden Place tomorrow night? And that we were most particularly asked on purpose to meet Lady Dalrymple, her daughter, and Mr. Elliot, all the principal family connections, on purpose to be introduced to them? How can you be so forgetful?'

Whilst she and Charles argued the point back and forth, he declaring no promise had been given, and she declaring it had, I watched Anne, to see if I could tell by her face whether she looked forward to meeting Elliot again.

Charles's final words, 'What is Mr. Elliot to me?' brought my eyes to Anne again, as I wondered, with all my soul: What was Elliot to Anne? I could read nothing from her expression, nor did it seem to change when Mrs Musgrove said that Charles had better go back and change the box for Tuesday.

'It would be a pity to be divided, and we should be losing Anne, too, if there is a party at her father's,' she said. 'I am sure neither Henrietta nor I should care at all for the play if Anne could not be with us.'

I awaited Anne's reply with bated breath.

'If it depended only on my inclination, ma'am, the party at home (excepting on Mary's account) would not be the smallest impediment. I have no pleasure in the sort of meeting, and should be too happy to change it for a play, and with you,' she said.

But Mary was adamant that the party could not be missed, and it was soon generally agreed that Tuesday should be the day.

I left my seat, overcome by what I had heard. She had no pleasure in that sort of meeting! No pleasure in Mr Elliot's company! She would rather go to the play!

I went over to stand by her, going by way of the fireplace so as not to draw attention to the fact, and tried to think of something to say.

'You have not been long enough in Bath to enjoy the evening parties of the place, then?' I asked.

'Oh! no. The usual character of them has nothing for me. I am no card-player,' she replied.

Here was my opening, no matter how slight, and I seized it.

'You were not formerly, I know. You did not use to like cards; but time makes many changes,' I added significantly.

'I am not yet so much changed,' she said, and her words, too, seemed significant.

She was not so much changed. And yet . . .

'It is a period, indeed! Eight years and a half is a period!' I said, not knowing I had spoken out loud.

I would have said more, but Henrietta urged Anne to go with her in order to fulfil her commissions.

'I am perfectly ready to go with you,' said Anne, but she did not look it. She looked as though she wished to stay.

And then something happened to delay her. Sounds were heard; other visitors approached, and the door was thrown open. Sir Walter and Miss Elliot had arrived.

I felt an instant oppression, and I could tell that Anne felt the same. The comfort, the freedom, the gaiety of the room was over, hushed into cold composure, determined silence, or insipid talk, to match the elegance of her father and sister.

I was surprised that they acknowledged me, and that they did so a little more graciously than before. I wondered what could have raised me in their estimation. Perhaps Lady Dalrymple had spoken well of me, for I was sure nothing else would have satisfied their pride.

'Captain Wentworth,' said Miss Elliot, smiling.

I made her a cold bow: I had not forgotten how she treated Anne.

It turned out that she and her father had called to give out invitations to their party.

'Tomorrow evening, to meet a few friends: no formal party,' Miss Elliot said.

She laid her cards on the table—*Miss Elliot at home*—with a courteous smile, and included me in the courtesy; indeed she made a point of handing me an invitation. I acknowledged it politely, but felt only disdain. They had not valued me eight years previously; would not value me now, if others had not shown them the way; and I knew their friendship would be lost the moment Lady Dalrymple, or some such other person, spoke against me. And yet it was an invitation, and it would give me a chance to see Anne, I thought, as I turned the card over in my hand.

'Only think of Elizabeth's including everybody!' whispered Mary very audibly. 'I do not wonder Captain Wentworth is delighted! You see he cannot put the card out of his hand.'

I felt myself growing red with contempt and, as I caught Anne's eye, I knew that her feelings echoed my own. That decided me. I would go to the party. It was not certain that Anne loved Mr Elliot; and I would not count her lost until an engagement was announced.

I made my bow and, feeling there was still hope, I left the ladies to their shopping.

Saturday 25 February

It was raining heavily when I awoke, but it would have taken more than rain to keep me from the White Hart this morning. I escorted my sister and Benjamin and we arrived there immediately after breakfast. To my disappointment, Anne was not there. Sophia was soon talking to Mrs Musgrove, and I fell into conversation with Harville. Mary and Henrietta kept walking over to the window and exclaiming on the rain. As soon as it cleared, Henrietta said, 'At last! Come, Mary, let us be off.'

'Will you not wait for Anne?' asked Mary.

'I will not wait for anyone, I am eager to be about my business. There is some lace I saw yesterday that I must procure, and a new bonnet that I must have. Mama, you must make sure Anne does not leave. Once she has arrived, you must keep her here until we return. I would not miss her for anything.'

I was gratified to see how much Henrietta valued Anne. She evidently had not forgotten that Anne had lent her her assistance at Lyme.

The two young ladies set out, and not long afterwards Anne arrived. I was immediately aware of her, but I could not break off from Harville as he had asked me to help him with a letter of business. I wanted it out of the way, and suggested I write it at once.

Paper and pen were laid out on a table at the side of the room, so I went over to it, and began to write. I consoled myself with the fact that I was not missing any conversation of great import, for Mrs Musgrove was telling Sophia about Henrietta's engagement, and was going into such detail that I am sure it took all of Sophia's patience to seem interested.

'And so we thought they had better marry at once, and make the best of it, as many others have done before them. At any rate, said I, it will be better than a long engagement,' finished Mrs Musgrove.

'That is precisely what I was going to observe,' said my sister. 'I would rather have young people settle on a small income at once, and have to struggle with a few difficulties together, than be involved in a long engagement. I always think that no mutual—'

I no longer heard her for I had to pay attention to my letter, but when I had come to the end of it, Sophia was still abominating long engagements.

I sanded the letter, and as I did so Harville left his seat, moved to the window, and invited Anne to join him with a smile. They had moved so close to me that I could not help overhearing what was being said.

'Look here,' he began, unfolding a parcel in his hand, and displaying a small miniature painting, 'do you know who that is?'

Anne took it and looked at it, and declared it to be Captain Benwick.

He agreed, and said it was for Louisa.

'But,' he went on sadly, 'it was not done for her. It was drawn at the Cape, in compliance with a promise to my poor sister, and he was bringing it home for her. And I have now the charge of getting it properly set for another! It was a commission to me! But who else was there to employ? I hope I can allow for him. I am not sorry, indeed, to make it over to another. He undertakes it,' he said, looking at me and referring to the letter I was engaged upon. 'He is writing about it now.' His voice dropped. 'Poor Fanny! she would not have forgotten him so soon!'

'No,' replied Anne, in a low, feeling voice, 'that, I can easily believe.'

Her ready sympathy won Harville's gratitude. I, too, was grateful to her, for giving solace to Harville's spirits.

'It was not in her nature,' he said, drawn on by Anne's manner. 'She doted on him.'

'It would not be the nature of any woman who truly loved,' said Anne.

I started, and I was glad at that moment that there was no one near enough to see it. Could I believe what I was hearing? Could Anne really be saying that a woman who truly loved would never forget a man so soon? And could she mean something by it? For I thought she glanced in my direction. Did she mean that she had not forgotten me? I felt my hopes stir—and then sink. The two cases were not alike. Fanny had been dead for less than a year, but Anne and I had been separated for eight years. That was a difference in time indeed.

Even so, I strained to hear what she would say next, for I felt sure there was more to her words than Harville could know, and my every nerve was on fire. I glanced at her, too, in the mirror that hung over the table, so that I could catch her expression. Next to her, I saw Harville smile and shake his head.

Anne spoke out more decidedly.

'We certainly do not forget you so soon as you forget us,' she told him. 'It is, perhaps, our fate rather than our merit. We cannot help ourselves. We live at home, quiet, confined, and our feelings prey upon us. You are forced on exertion. You have always a profession, pursuits, business of some sort or other, to take you back into the world immediately, and continual occupation and change soon weaken impressions.'

Is that what she thought? I wondered. Did she believe that occupation and exertion had weakened my impressions? That I had forgotten her in the press of other concerns?

It was a new idea to me, and one that troubled me greatly.

'Granting your assertion that the world does all this so soon for men (which, however, I do not think I shall grant),' said Harville, his words putting new heart in me, for he was speaking up for all men, 'it does not apply to Benwick. He has not been forced upon any exertion. The peace turned him on shore at the very moment, and he has been living with us, in our little family circle, ever since.'

'True,' said Anne, 'very true; I did not recollect; but what shall we say now, Captain Harville? If the change be not from outward circumstances, it must be from within; it must be nature, man's nature, which has done the business for Captain Benwick.'

I longed to speak but I could not, for I feared what I would say; that I would blurt out my feelings before everyone, astonishing them with the fervour of my passion.

'No, no, it is not man's nature,' said Harville. 'I will not allow it to be more man's nature than woman's to be inconstant and forget those they do love, or have loved. I believe the reverse. I believe in a true analogy between our bodily frames and our mental; and that as our bodies are the strongest, so are our feelings; capable of bearing most rough usage, and riding out the heaviest weather.'

'Your feelings may be the strongest,' replied Anne, 'but the same spirit of analogy will authorize me to assert that ours are the most tender. You are always labouring and toiling, exposed to every risk and hardship. Your home, country, friends, all quitted. Neither time, nor health, nor life, to be called your own. It would be too hard, indeed, if woman's feelings were to be added to all this.'

As she spoke, she faltered, overcome with emotion, and I dropped my pen on the floor, so agitated was I, and nearly bursting with all I wanted to say.

'Have you finished your letter?' Harville asked me, his attention attracted by the noise.

I was about to admit that I had when an idea occurred to me, and saying, 'Not quite, a few lines more. I shall have done in five minutes,' I pulled another sheet of paper towards me, picked up my pen, dipped it in the ink, and began to write. My pen scrawled across the paper in my haste as my feelings poured out of me.

I can listen no longer in silence. I must speak to you by such means as are within my reach. You pierce my soul. I am half agony, half hope. Tell me not that I am too late, that such precious feelings are gone forever.

And as I wrote, I heard more and more words that almost overpowered me.

'I do not think I ever opened a book in my life which had not something to say upon woman's inconstancy. Songs and proverbs, all talk of woman's fickleness. But perhaps, you will say, these were all written by men,' Harville was saying.

'Perhaps I shall,' said Anne. 'Men have had every advantage of us in telling their own story. I will not allow books to prove anything.'

Men have had every advantage of us in telling their own story, I thought. And I was determined to tell Anne mine:

I offer myself to you again with a heart even more your own than when you almost broke it, eight years and a half ago. Dare not say that man forgets sooner than woman, that his love has an earlier death. I have loved none but you.

'But how shall we prove anything?' Harville asked.

'We never shall,' admitted Anne. 'We each begin, probably, with a little bias towards our own sex; and upon that bias build every circumstance in favour of it which has occurred within our own circle; many of which circumstances (perhaps those very cases which strike us the most) may be precisely such as cannot be brought forward without betraying a confidence, or, in some respect, saying what should not be said.'

With every word, I was more and more convinced that

she had not forgotten me, that she loved me still, for what else could her talk about betraying a confidence mean?

Unjust I may have been, weak and resentful I have been, but never inconstant. You alone have brought me to Bath. For you alone I think and plan. Have you not seen this? Can you fail to have understood my wishes?

'Ah! if I could but make you comprehend what a man suffers when he takes a last look at his wife and children, and watches the boat that he has sent them off in, as long as it is in sight, and then turns away and says, ' "God knows whether we ever meet again!" ' said Harville.

'Oh! I hope I do justice to all that is felt by you, and by those who resemble you. God forbid that I should undervalue the warm and faithful feelings of any of my fellow-creatures! I should deserve utter contempt if I dared to suppose that true attachment and constancy were known only by woman,' said Anne.

Then she knew that men could be constant! And, knowing it, must know that I could be constant, too!

My pen responded to her, as my voice, at the present time, could not:

I had not waited even these ten days, could I have read your feelings, as I think you must have penetrated mine. I can hardly write. I am every instant hearing something which overpowers me. You sink your voice, but I can distinguish the tones of that voice when they would be lost on others. Too good, too excellent creature! You do us justice, indeed. You do believe that there is true attachment and constancy among men. Believe it to be most fervent, most undeviating, in F. W.

I was about to put down my pen when I realized that Anne was still speaking.

'I believe you capable of everything great and good in your married lives,' she said. 'I believe you equal to every important exertion, and to every domestic forbearance, so long as—if I may be allowed the expression, so long as you have an object. I mean while the woman you love lives, and lives for you. All the privilege I claim for my own sex (it is not a very enviable one: you need not covet it), is that of loving longest, when existence or when hope is gone!'

Is that what she thought? That she loved longest when hope was gone? Nay, for I would love her forever, with or without hope.

'You are a good soul,' said Harville affectionately.

A good soul, indeed.

Sophia was taking her leave, saying that we would all meet again at the Elliots' party, and I added a postscript in haste.

I must go, uncertain of my fate; but I shall return hither, or follow your party, as soon as possible. A word, a look will be enough to decide whether I enter your father's house this evening or never.

I folded my letter, made some answer to Sophia, though I had not caught her question, and told Harville I would be with him in half a minute. I sealed the letter, slid it under the scattered paper—for I had time to do no more—and hurried from the room. She would find it there, I was sure.

But a minute later I was not sure, and I decided I must find a way of delivering it into her hand. I returned, saying I had forgotten my gloves, and to my relief I found Anne standing by the table. So she was curious as to what I had been writing, as I had hoped! Standing with my back towards Mrs Musgrove, I pulled out the letter and gave it to Anne, and was out of the room in an instant.

What would she think when she read it? I asked myself. I had written in such haste, I scarcely knew if it was intelligible. I had blotted the ink once to my certain knowledge. Would she be able to make out the words?

I went out into the street. I walked, I turned, I walked again, until at last I found myself in Union Street, and there in front of me was Anne! She was going home, then, and I might have a chance to speak to her. But she was accompanied by Musgrove. I wished him a hundred miles away. I joined them, hoping that, by a word or a look I could read her thoughts, and yet she did not look at me. What did it mean? Was she embarrassed? Yes. But embarrassed because she was pleased with my letter, or embarrassed because she was alarmed by it? I did not know.

I was irresolute. I did not know whether to stay or pass on. I looked again, and this time Anne returned my look. It was not a look to repulse me. Her eyes were bright and her cheeks glowed. I had seen that look before, when we had walked by the river in the first days of our courtship, and it encouraged me to walk by her side.

And then Musgrove said, 'Captain Wentworth, which way are you going?'

'I hardly know,' I said, surprised.

'Are you going as high as Belmont? Are you going near Camden Place? Because if you are, I shall have no scruple in asking you to take my place, and give Anne your arm to her father's door. She is rather done for this morning, and must not go so far without help, and I ought to be at that fellow's in the market place. He promised me the sight of a capital gun he is just going to send off; said he would keep it unpacked to the last possible moment, that I might see it; and if I do not turn back now, I have no chance.'

'It sounds too good to be missed. I should be glad to escort Anne; it will give me the greatest pleasure to be of service to her,' I said, hoping I did not sound too rapturous, for my spirits had soared at the thought of being alone with Anne.

Musgrove left us, and we bent our steps to the gravel walk, where we could talk to our hearts' content. As soon as we reached it, the words tumbled out of me, for I could contain them no longer.

'I cannot be easy . . . I cannot be still . . . Anne, tell me, is there hope for me?' I said, scarcely daring to breathe.

'Yes, there is hope, more than hope,' she said, in accents as breathless as my own. 'I have been so wrong . . .' she said.

I wanted to shout for joy, but I said only, 'Not wrong, never wrong.'

'If you could only know what my feelings have been since the day you left Somerset eight years ago.'

'Did you regret me at once?' I asked.

'I did, though at the time I still thought I was right to have refused you.'

'How could you have done it, when you were so much in love with me? The times I spent with you that summer were the happiest of my life. Do you remember them, too?'

'Every day. I remember the way my heart lifted every time I saw you, looking so much more alive than anyone I knew. Your spirit captivated me, and so did your tales of foreign shores, your zest for life, and your love of me,' she added with a blush. 'No one had ever looked at me like that, and if they had, I would not have wanted them to. But with you, everything was different. With you, the world was a bright and wonderful place.'

'I asked you once before if you would marry me. I ask you again. Will you marry me, Anne?'

'I will,' she said.

A slight shadow crossed my face.

'You need not be afraid that I will change my mind,' she reassured me. 'Then I was a young girl, persuaded by friends who knew more of the world than I did, who told me that it would lead to unhappiness; that I would stand in your way; that you would not be free to pursue your goals; that your ambitions would be frustrated because of me; that you would come to regret your decision; and that I, worn down by anxiety, would come to regret mine. Now I am a woman who knows her own mind and heart, and a woman who knows yours. I have no fears, no apprehensions, and I will not be persuaded out of my future happiness by anything anyone can say to me.'

I clasped her hand in mine, oblivious of the passersby as we paced the gradual ascent.

'When you came back to Bath, was it to see me?' she asked.

'It was. I came only for you.'

'I wanted it to be so, but at the same time I thought it was too much to hope. Your affection for Louisa . . .'

'Do not say any more. My conscience upbraids me. I should never have sought to attach myself to her, but I was angry with you, and full of wounded pride. After you rejected me, I told myself I would forget you. I gave my attention to my career and put my energies into defending my country. I commanded some fine ships and I made my fortune, but all the time you were there, like a heart's bruise that would not fade. When I met you again, I was still angry. I was unjust to your merits because I had been a sufferer from them. It was only at Uppercross that I began to do justice to them, for you shone there as you had shone before. And at Lyme, I learnt a painful lesson: that there is a difference between the steadiness of principle and the obstinacy of self-will; and that you had the former and Louisa the latter.'

'I will never forget the moment she fell,' said Anne.

'Nor I. I was in an agony of despair, for I felt I was to blame, for I had told her how much I valued a resolute character.'

'You could not have known where it would lead.'

'No, but I was overcome all the same. Yet whilst Henrietta swooned and Mary was hysterical, you, Anne, kept your head, and arranged for practical matters to be attended to.'

'I was the least affected,' she said. 'It was easier for me than for the rest.'

'Only you could say that,' I returned with a smile. 'But you saw to everything. And when we eventually reached Harville's house, and Louisa was put to bed, then the full force of my thoughts hit me, for I had nothing else to do in the succeeding days but think. I began to deplore the pride, the folly, the madness of resentment which had kept me from trying to regain you at once, as soon as I had discovered that Benjamin had rented Kellynch Hall.'

'My feelings when I heard that he had done so . . .'

'Yes?' I asked, eager to hear.

She shook her head.

'I was almost overpowered. I listened to every detail, then left the room, to seek the comfort of cool air, for my cheeks were flushed. I walked along my favourite grove, thinking that, in a few months, you might be visiting there.'

'And did you want me to come?'

'More than anything. When you left Somersetshire, after I had told you I could not, after all, marry you, I could not forget you. My attachment to you, my regrets, clouded every enjoyment. My spirits suffered, and everything seemed dull and lifeless. I did not blame Lady Russell for her advice, nor did I blame myself for having been guided by her; but I felt that, if any young person in similar circumstances were to apply to me for counsel, they would never receive any advice which would lead to such certain immediate wretchedness for the benefit of such uncertain future good.'

'Then you wished the choice unmade!' I said, much struck. 'And so soon.' My heart was warmed. 'I never knew. I was angry and I could see only that you had betrayed me. I was a hotheaded young man, though I thought myself so experienced. Did you, then, believe that even with the disadvantages of your family's disapproval, and the uncertainties of a long engagement, that you would yet have been happier with me than without me?'

'I did.'

'And did you hope my professions might be renewed when I came to Kellynch?'

'I hardly dared hope for anything of the kind, but I longed to see you, to discover how you looked, and if you remembered me. I told myself it could not be, and many a stroll, and many a sigh, were necessary to dispel the agitation of the idea. I told myself it was folly, that we would meet as strangers, that we could never be to each other what we once had been, but still, I could not be easy. I thought of you constantly.'

Better and better!

'I was relieved that the past was known to so few people—only you, myself, Lady Russell, my father and my sister—for

I could not have borne conscious looks from others. Your brother I supposed you would have told, but he had long since moved out of the neighbourhood, and I was sure that his discretion could be relied upon, so I was spared the trouble of it being common knowledge, at least.'

'And so you thought of me, even on that first day,' I said, pleased and yet angry with myself at the same time. 'If I had only spoken . . . if I had only put aside my pride and my anger, we could have been spared all that followed.'

'When did you put it aside?' she asked.

'That day at Lyme. I saw myself in a different light, because I saw that you had been right to be cautious, and to listen to the counsel of those older and wiser than yourself. I do not say that their counsel was good, only that you had been right to listen to it. I was about to tell you so, to go to you as soon as Louisa was out of danger, and tell you of my feelings, but no sooner had she been pronounced out of danger than Harville made it clear he thought that Louisa and I were engaged. That was a bitter time,' I said, shaking my head, 'for if those about us thought we were engaged, and if Louisa herself felt it to be so, then I knew I could not in honour abandon her. I would have to marry her. Never had I regretted my foolish intimacy with her more. I had been grossly wrong, and must abide by the consequences. I decided to leave Lyme, for I decided I could, in all honour, try to weaken her attachment, if it could be done by fair means.'

'I knew nothing of this. I thought you were in love with Louisa. I thought her youth and gaiety had captivated you. I knew that, beside her, my looks were faded and my spirits were low. You did not return to Kellynch, and I presumed it was because you were worried about Louisa.'

'And so I was, but only in the way I would worry about any girl who had had such an accident. I stayed with Edward. He enquired after you very particularly, and it gave me some relief to talk of you. I believe he guessed my feelings, for he even asked if you were personally altered, little suspecting that to my eye you could never alter.'

She smiled.

'And then, I was released from my torment by Louisa's engagement to Benwick. Within the first five minutes I said, "I will be at Bath on Wednesday," and I was. Was it unpardonable to think it worth my while to come? And to arrive with some degree of hope? You were single. It was possible that you might retain the feelings of the past, as I did: and one encouragement happened to be mine. I could never doubt that you would be loved and sought by others, but I knew to a certainty that you had refused one man, at least, of better pretensions than myself; and I could not help often saying, ' "Was this for me?" ' I turned to look at her. 'Was it, Anne? Did you refuse Charles Musgrove for me?'

'Yes,' she acknowledged, and the thought made me very happy. 'Lady Russell liked the match, but I was older by then, and wiser, and I did not take her advice. I had been persuaded by her out of marrying the man I loved. I was not going to be persuaded by her into marrying a man I did not love.'

I smiled.

'I was jealous of him, when I met you in the year six.' I shook my head as I remembered the feeling. 'You seemed fond of him, but once I learned he was a family friend, I forgave him! But I had someone else to be jealous of this year. Mr Elliot. I could not help but see that he admired you when we saw him in Lyme, and once I discovered who he was, and how eligible he was, and how desirable the connection, I was afraid. I had come to Bath to speak to you, to tell you I loved you, and yet, when I saw you, you were always with Mr Elliot. You smiled at him—'

'Through simple courtesy.'

'I did not know that. I thought you favoured him, and so I was silent. The meeting in Milsom Street was exquisite in its pleasure and its pain, and the concert was worse. You stepped forward to greet me, which gave me hope, but then you sat with Mr Elliot. Your heads were always together, as though you were having a private conversation—'

'I was translating the words of the songs for him. Mr Elliot does not speak Italian.'

'Ah,' I said, much gratified.

'Is that why you left?' she asked.

'Yes, I could bear it no longer. To see you so close to him . . . I had to leave, for to see you in the midst of those who could not be my well-wishers; to see Mr Elliot close by you, conversing and smiling, and feel all the horrible eligibilities and proprieties of the match, was terrible for me! To consider it as the certain wish of every being who could hope to influence you! Even if your own feelings were reluctant or indifferent, to consider what powerful supports would be his! Was it not enough to make the fool of me which I appeared? How could I look on without agony? Was not the very sight of Lady Russell, who sat behind you, was not the recollection of what had been, the knowledge of her influence, the indelible, immovable impression of what persuasion had once done—was it not all against me?'

'You should have distinguished, you should not have suspected me now; the case so different, and my age so different,' said Anne. 'If I was wrong in yielding to persuasion once, remember that it was to persuasion exerted on the side of safety, not of risk. When I yielded, I thought it was to duty, but no duty could be called in aid here. In marrying a man indifferent to me, all risk would have been incurred, and all duty violated.'

'Perhaps I ought to have reasoned thus, but I could not. I could not derive benefit from the late knowledge I had acquired of your character. I could not bring it into play: it was overwhelmed, buried, lost in those earlier feelings which I had been smarting under year after year. I could think of you only as one who had yielded, who had given me up, who had been influenced by any one rather than by me. I saw you with the very person who had guided you in that year of misery. I had no reason to believe her of less authority now. The force of habit was to be added.'

'I should have thought that my manner to yourself might have spared you much or all of this.'

'No, no! your manner might be only the ease which your engagement to another man would give. I left you in this belief;

and yet, I was determined to see you again. My spirits rallied with the morning, and I felt that I had still a motive for remaining here.'

We had by this time reached Camden Place, and I was forced to relinquish Anne.

'I do not want to part from you,' I said.

'It is only until this evening.'

'Ah, yes, your sister's card party. I am surprised she invited me.'

'You are well spoken of in Bath. She has at last, through the opinions of others, discovered your worth,' she said.

I let her go, reluctantly, and watched her go inside, then I returned to my rooms, more happy than I had ever been.

As I dressed for the evening, I thought I might have spared myself much misery by speaking to Anne as soon as I came to Kellynch Hall.

I finished dressing and made my way to Camden Place.

The party was insipid, as all such parties are, but it gave me an opportunity to see Anne. I watched her as she moved amongst her father's guests, glowing with happiness, and knew her happiness was for me.

I talked freely to Mr Elliot, my jealousy banished, and replaced with an excess of goodwill. I ignored the superior attitude of Lady Dalrymple and Miss Carteret, and instead I talked to them of the sea. I even exchanged pleasantries with Sir Walter and Miss Elliot. The Musgroves were there, and

Harville, and we had free and easy conversation. Louisa engaged, Anne and I coming to an understanding—I had had no idea, at the start of the year, that such a happy conclusion could be reached.

I saw Anne talking to my sister and brother-in-law, and I was delighted to see how well they all got on together, for even though I had not told Sophia my news, I knew she would be pleased.

And every now and then I managed to snatch a few moments with Anne. Her shawl slipped, and I helped her with it. A fly settled in her hair, and I wafted it away, feeling the soft strands of her hair brushing my fingers.

And when I could not talk to her, I watched her.

But I could not bring myself to talk to Lady Russell. Anne noticed it, and joined me by a fine display of greenhouse plants. Pretending to admire them, so that she could speak to me without drawing watchful eyes, she asked if I had forgiven her friend.

'Not yet, but there are hopes of her being forgiven in time,' I said. 'I trust to being in charity with her soon. But I too have been thinking over the past, and a question has suggested itself, whether there may not have been one person more my enemy even than that lady?'

I told her of the time, in the year eight, when I had almost written to her, but that I had been held back by fear.

'I had been rejected once, and I did not want to take the risk of being rejected again,' I told her, 'but if I had then written to you, would you have answered my letter? Would you, in short, have renewed the engagement then?'

'Would I?' she answered, and her accent told me all.

'Good God! you would! It is not that I did not think of it, or desire it, as what could alone crown all my other success; but I was proud, too proud to ask again. I did not understand you. I shut my eyes, and would not understand you, or do you justice. This is a recollection which ought to make me forgive everyone sooner than myself. Six years of separation and suffering might have been spared. It is a sort of pain, too, which is new to me. I have been used to the gratification of believing myself to earn every blessing that I enjoyed. I have valued myself on honourable toils and just rewards. Like other great men under reverses, I must endeavour to subdue my mind to my fortune. I must learn to brook being happier than I deserve.'

She smiled, but could do no more, for she was borne away by the Musgroves, and I had to make do with Harville's company until the party came to an end.

Monday 27 February

I rose early and went to Camden Place where, once again, I found myself asking Sir Walter for Anne's hand in marriage. He was a little more gracious than last time, for his friends esteem me. He expressed his surprise at my constancy and then enquired as to my fortune. On finding it to be twenty-five thousand pounds he said that it was not as large as a baronet's daughter had a right to hope for, but declared it to be adequate. I was angered by his attitude, but I resisted the urge to say that my fortune was at least better than his, for he had nothing but debts. He gave his consent at last, then our interview was at an end.

I smiled at Anne as I returned to the drawing-room. Anne smiled back at me, and we told her sister the news. Miss Elliot showed no more warmth than formerly. She managed only a haughty look, and a slightly incredulous, 'Indeed?'

I was angered on Anne's behalf, for it was ungenerous of her sister not to congratulate her, but I soon saw that Anne did not care. And why should she? We had each other, so what did we care for anyone else's approval?

'And when will you tell Lady Russell?' I asked Anne, as her sister left us alone.

'Soon. This afternoon,' she said. 'She has a right to know, indeed, I am longing to tell her. It will be very different this time, and I hope she will be happy for me.'

'I hope so, too, but tell her tomorrow instead. For the rest of the day, I want you to myself.'

She agreed, and we spent the time in free and frank conversation, opening our hearts to each other as we had done in the past, until it seemed that we had never been apart.

We spoke to no one, except at mealtimes, when it could not be avoided, and parted at last, reluctantly, at night.

I was longing to tell Sophia and Benjamin about my

engagement, but they were away, visiting friends, and so I nursed my secret to myself.

Tuesday 28 February

I arrived at Camden Place early this morning and found that Anne was out. I waited for her, and when she returned, she told me that she had been visiting Lady Russell.

'And how did she take the news?' I asked Anne.

'She struggled somewhat, but she told me that she would make an effort to become acquainted with you, and to do justice to you.'

'Then I can ask for no more,' I said. 'I know she wanted to see you take your mother's place. I cannot give you a baronetcy, but I can give you the comforts I could not provide you with eight years ago. And how has Mr Elliot taken the news? Has he heard it yet?'

'I neither know nor care. I have just learnt that he is not the man we thought he was. We have been sadly deceived in Mr Elliot,' she said.

I was astonished, and asked her what she meant.

'He did not seek us out in order to repair the breach that had come between us as he claimed. Instead, he came to Bath in order to keep watch on my father. He had been warned by a friend that Mrs Clay, who accompanied my sister to Bath, had ambitions to be the next Lady Elliot.'

'He knew that if Sir Walter married and had a son, he would lose his inheritance,' I said, nodding thoughtfully.

'He did. He declared that he had never spoken slightingly of the baronetcy, as my father had heard, and protested that he had always wanted to be friends. He made himself so agreeable that my father and sister were completely taken in, cordial relations were restored, and he was made welcome in Camden Place at any time.'

'So he achieved his object of keeping a close watch on Mrs Clay.'

'And put himself in a position to intervene if he felt it necessary.'

'But are you sure?' I asked.

'I am. I learnt it from an old school friend, a Mrs Smith, who is in Bath at present. She was, once, a wealthy—comparatively wealthy—woman, and she and her husband knew Mr Elliot in London, but now she has fallen on hard times.'

I thought that this must be the same friend Mrs Lytham had told me about, and I honoured Anne for her continued friendship, even through adversity. I thought how fortunate I was to be marrying a woman who knew as well as I did that the important things in life—love, affection, friendship—had nothing to do with wealth.

'It is largely because of Mr Elliot that my friend has suffered. He borrowed money from her husband, which he did not repay, and, even worse, he led her husband into debt. When Mr Smith died, he should have seen to it that she was able to claim some property to which she was entitled in the West Indies, for he was the executor of the will, but he ignored his duties, and as a result, my friend is living in poverty,' she said with a sigh.

'But this is terrible!'

'It is indeed. If he would only bestir himself, the money raised from the property could provide her with a degree of comfort that would improve her life immeasurably.'

'I am very sorry to hear it,' I said. I thought for a moment, and then said, 'I am indebted to her for opening your eyes about Mr Elliot, and I owe her my friendship because she is your friend. I have some knowledge of the West Indies, and I would be glad to help her.'

She gave me a look of heartfelt gratitude, and expressed her desire that we should go and see Mrs Smith this afternoon. This I agreed to, and when we arrived at Westgate Buildings, I was shocked to see how Anne's friend was living. Her accommodations were limited to a noisy parlour and a dark bedroom behind. She was now an invalid, with no possibility of moving from one room to the other without assistance, and Anne told me her friend never quitted the house but to be conveyed into the warm bath.

I was sorry for her indeed. However, I soon found that her spirits had not been crushed, for she expressed her pleasure at meeting me, and she congratulated me heartily on my engagement.

'Anne was good enough to visit me this morning and tell me the news,' she said. 'I am delighted for her, and for you, too. You are lucky to have won her.'

I assured her I knew my luck, and she declared that she was sure we would be very happy together.

'I have brought Frederick here for more than one purpose,'

said Anne. 'I have brought him here to help you. You mentioned a property in the West Indies?'

'Yes, indeed. If you could do anything to help me I would be most grateful,' she said to me.

I asked her for particulars and on hearing the details I felt she had a good chance of success. I offered to act for her, and we parted with goodwill on both sides.

I walked back to Camden Place with Anne, and there I left her, for I had promised to look into Mrs Smith's affairs right away. We did not meet again until later that evening, when we went to the theatre with the Musgroves.

They were, as always, a happy family party. Benwick was missing, for he had promised to dine with an acquaintance, but the rest of the party was there. As we assembled in the box, Henrietta and Louisa were full of their forthcoming marriages; Musgrove was eager to talk of the gun he had seen; Hayter was talking of his living, and Mr and Mrs Musgrove were wanting to talk about their children, the shops and their delight at being in Bath. When there was a pause in the conversation, Anne and I gave them our glad news. They looked stunned, but Mary recovered almost at once and congratulated us heartily.

'I always felt you were meant for each other,' she said, though it was obvious the idea had never occurred to her before that moment. 'I am sure you have me to thank, for I was greatly instrumental in bringing you together.'

'Ay, a happy chance,' said Mrs Musgrove, beaming with delight. 'I am very happy for you. You would have always been welcome in our family, Captain Wentworth, for your kindness to Richard, but you will be doubly welcome as the husband of Anne.'

Whilst Anne accepted everyone's congratulations, and sought to answer Henrietta's and Louisa's questions about wedding clothes, Mary, who was sitting next to me, turned to me and said, 'If I had not kept Anne with me in the autumn, she would have gone to Bath with Lady Russell, and you would never have met. You owe it all to me. I will be very glad to have a sister married. I do not see why Charles should have two sisters married this year, and I not one. And Anne has caught the best husband, after all, for you are far richer than either Captain Benwick or Charles Hayter. Yes, I am glad that my own sister has won the best husband of the three.'

I could not help my grimace, and later, when Anne joined me, she asked what my expression had meant.

'One member of your family is glad to have me, at least, but it is only because I am richer than either Hayter or Benwick,' I told her.

She was embarrassed, and blushed, but she was too happy to be troubled by Mary's vulgarity for long, and we passed a joyful evening. The play, I believe, was good, but neither of us paid any attention to it, for we were too busy looking at each other.

MARCH

Wednesday 1 March

I called on Lady Russell this morning. There must inevitably
be some awkwardness about our first meeting, and I thought
it best it should be conducted in private. I was shown in, and
there before me I saw the woman who had blighted my hopes
eight and a half years before.

She looked conscious, and I felt a moment's resentment . . . and then it was gone, pushed aside by happiness.

I went forward and greeted her.

'Lady Russell,' I said, for she did not seem to know how to
begin. I took pity on her confusion, and I went on kindly,
'Once before you offered me your hand and suggested we be
friends. I refused to take it, for I was not ready to make my

peace with you then, but I am ready now. This time, *I* will offer you *my* hand, and say, "What is done is done, let us be friends."'

I held out my hand. She hesitated a moment, seemed about to speak, and then took it.

'I told you, a long time ago, that I would never do anything to harm Anne, and I repeat it now. More, I will tell you that her happiness is, and always will be, my first consideration. I hope this will reconcile you to the marriage.'

'You are very generous,' she said, 'and I will endeavour to be the same. Though I do not believe my advice was wrong at the time, it proved wrong in the event. I believe you love each other sincerely and deeply, and though I wished for a better match for her in terms of rank—I am being honest, you see—I think she could not make a better match in terms of mutual loyalty and affection.'

I made her a bow, and assured her again of my determination to make Anne happy, and we parted, if not friends, then, at least, as two people who had reached a point of understanding and respect.

I told Anne of our meeting when we dined together at the house of some of our Bath acquaintance.

'Lady Russell told me about your visit. I am glad you went,' said Anne. 'In time, she will come to love you as much as I do, and then my happiness will be complete.'

News of our engagement had spread, and we found ourselves being congratulated on all sides. Benwick looked at me with a sense of relief and satisfaction, and when we were sitting over the port, he said to me, 'This takes a weight off my mind, Wentworth. I was not sure, when you came to Lyme in November, if you were in love with Louisa. I held back at first, for I did not wish to cause you harm, but when you went away and did not come back, I began to understand that there had not been a serious attachment, and so I allowed myself to fall in love with her. She is such an intelligent girl, with such expressive eyes and such a gentle character. Moreover, she does not remind me of'—his voice became low and wistful—'Fanny.'

I gave him an understanding look, for I began to see how it had been for him. Another girl like Fanny would have reminded him too much of his first love. A girl who was the opposite would not.

'I still remember her, Wentworth, but now it is not with pain, it is with warmth,' he said. 'I am grateful that I was fortunate enough to know her. God knows, I suffered when she died . . . well, you know, you were there,' he said, gripping the stem of his glass, as his feelings overcame him. 'But all things must pass, or at least lessen, even grief. It is still there, but not as strong, and although I will miss her always, I have other joys now to attach me to life. I am persuaded that Fanny would have wanted it that way.'

'She would,' I said fervently. 'She was an intelligent young woman who enjoyed life. She would not have wanted you to waste yours in painful memories.'

He smiled gratefully.

'That is what I think. Harville is finding it difficult to accept this new love—no, do not protest, you know it as well as I. And so he should. He was Fanny's brother. I do not say he was glad to see me in pain, but it is only natural that someone who loved her as much as he did, should want to know that she is missed by others who loved her as well. But he is a good fellow, and glad to see me emerge from despair. He likes Louisa, and the circumstances of our romance are such as to touch the coldest heart.' He shook his head, recalling the circumstances. 'When I think that Louisa, too, might have been dead. She looked so lifeless when she was taken up after the fall.'

I remembered that moment well. It had affected us all.

'But a strange thing happened,' he said, his voice becoming stronger. 'As I saw her recovering from her deathlike state, so, too, I felt myself recovering from mine. I found myself, at last, able to love again. I am a lucky man to have been give a second chance, Wentworth,' he said.

'A second chance!' I said, much struck, knowing that I, too, had been given a second chance with Anne.

'What is it?' he asked, sensing a change in my manner.

I simply smiled, for he had never known of our first engagement.

'Nothing, save that I agree with you. To second chances,' I said, raising my glass.

The general conversation having died down at just that moment, the words were taken up as a toast. Glasses were raised, and all about me I heard the cry, 'To second chances!'

Sunday 5 March

Anne and I found ourselves much looked at in church this morning, for our engagement is the talk of Bath. We were congratulated by those who had not yet had an opportunity to give us their best wishes, and even Mr Elliot managed to bow from the other side of the church, though he could not bring himself to wish us happy.

Mrs Clay was very pleased, for Mr Elliot's fall from favour meant she was free to catch Sir Walter if she pleased. I asked Anne if she thought it prudent to warn her father of Mrs Clay's intent.

'It would do no good,' she said. 'I tried to warn Elizabeth last year, but she dismissed the notion. My father would only do the same. Worse, it might put the idea into his mind.'

'Then you are right to say nothing.' I did not like the idea of Mrs Clay living at Kellynch Hall, if she managed to marry Sir Walter, and so I voiced an idea that had been in my mind for some time. 'I have been thinking about Kellynch, Anne. Do you think your father would sell it to me? If it is not an inalienable part of the estate, then he can sell it if he wishes. It would clear his debts at once, and Kellynch would still remain in the family. Moreover, you would be able to take your mother's place as the mistress of Kellynch Hall.'

'I doubt if my father would sell it. Besides, I would not like to live at Kellynch Hall. Lady Russell would like to see me there, I know, but I have not been happy there. I have my heart set on an estate by the sea.'

'The one we talked about when we were first engaged all those years ago?'

'Yes. I have thought it a model of perfection ever since, with its stretch of coastline and its sandy coves, its countrified aspect to the rear and its view of the sea to the front.'

'Then we must set about finding it. I will start making enquiries with the land agents tomorrow, and see if there is anything we can view.'

We fell into a happy discussion about the number of rooms and size of grounds we wanted in our new home, and did not let up until recalled to our company.

Tuesday 7 March

I had a letter from Edward this morning, thanking me for mine, and telling me he was delighted to learn that Anne had accepted me. He invited us to visit him on Thursday. Anne agreed to the idea and I wrote back to accept Edward's invitation.

Wednesday 8 March

Sophia and Benjamin returned from spending a week with friends, and I told them of my engagement.

'At last!' said Benjamin. 'Sophia and I were beginning to think you would never marry. You took your time, but you have chosen well in the end. She is a pretty little thing. Not as lively as the Musgrove girls, perhaps, but there is an air of quiet refinement about her that I like.'

'I am very pleased for you,' said Sophia, 'and I am pleased for myself. There is an air about her that is most pleasing, and I like her better than either of the Musgrove girls. I wonder you did not notice her when you were here before, visiting Edward. You must have seen her?'

'Never mind what Frederick did or did not do eight years ago, Sophia, he has brought the girl home now.' He turned to me. 'You must bring her to see us this afternoon.'

I did as they suggested, and I was warmed to see how well they all got on together. Anne Elliot as the daughter of their landlord they could like: Anne as my future wife they could love.

'And have you told Edward?' asked Sophia.

'Yes, I wrote to him and gave him the news. We are to pay him a visit tomorrow.'

Thursday 9 March

Our visit to Edward was one of great enjoyment. He welcomed Anne with warmth, and Eleanor did likewise. Edward and Anne remembered each other from the years he had lived at Monkford, and spoke of those days affectionately.

'You were at the ball where Frederick and I first met,' she said.

'It was a very propitious meeting,' he remarked with a significant look.

'Ah. I wondered if Frederick had told you,' said Anne, colouring slightly.

'He did indeed, many times over. He would not be silent. He spoke of nothing but you: your loveliness, your intelligence, your tenderness and your charm. He told me how happy he was to be engaged to you.'

Eleanor smiled benignly, and Anne blushed, for it became obvious that Eleanor knew about it, too.

'I can keep a confidence, but no man can keep such a thing from his wife,' said Edward. 'Eleanor soon guessed there had been something between you, and I told her the whole. I give you my word I have never mentioned it to anyone else, and I only hope you will forgive me for my one small lapse.'

We granted him our pardon, and indeed, it made it easier that Eleanor knew, for conversation was then much freer. We spoke of the past, and recalled the summer of the year six with much affection. As everything had turned out so well, I was able to think of those times without pain, indeed, with the greatest of pleasure.

Monday 13 March

Mr Elliot has left Bath! I am surprised. It is true that, now Anne and I are engaged, he has no excuse to visit Camden Place, and therefore he cannot watch over Mrs Clay, but I would not have expected him to give up so easily. He has left the way clear for Mrs Clay to marry Sir Walter, if she can catch him. I think it not unlikely, for Sir Walter speaks very well of her. It is not a match I would like to see, but it cannot be helped, and at least I will be taking Anne away, so that she will not have to see Mrs Clay in her mother's place.

Wednesday 15 March

Camden Place was in a state of shock this morning when I called, for Mrs Clay had left!

'Where has she gone?' I asked Anne.

'No one knows,' she said. 'I am as much in the dark as you. She left a letter for my sister saying she had been called home, without giving further particulars.'

Elizabeth entered the room at that moment, with Lady Russell.

'Base ingratitude,' she said angrily. 'I took Mrs Clay up, made her my confidante, and this is how she repays me.'

I saw Lady Russell open her mouth and then close it again, obviously wanting to say that she had warned Elizabeth, but thinking it would be better not to say anything.

'To leave without giving me a moment's notice, without even telling me to my face that she intended to go,' Elizabeth went on. 'I hope it is something serious that has called her away, and not anything trifling.'

Anne and I decided on a walk, as the atmosphere in the house was very uncomfortable. Once out of doors, I asked Anne what she made of Mrs Clay's abrupt departure.

'Do you think she has realized that Sir Walter will never marry her, and therefore she has decided not to waste any more of her time, or do you think Mr Elliot could have had something to do with it?'

'The latter, I suspect,' said Anne.

'Perhaps he has bribed her to stay away from Sir Walter. He is determined to be the next baronet, and, as the money is nothing to him, it would be a small price for him to pay in order to ensure his succession.'

I wondered what Mr Elliot could have offered her to tempt her to forgo the chance of such a prosperous future, but I did not wonder for long. Mrs Clay was of very little interest to me. My interest lay in Anne.

Friday 17 March

I had a letter regarding Mrs Smith's property in the West Indies this morning, and the news seemed so promising that I went to tell her. To my astonishment, she told me that Mrs Clay had joined Mr Elliot in London, and was living there under his protection.

'As his mistress?' I exclaimed in astonishment.

She nodded.

'But Mrs Clay is a clever woman. I think she will not be content to remain his mistress for very long.'

'You mean she has her sights set on marriage?'

'I think she has set her sights on a baronet, and the future one will do as well as the present.'

'I cannot believe he will marry her.'

'No? If he refuses, she can go straight back to Sir Walter. She would only have to make a few protestations of innocence, and voice her outrage about the lies that have been spread about her, then proceed to flatter him, and the thing would be done.'

I began to smile.

'I like the idea. I think Mrs Clay and Mr Elliot will suit each other very well. They are two greedy, self-seeking people who have not a decent standard or value between them.'

'And two people who are better away from the Elliots. Anne's father and sister were always proud, and I would not care what became of them, but I would not wish to see Anne distressed in any way.'

On this we agreed, and I went on to Camden Place, where I found Anne ready to go on our arranged drive. As we went out into the country, we discussed everything Mrs Smith had said. She expressed her surprise, but before long she had come to think, as Mrs Smith did, that Mrs Clay might persuade Mr Elliot to marry her after all.

'Would you mind?' I asked her.

'I would not like to see her as the next Lady Elliot, but then, I doubt if I will have to, for we will have moved out of the neighbourhood by then.'

'As to that, I have heard of a promising property. Would you like to see it?'

She expressed her delight at the idea, and after I had left her at Camden Place I made the arrangements.

Monday 20 March

We have found our estate. It is exactly as we imagined it, a Queen Anne house set amidst verdant countryside with a long stretch of coastline, and three sandy bays. We were both delighted with it and I closed with the agent at once.

We returned to dinner with the Musgroves, where we found that our news met with a mixed reception. The Harvilles were delighted; Henrietta and Louisa asked if this meant we would be married before them; and Mary looked ill-used.

'You are wondering why Mary is so put out,' said Henrietta to me after dinner. 'It is not really surprising. She liked you well enough to begin with because you were rich enough to do her credit, but not wealthy enough so that Anne would eclipse her. She had Uppercross Hall before her, a substantial property that Charles would inherit in due course, whereas Anne had no such property to look forward to, therefore Mary could consider herself superior. You have now taken that source of gratification away from her by your purchase of an estate. However, as long as you are not made a baronet, I think she will rally.'

Sure enough, Mary soon regained her spirits.

'You can set a date for the wedding, now,' said Benjamin.

'Make it an early wedding. We will be marrying in May,' said Henrietta.

'And so will we,' said Louisa. 'Why do we not all three marry in May?'

'I have a fancy to marry in June,' said Anne.

I was pleased, for although I liked the Musgrove girls, I did not want to share my wedding day with them.

'That is a good plan,' I said. 'I have a suggestion to make. I think we should marry on the ninth.'

Anne flushed, for that was the date when we first met.

'It seems to suit the lady,' said Benjamin with a smile.

'Then it is settled?' I asked, looking at Anne.

'It is,' she agreed.

JUNE

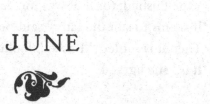

Friday 9 June

Today, Anne and I were married. As I saw her walking down the aisle on her father's arm, I no longer thought of the years we had wasted, but the years we had to come. She was attended by her sisters, and the church was full of the Elliot tenants, who had come to see her married. Lady Russell was there, and Mrs Smith, too. Edward and Eleanor were sitting beside Sophia and Benjamin. Harville was there, and the Musgroves, all come to wish us well.

After the ceremony, we returned to Kellynch Hall for the wedding breakfast.

'Have you seen?' asked Mary, as we emerged from the dining-room. 'Papa has been writing in the *Baronetage*.'

Anne took up the book, and there it was, the news of our

marriage, written in Sir Walter's hand, after the date of Anne's birth.

It was something I had never expected to see, but, under Lady Dalrymple's influence, Sir Walter had come to value a captain, or, at least, to realize that others valued him, and for Sir Walter, that was enough.

But was it enough for me?

As we went out to the carriage, I found myself thinking of the future.

'What are you thinking about?' Anne asked me.

'I am thinking that I am still young, and that there is time for me to go further in the world. How do you like the sound of Sir Frederick and Lady Wentworth?'

'I am content to be Mrs Wentworth, but since you achieve everything you set your mind to, I believe I must accustom myself to being Lady Wentworth before very long.'

'You believe in me!' I said, touched to the depths of my being.

'I always have done,' she said.

'Then I have nothing left to wish for.'

'Except a knighthood,' she teased me.

'A knighthood to begin with, and then, who knows?'

I handed her into the carriage and we set out for the future.

Amanda Grange lives in Cheshire. She has published many novels, including *Lord Deverill's Secret*, *Mr. Knightley's Diary* and *Harstairs House*. Visit her website at www .amandagrange.com.